COOL FOR Cats

a novel

ANDREW ORDOVER

- CFC Books -

ISBN: 0615532098
ISBN-13: 978-0615532097 (C4C Books)

For Heather

"I'm not a star; I'm just backing up the cats."

Jaco Pastorius

1

It's hot.

My leg itches, right down where I can't reach it, deep inside the cast. It's driving me crazy. Like grind your teeth crazy. I've been sitting here all morning, trying to remember every detail about how this whole thing got started, but all I can think about is my goddamned leg.

And the heat.

It felt just like this, though—exactly like this, the day he called me. I remember that. I remember sitting in my office all morning with my eyes closed, trying to work out a Mingus tune in my head and ignore the sweat dripping down my back. It was like that joke about trying not to think about elephants. Big, sweaty elephants. Sitting right next to me. Breathing on me.

Mingus didn't stand a chance.

What I don't remember is why I bothered going in to work that day, knowing how gross it was going to be. It's not like I have a drop-in business at the damned place. If I stopped going in, no one would even notice. Nine times out of ten I meet clients in their own offices, or at a Starbucks somewhere. The rest of my clients, I don't ever meet. They just call me. Or they email. They fill out a form online and press "Submit." I could be in Mumbai for all they know. Or at home, in my underwear.

What I'm saying is, mysterious blondes do not drift through a curtain of cigarette smoke and lean against my door, begging me for help. I am 100% not that guy. The office is just a place to keep my files, because my wife hates it when I leave photos of naked salesmen and botched surgeries on our dining room table.

The problem with the office, besides the lousy air conditioning, is that it's a dark, little hole carved into a grim, old building on a totally nothing, downtown street. It's got smeary windows, yellowing walls, and floors so old you could do an archeological dig on the dirt that's wedged in the crevices. It's very film-noir, if you like that kind of thing, but it's depressing as hell to sit in all day.

But I go there, and I sit there, if only to feel like I'm a grown up with a real job—and I was sitting there on that August morning, for whatever reason, when the phone rang and shattered about three solid hours of silence.

It was a guy named Palmer. Middle aged from the sound of his voice. Baritone-ishly self-important. One of those "I have just enough time to tell you I have no time" voices. He wanted me to investigate a hit-and-run accident that had never been solved. His daughter had been skating in her neighborhood and had been hit by a car. Killed on the spot, with no witnesses and no

2

evidence worth speaking of. Case closed. Except he couldn't live with the case being closed without answers—even three years later. He wanted to see if I could dig up anything the police hadn't. He wanted closure. His words.

Not that I'm trying to make fun—it was a totally reasonable request, and closure is a fine and good thing. I'm all for closure. The problem is, I'm not that kind of private investigator. You know, the kind that solves crimes, gets in car chases, and sleeps with mysterious blondes. I don't even own a gun. I'm just a low-level grind. A process server. A snoop, basically. I snoop on a lot of nasty, petty shit that ordinary people do to each other, then I write down what I see and somebody hands me a check. It's usually not a big check, and they're usually not happy when they hand it to me. But they're satisfied, somehow, to learn whatever it is I've taught them about their loved ones. So I guess it's a public service. Anyway, it's what I do, and I'm pretty good at it.

What I *don't* do is solve murders, or manslaughters, or whatever the hell this thing was going to be.

So I said *No*, very politely, and he said he understood, also politely, and I started looking for the number of another agency in town to refer him to. And then, out of the blue, he told me his girl's name. I don't know why he did it. I didn't ask for it. But he told me his daughter had been named Giselle.

Giselle.

I stopped scrolling through my contact list and looked at the caller ID on the phone. It was a 516 number: Long Island. Suddenly I was 17 years old again.

I put one and one together and said, "This is Giselle Palmer you're talking about? From Great Neck?"

He paused for a second, taken aback.

"I'm sorry, do you...did you know my daughter?"

I barked out something like a laugh that wasn't really a laugh. "Mr. Palmer," I said, "This is Jordan. Jordan Greenblatt."

"Jordan? I thought your name was Barnes."

"It *was* Barnes. I mean, the office is Barnes. I'm...Jesus. *Giselle*? She's dead?"

"Jordan...my god."

"You remember me?"

"Of course," he said quickly. Then he said it again, but differently.

It was exactly the reaction I had when I heard *her* name. Giselle! And then: Giselle.

Giselle Palmer. Right here, in the same city as me. And then gone. Gone before I could even...

I took the job.

That's right: I took the job even though I wasn't that kind of investigator. I took the job even though I knew I shouldn't. In other words, I was a schmuck.

And that, ladies and gentlemen, is why I'm sitting here at home, trying to scratch a hopeless itch and write about what happened a year ago, instead of sitting in my office, doing something useful. Because even now, still, I see my face plastered in newspapers or on local TV shows as some kind of Authority on bad behavior.

Which you'd think would be great for business, right? But you'd be wrong. To be an investigator, even a bottom-feeder like me, you need two things: stealth and silence. And being a minor celebrity has destroyed both of those things. The last thing you need on a stakeout is some chowderhead spotting you in your car and yelling, "Hey! You're that guy on TV!"

I forgot patience. You need a lot of patience. Which I'm rapidly running out of.

So here I am, holed up at home with Eliot the cat, waiting for the Big Spotlight to pass on to someone else so I can get back to work and pay some bills.

And no, Susannah, I'm not going go back and capitalize the *g* in "god." And I'm not going to fix those dangling prepositions, either. And stop reading over my shoulder.

Susannah is the aforementioned wife, and she's just home from work, which means I've spent the whole day writing what amounts to about three pages. At this rate, I should be finished just in time to retire.

It's not that I don't want to tell the story. I do. The whole thing has gotten so distorted that I don't even recognize it anymore. And I lived it.

But I'm obviously not going to finish tonight. My big bass fiddle is leaning against the wall, waiting patiently for its turn under my fingers. And Susannah is splayed across the couch, waiting slightly less patiently for *her* turn.

Yeah, celebrity's a bitch.

2

I got into this whole business kind of sideways. I was looking for some temp work after college so I could support myself while pursuing fortune and glory as a rock star. I had sworn to myself that I was never going to work as a waiter, so office work was pretty much all that was left. After a couple of years of secretarial gigs for lawyers and bankers, I stumbled into a job working for an old-time private investigator.

His name was Billy Barnes, and he could have walked straight out of a 1940s movie, right down to his fedora. He drank and smoked constantly, and he had a nasty, mucous-y cough that swore me off cigarettes for life. He said he only wanted someone for a few days to straighten out his files and answer his phones, but we hit it off pretty well and he ended up keeping me on full time. Before the year was out, I was doing a lot of the basic investigative work for him. It was all pretty intuitive, and I liked it a hell of a lot better than filing. As far as Billy was concerned, he was thrilled to get off his feet and re-read his favorite Raymond Chandler novels.

I was playing with an all-bass band at the time. We called ourselves Fuck Guitars, which we thought was a really clever name until we tried running newspaper ads. The egos were another problem. Imagine trying to work with three guys who've spent their whole lives standing quietly off to the side—three sidemen who suddenly wanted to be rock stars. I mean, I wanted to be a rock star, too, I guess, but these guys were obnoxious.

Being a bass player is not a job for egomaniacs, because most of the time, you're just laying down support. Someone else is always calling the tune, and that's the way it should be. Your job is to listen and respond. Your job is to be there when you're needed. And to do that well requires two things: stealth and silence. And patience, of course. Basically, it requires a stable personality. Any bass player who wants to be out front as a star, I don't trust him. Except for Paul McCartney. I don't know why he gets a pass, but he does.

As for me, I never had a problem standing off to the side. All the things my band mates hated about playing bass were the things I loved. I loved having to watch and listen to figure out where the music was going. I especially loved sitting in with other bands whose songs I didn't know, or accompanying gospel choirs around town. I always dug the challenge: how fast can you pick it up? How seamlessly can you follow?

Music lays down structures and sets up equations, and if you know the math and can follow the logic, you can anticipate the next move and be right there supporting it, hitting the perfect note just when the piano needs it, shifting into a new key right when the singer goes there. And everybody looks at you like you're a magician. But you're not a magician. You just know how to read the signs and follow the trail.

Which I guess is what led me to jazz. When you're playing jazz, everybody's working like I work—watching each other, listening to each other, picking up cues and clues and taking the line of music further on in that direction, or maybe in a new direction, and always without words. It's a simultaneous thing, a group investigation, and the results are never the same.

So I traded my electric bass for a big bull fiddle and traded my dreams of fortune and glory for the more sedate reality of hanging out with some cool cats on my front porch a couple of times a week, drinking beer and making music. And I've never regretted it.

I made that switch at about the same time Billy Barnes decided to surrender his lungs permanently to the cancer farm he was growing there. By the time he cashed out, I was pretty much doing his job for him anyway, and I realized I was pretty good at it. It wasn't my heart's desire or anything, but it beat temp work. So I took the test, got my license, picked up his lease and kept the place running. I knew all the lawyers he'd been working with and had pretty good relations with the people at the DA's office and the local precincts. Everyone had liked old Billy, so I just kept his name on the door. I figured it carried more weight than my name. Plus, "Billy Barnes" played a hell of a lot better than "Jordan Greenblatt" with the older crowd of Atlanta cops.

Looking back, I guess it was entropy more than anything else. Or maybe it just seemed like the next place the music was going. I don't know anymore.

Anyway, that's my life and times, or as much of it as you need to know. I've been doing the work for about six years now, which sometimes feels like ten and sometimes feels like a week. And I can honestly tell you that in all that time, not one genuinely interesting thing has ever happened to me.

All right—*one*. And it turned out to be more than I ever wanted.

3

Palmer wanted me to get started right away, which was fine by me. He was all business, which you'd expect from a guy like him, but I was grateful for it, since I didn't really want to dredge up our Long Island past and talk with him about...well, much of anything. He said he couldn't fly down to meet with me, money being tight, but he'd send me a packet of news clippings and photos and other information, and he'd be available by phone or email whenever I needed him. I decided not to press him on the money issue, which I thought was weird, but I filed it away for a future conversation.

Did he just not want to see me face to face? That was totally possible. More than possible. I mean, why the guy hadn't just hung up when he realized who I was, I had no idea. There were other PIs in town, and any one of them would have been happy to overbill him for a hopeless case. So that wasn't it.

Was it the money? Was it just that my rates were the lowest in town and I was all he could afford? Could the Palmers have sunk *that* low since I first met them? I mean, I know a family's fortunes can change over the course of fifteen years or so—but man…if Ted Palmer couldn't afford one plane ticket to Atlanta, that was a big deal. Back when I knew the family, they had *money*—the kind you italicize even when you say it out loud. Even their names had money. I mean—*Giselle?* Who did I know with a name like Giselle? Or Palmer, for that matter. Everyone I knew, growing up, had names like Silverman or Horowitz. And first names like Lori—with an "i."

As it turned out, Giselle's family *did* have that kind of last name—Plotnick—but her parents had buried it a long time ago. When my earliest detective work, back in high school, uncovered this fascinating little tidbit (a quest undertaken out of pure spite, I admit, because the asshole wouldn't let me talk to his daughter), old Ted yelled at me, "The P is for Palmer!"

Right. Actually, Ted—the P was for Pretentious.

Anyway, something had happened, and I was itching to find out what it was. And that was a bad move.

See, my first instinct was to snoop into Ted's life and see what was going on, because that's what I did for a living. That was my comfort zone. It's just where I went, automatically. You give me a picture of your wife and tell me to follow her; I follow her and tell you what she's doing. If she's doing something wrong, sooner or later I'm going to catch her doing it. For a little extra, you can get pictures. You give me your husband's social security number; I follow it and tell you what *it's* been doing. The only difference is I don't have to sit in my car all night. All I need is a little stealth, a little silence, a little patience.

12

Now, I'm told the really big crooks know how to cover their tracks, and it's hard to track them down. But I've never had to follow a really big crook, so I don't know. The idiots I'm paid to snoop on are…well, they're idiots. They always leave a trail to follow—mostly because they never think anyone is going to follow them.

But now, all of a sudden, I'm dealing with a three-year-old hit-and-run case. That's a whole different ball game. I couldn't just go to my happy place and run on auto-pilot. In fact, I didn't even know where to start. The accident itself—that wasn't the problem. I could handle that. With or without Palmer's box of clippings, there was going to be a trail I could follow. There was Google. There were newspaper archives. That's my home field. Plus, the fact that it *was* an accident, not a premeditated thing, meant no one planned it or thought it through. So most likely, the guy who did it hadn't covered his tracks. After all, it wasn't called hit-and-clean-up-your-mess-before-running.

No, what worried me was the fact it was three years old, and abandoned by the police. Those were two bad things. First, there was no reason to assume the cops had screwed up. After all, this was a pretty, young woman—a pretty, young, *white* woman—from a family that knew how to make trouble and get what it wanted. If the police hadn't found anything back then, didn't it mean there was nothing to find? *I* sure as hell thought so; why didn't Palmer? Or was he just not able to think straight?

And three years? That's a pretty cold scent to pick up and follow for an inexperienced bloodhound like me. I mean, you give me a picture of your daughter and tell me to follow her, fine. But when she's been dead for three years, where the hell am I supposed to start?

Not with her father, that was for sure. That was just me, nursing an old grudge and defaulting to what I knew how to do. So I looked myself in the mirror and reminded myself: Palmer isn't the case. Stirring up loose dirt isn't the case. You're doing archeology here. So get out your little spoon and your little brush and start digging.

I complained about all of this to Susannah that first night in my inimitable New York whine as we walked through the heavy, humid evening towards dinner. (I could have said, "I opened my heart to my soul-mate and best friend," or some crap like that, but I'm trying to be *honest* here. I want some credit for that. Also, she's reading this every time I leave the room.)

Her first question was, "So why did you take the case?" Now, that was a first-rate question, and it was one I really couldn't answer. I didn't *have* to take the case, and she knew it. August makes people pissy, and pissy makes people stupid. So there's always work for me in the summertime if I want it. And I never want *much* of it, because August makes *me* pissy, too, and all I really want to do is open a beer and play some music till the weather cools off. The truth is, if it had been anyone but Giselle, I wouldn't have taken the case, but because it *was* Giselle, I had to. And I wasn't sure how to explain that.

"It was an old friend who got killed," is what I ended up saying. "A girl I knew in high school." Which was true enough.

"Ahhh, an old girlfriend." she teased, punching me in the arm in that country, tomboyish, Daddy-kept-cars-up-on-blocks-in-the-yard way she has.

"Not even," I said, trying for Bogart but managing only Eeyore. "Just someone I used to know. It's a favor for her dad."

"Which means you're stuck," she said.

I nodded and put my arm around her. "Big stuck."

4

I met Giselle Palmer at the Kaplan center near Hofstra University on Long Island, where I grew up. I used to take the bus down there for my SAT class and then catch a ride home with my dad, who taught at the law school. Giselle was there for SAT too, though she had a much longer drive to get there. When I found out where she lived, I wondered why she wasn't taking classes closer to home. But then I met her prick of a father and realized exactly why she wasn't taking classes closer to home— Daddy didn't want her classmates to know she needed help. Which was ridiculous, because you've got to figure every kid in Great Neck was taking SAT prep *somewhere*. But then, you've also got to figure every kid in Great Neck also knew that "Palmer" was a bullshit, made-up name, and that hadn't stopped old Ted either.

Giselle was a classic Jewish American Princess—bought blonde hair, all the right clothes, and a casual haughtiness that you took for charm as long as she was smiling at you. And she *did* smile at me. I was the class clown at our SAT gig—smart enough to do the job but massively unmotivated. First off, I knew I had a free ticket to Hofstra, since my father taught there.

Second, I had scored just fine on my PSATs, even if I had blown my first shot at the SAT by being hung over. I figured with a prep class and me showing up sober, I'd do well enough the next time, without having to sweat it much. And third—well, I was no genius student, but I picked up stuff pretty quickly, especially stuff like how to outsmart multiple-choice tests. So every week, after about ten minutes, I just sat there saying, "I get it, I *get* it. Let's move on." Which left me lots of time to mouth off and be a pain in the teacher's ass. But the girls liked it.

It wasn't that I was un-ambitious. I mean, I *was* planning on being a doctor back then, and I knew (more or less) what it was going to take. I just wasn't plugged in to that whole world yet. It was a cool *idea*. But I wasn't even close to competitive enough to face a pre-med program. I figured I'd have time to ramp up my game later, once I got to college. I didn't have a clue. I mean, I was doing well enough at West Hempstead High School, wasn't I? And it wasn't like I was aiming for Harvard. As long as I didn't end up living at home and going to Hofstra (please, God) I'd be happy wherever I landed. I figured it'd be a cakewalk.

Giselle, on the other hand, was *definitely* aiming for Harvard. Or Yale. I think Columbia may have been her safe school. And that was probably true of every kid in her class. Me—I had to reach to get into Candler College, down in Atlanta. And it kicked my ass once I got there.

So Giselle was slumming in Uniondale with us South Shore, heavy-accent types, and she was having herself some fun. For the first time in a long time, she was outside the gaze of her classmates *and* her father, and she could relax. She started holding court after class at a bar that served kamikazes by the pitcher. Giselle's court was invitation only—and, of course, you had to have a fake ID. My dad was disappointed when I blew him off for the ride home, and I was, too, a little bit. We had just started having some really good and honest talks during those rides home, and I felt like I was finally starting to learn who he was. But I was being invited to hang out with royalty, and that was something new for me. I couldn't resist.

In retrospect…

Well, fuck retrospect. I did what I did.

Meanwhile, where *had* Giselle gone? I didn't know anything about her after high school. Had she gone to Harvard after all? If so, what was she doing in Atlanta? How long had she been here, just minutes away from me? Where was she going, that morning when she got mowed down—and why hadn't she been paying attention?

I had no idea if her daily life or routine would give me any leads or clues, but learning more about her would at least give me some answers that *I* wanted, case or no case. And I had to start somewhere.

5

The box from Palmer arrived at my office the next day. It was an old copier-paper box, filled to the top with bits and pieces of Giselle's life and death. I started pulling things out and piling them on a long table I used for evidence. There were photo albums, loose pictures, news articles about her accomplishments and, of course, several accounts of the accident from *Newsday*, the Long Island newspaper. It was obviously the family's memory box—all they had left of their only child.

All of a sudden, I felt the weight of this thing that had been handed to me—the responsibility Ted Palmer had entrusted to me. This was their little girl, gone. This was an open wound that needed healing. And I was supposed to be the one to close it. Me—the last person in the world they should have turned to.. And yet, here I was.

I put the items carefully back in the box and sat down at the table, unsure what to do. I had been looking forward to this moment—looking forward to digging into Giselle's life and

19

finding out what had become of her after high school. Now it all just seemed wrong. Dirty, somehow, and selfish.

I'm usually a pretty even-tempered guy—hard to ruffle, hard to excite. Bass player. Not for me the Pete Townsend windmill guitar, or the Roger Daltrey microphone swing. Even playing jazz, I'm less of a showman than some of the guys I play with. I keep an even keel. I maintain an even strain. I stay cool.

But when something gets to me, it gets to me bad. It can send me down into these spirals of depression and self-loathing that are really shitty. I usually hide from Susannah when they hit me, and go off by myself somewhere, because when I think about other people having to deal with me when I'm like that, it just makes me hate myself even more. Better to be alone.

Well, I was alone that morning, and I felt more alone and more wrong than I had felt in a long time. Wrong in my skin. Wrong about everything. I don't know if you get moods like this, but they can pollute your whole world. Suddenly you start questioning everything you've ever done, every decision you've ever made. Everything feels false and hypocritical, small and stupid. You're a fraud, a loser. Here I was, well past thirty, fucking around with music—still—and pretending to be this private investigator that I wasn't. It was bullshit—all fake and all unearned. Even the name of the business wasn't mine. It was a stupid little game. And now somebody *expected* something from me—something important. Someone actually believed that I knew what I was doing. Well, I didn't. Figure out why somebody *died*? When the police couldn't even figure it out? Again, I thought to myself that I was the *last* person they should have turned to.

But that made me stop and look up out of the little hole I was digging for myself. And I said: shit, what if I *was* the last person they could turn to? Was that the gig here? Had everyone else given up on them? I mean, if old Ted Palmer hadn't hung up on me—*me*, of all people—maybe it was because he couldn't afford to—beyond the money. Maybe there was just no one else who gave a damn.

And if that was the case…man. If that was the case, I had to do whatever I could, however stupid or meager my efforts might be. I had to try. I owed them that. I owed her.

So I took everything out of the box again and I started to read.

6

Here's what I learned out about Giselle's life and times, circa three years ago:

- Age 32
- BA in psychology, Harvard
- Harvard law school
- 2 years clerkship with federal judge, Atlanta
- 3 years Associate at Wilkins, Frewell, Byrd, Atlanta
- Married at age, 28 to Brett Jacobson, Atlanta
- Divorced at age 31, reason unknown
- At time of death, living in a Virginia Highlands apartment with roommate Catherine Socolow

So she'd been in Atlanta for years. Around the corner from me, basically. For years. Atlanta is not that big a town—especially not post-college, yuppie Atlanta. I stared at the photos of her, wondering if I had ever seen her on the street or in a bar somewhere or…Jesus…at one of the law firms where I had temped. But I hadn't. I couldn't have. She looked like Giselle. She looked like herself. I would have known her anywhere.

Here's what I learned about the accident:

- Occurred February 16, sometime between 5:30 and 6:00 AM
- Weather was grey, rainy, in the mid 30s
- Accident occurred on Monroe Drive, just above Virginia Avenue
- Placement of the body indicates that Giselle was travelling north on Monroe. She was hit by a car that was also traveling northward at a speed of at least 60 MPH (well over the speed limit).
- Witness (on bicycle) saw the body on the side of the road and called it in (6:15 AM). Did not see the accident itself, or any car in the area.
- Unlikely had occurred more than 15-20 minutes earlier, given sight lines at that intersection and the time of day

I started a list of questions to ask my friends at the police department, hoping enough time had passed that they wouldn't mind talking about a cold case.

1. Was any physical evidence found at the scene?
2. Since it was a rainy day, were any identifiable tire tracks left behind? If there were, can I see the photographs that were taken?
3. Will they give me the evidence file? Worth asking—not much to lose from their POV at this point.

4. Since it was a rainy day, do they have any idea whether the car hit Giselle, or Giselle hit the car? The "run" was the driver's fault, but what about the "hit"?

And I made a list for myself:

1. Interview the roommate? Why? What would she know? State of mind, maybe? If Giselle was at fault, maybe there was a reason she was distracted that morning.
2. Interview the ex-husband? Anything he could shed light on? No. You're just nosing around. On the other hand, state of mind. You never know what their relationship was.
3. Bad weather? Drunk driver? Broken streetlight?

Granted, nothing in these lists was rocket science. Not a Sherlock Holmes insight or Hercule Poirot question in the bunch. A high school kid could have come up with these gems after looking at the evidence. They were no-brainers. But sometimes the no-brainers are where you have to start.

Not that it really mattered. I could already tell where this was going to end. I was going to put in a week of useless leg-word and dumb questions, followed by a sheepish phone call to Ted Palmer. I would do the best I could, and it would be shit. It was a bad accident on a rainy day, and it involved a nobody from nowhere, who nobody cared about. God himself wouldn't remember what had happened on that dark street, three years ago. The best I could do—if I could do it—was give Ted a better picture of the woman Giselle was on that morning—where she was going, what she was doing, how she was feeling.

It wasn't much, but it was worth a few questions, at least.

7

I had a gig that night at a club up in Buckhead, which is a neighborhood I really hate. Buckhead is basically a long street in the north part of town lined with meat-market bars and chain restaurants. It attracts exactly the kinds of guys I hated from college—the preps and the frat boys—grown up just enough to have spending money and fancy toys. They all look exactly the same, dress exactly the same, drink whatever is hip, and dream about hooking up with some hot chick so they can brag about it to their clone friends the next day at work. I didn't like them in school and I don't like them now.

Unfortunately, there was one fairly decent jazz club in Buckhead, and they paid. So up to Buckhead we went.

"We" was my band, or what passed for a band, since the shape and personnel were always pretty fluid. That night there were four of us: Oticha on trumpet, Peter on keyboards, me on bass, and, tonight, Ray on drums. Oticha was the main attraction; the rest of us just provided fill and color for him.

Oticha has been one of the main attractions in my life for a few years now. He's a six foot, four inch, Proud Black Man, but African in no way beyond ancestry, despite the exotic name. He was born in Detroit with a perfectly normal, American name, but adopted the name Oticha when he gave up teaching high school and decided to dedicate his life to music. The name is Bullshit African—it's actually just a creative spelling of what his students used to yell across the room at him when they needed help, "Yo, Teacher!" He says he got so used to hearing it all day, he decided it must be his True Name.

Oticha is the main reason Susannah and I wound up living in Candler Park. He and his wife, Melanie, have been there for years, and we used to practice at his house before they started having babies—mostly because he alone was stable enough to own a house. So I knew the neighborhood pretty well, and I knew I'd have a friend nearby, which was good. Two friends, really—Melanie has always been kind and generous to me and Susannah. Of the four of us, she's the official grown up, being a registered nurse. She works crazy hours at St. Joseph Hospital, which is one of the things that made it okay for Oticha to stop teaching. He stays home with their two little girls. Melanie gets to work, and he gets to play music…as long as nobody is taking a nap.

Peter, the keyboardist, makes his money as a sound designer for local theatre companies and video production houses. He's a decent jazz pianist, but his real genius is in using his roomful of weird computer equipment to recreate every sound known to man, and a whole lot man has never heard. He's painfully skinny and has the kind of raccoon eyes that make you think he probably never sleeps. I've never seen him with a date of any kind—male, female, or cyborg. No woman I know would ever risk setting foot in his apartment, even if she were invited—and no woman I know of has ever been invited. I've been there, though, and aside from the roomful of computer and sound equipment, the most striking feature is the Captain's Bridge he's set up for himself in his living room. He has an enormous, plasma-screen TV, in front of which he's set up a huge recliner chair with custom-made drink holders, remote holders, and snack trays. There's usually an orange circle of Cheetos-dust on the carpet surrounding the chair, which is the only evidence I've ever seen that he eats. Pete is profoundly singular and single.

Ray is the one I know least well. We tend to cycle through drummers for some reason, like the Great Rock Bands of Yore. Except ours don't die; they're just too busy to hang with us consistently. I think Ray lives out by Stone Mountain. He's got the Stone Mountain look—pickup truck, mullet haircut, sleeveless T-shirts. Whenever he plays with us in town, he's always late. Thus I assume he lives some distance from town, in the redneckier outer boroughs. Of course, I could be totally wrong. He could live two streets down from me, for all I know, and just be the kind of guy who always shows up late.

I told you I'm not much of a detective.

So: off we went to Buckhead. I remember this particular gig very well, because I sucked. I was way too preoccupied with Giselle and the hopeless task I had agreed to. Instead of following the music, I kept going over the obvious and ordinary lists I had made that afternoon, trying to think of other angles, other lines of inquiry I could pursue, other ways in. Even though we were playing songs I'd played a hundred times, I fell behind again and again. The customers couldn't have cared less; they were barely listening and probably couldn't hear my bass-line over the white noise of bar talk—the office war stories, the TV show recaps, the sad pickup lines. But my boys knew. Pete and Ray kept shooting me ugly looks, wondering why they had to play in public with such a fuckup. Oticha just looked worried, wondering what was wrong.

We launched into "Imagination," the Chet Baker version. It's a great piece for Oticha, who's as warm and fluid a horn player as I've ever seen. I love playing with him because I get to be intuitive—I can leave the math behind and just follow the emotional line, working from a deeper, more subconscious place. I can stop thinking and just feel. This song, in particular, has always felt very haunting and melancholy to me, and on that night, I got hopelessly lost in it. I didn't even know what I was playing—it might have been completely off target and off key and wrong. I have no idea. All I could hear was the horn sighing the melody, and all I could think about was Giselle.

8

I fell in love with Giselle because she was beautiful and rich, with a rich, beautiful girl's power to bestow grace and blessing on anyone she smiled at. Why she smiled at me, I don't know. I may not have been crude or poor in any global sense, but in the limited life I knew on Long Island, I was definitely both. I was South Shore. I was heavy accent. I was not in her league. And as far as I could tell, I wasn't all that interesting. I mean, I played bass, sure, but other kids at her school must have been in lousy rock bands. I wanted to be a doctor, but...come on, she was from Great Neck. Were there any kids at her school who *didn't* want to be doctors?

Still, she invited me out to the bar with her other acolytes after SAT class, and I was grateful. I got to sit at the princess' table in the corner. Maybe I made her laugh. Maybe she thought she was being daring. I didn't know and I didn't really care—I was just glad to be there.

I didn't fit in with her crowd, but she was far from home and the conversation wasn't exactly challenging. None of us really knew each other—the only thing most of us shared was SAT prep, and that didn't give us much to talk about. So we talked about TV, and music, and drugs. It wasn't anything I couldn't navigate.

It helped that I could hold my liquor better than anyone else at the table. And since this bar served kamikazes by the pitcher, as I think I've said, this skill turned out to be a real asset. It's easy to seem smart and witty when everyone around you is sloppy and drunk.

Giselle was a lousy drunk. Or a glorious drunk, depending on your point of view. She pounded down whatever was in front of her, and within ten minutes she was hammered—on one drink. But there wasn't a mean bone in her body. She was everybody's friend and everybody was fascinating. She moved around the table, plopping down next to one person and then another, hanging her long arms wonderfully across the shoulders of whoever she was talking to.

Once I stopped going home with my dad after class, I found myself stranded at the bar every week. But since the class and the bar were both close to home, it was easy to catch a ride with one kid or another. I usually did the driving, at least to my own house. After that, they were on their own. Fortunately, no one ever got killed, or even arrested. Although, looking back, God knows they should have been.

Giselle gave up trying to drive herself home. She did it once and scared herself half to death. The next week, she called her father to come pick her up, and then had to return to Uniondale with him to rescue her car the following morning. After that, she just let her father drop her off, and then called a cab to take her home.

I was desperate to get more time with Giselle—alone time, where I wouldn't have to share the light and heat with a table full of people. And giving her a lift home seemed like the perfect opportunity. So I convinced my mother that I needed to borrow her car for SAT class. I told her I was nervous about having to beg rides from irresponsible drunk teenagers at the bar, and would feel much safer driving myself. She didn't put up a fight, and she never checked the odometer.

The next week, I gallantly offered to drive Giselle home, even though it was miles out of my way. She accepted, and from then on, I had half an hour of heaven every week—just me and Giselle, riding and talking, Bon Jovi on the radio and the windows rolled down to let the cold air wake us up from our boozy reverie.

There was nothing complicated or tense about our time together. I was in awe of her and in love with her, but I never dreamed of doing or saying anything about it. She was way too unreachable. She was my friend once a week, nothing more, and I was grateful for her friendship. And that kept things simple between us. Simple and light.

So crazy long ago.

Oticha's music seeped into my dream, and I heard the end of the lyric I knew so well, even though nobody was singing it that night:

> *Have you ever felt a gentle touch*
> *And then a kiss, and then and then*

Find it's only your imagination again?
Imagination is silly
You go around willy nilly
For example I go around wanting you
And yet I can't imagine that you want me too

And even though, back then, I never listened to music like that—didn't know music like that existed—the song inserted itself into my memory as though I was listening to it fifteen years ago on those long drives home after dropping off Giselle. I watched my dreamy young face behind the wheel and thought: weren't those happy dreams, and pure? Wasn't I content? I remember feeling happy, and lucky, and blessed back then. I don't think it was a lie. And look—there was no malice, no meanness in that face. No pent up…anything.

And yet, it all turned to shit so fast.

9

I drove back up to Buckhead the next morning, slightly hung-over, to harass a cop named Carter Wiggins for some information. Carter is a friend—I met him during my first year of investigative work, back when I was just running errands for Billy Barnes. He was a freshly minted cop from a small town in southern Georgia who was also running errands for his seniors, so the two of us went out for coffee from time to time, to gripe. We had nothing in common other than our flunkydom, but we got along and enjoyed each other's stories. Since then, he's been moving up through the ranks pretty steadily.

He had just recently transferred to the Zone 6 precinct covering Midtown and Buckhead. It was a much cushier assignment than the downtown precincts he had started in— a fratboy fight, a public bathroom sex thing in Piedmont Park, maybe a drug deal here or there. At worst, he had to deal with car thefts and vandalisms at the office buildings, the art center, or the High Museum. Last time I had talked to him, he couldn't decide if he was lucky or cursed. Half of him liked not being in danger, and the other half was bored.

He was a sergeant now, which meant he was supposed to be above bitching and griping—at least in earshot of his field officers. But he was also new to the precinct, which meant he didn't have to claim responsibility for anything that had happened pre-him. Unsolved hit-and-run accidents are pretty low-stakes anyway—they tend to fall in the "shit happens" category. Shit *does* happen, and the police can't be expected to stop it all, control it all, or have answers for it all. When I told Carter that this girl's father wanted some closure, he understood. He didn't think I'd find any, frankly, but he didn't mind digging through the evidence cabinet for me.

He found me an unoccupied interrogation room and went off to search for the box. He came back just a few minutes later, amazed that he had found it so easily.

"Damn, son, this is your lucky day." He grinned lopsidedly and plopped the box down on the table. "Case this old, I'd usually have to dig around for hours, but this old baby was sitting right there for me."

He left me with the box, saying he'd take me out to lunch if I was still digging through the stuff when he came back. He shut the door and left me—and there I was, with another box of Giselle.

This one was much worse than the first. Instead of prom photos and newspaper articles, I had forensic reports and autopsy photos—garish pictures of a naked, smashed body and a broken, once-beautiful face, detailed descriptions of how and where the car hit the body, how the body had likely been thrown into a nearby telephone pole, how the head-on impact with the pole was probably what killed her. Suddenly the room felt very hot and close, and my breakfast churned in my stomach. I got up from the table and left the room, looking for some fresher air. There was none to be found inside, and I didn't want to risk leaving the building with everything in the room. I splashed some cold water on my face and went back in. I turned the photos over and pushed them away, and concentrated on the other papers.

When Carter came back, I still had papers strewn across the table and a cold cup of coffee in my hand.

"Still at it?" he laughed.

"It's not funny."

"Why? What's the matter?" He sat down across from me.

"There's too much stuff here."

"Too much? Shit, I never heard no one complain about *that* before."

I pushed some photos and notes across to him. "Look at this. Here's a picture of some tire treads—clear as day. No mention of them in the newspapers. At least not New York papers I looked at."

He looked at them and shrugged. "We don't tell the papers everything."

"They're like six inches deep, though. That should have been a solid lead. And look at this—a hood ornament from a Mercedes. Found at the scene. No mention of it anywhere."

"Like I said—"

"Yeah, no, I get you. You don't tell the papers everything. But look at it."

Carter took the baggie holding the Mercedes insignia and turned it around in his hand. It had been a clear break, but there was a piece of transparent tape attached to the side of it. He held it up to the light and said, "Black paint?"

"Yeah. Car paint. The thing didn't just snap off—it got dragged across the hood of the car somehow. The forensics notes corroborate that. There's all sorts of evidence here."

"Yeah, maybe. Mercedes with a gash on the hood. Coulda been something."

"But nobody followed up on it."

"Maybe it didn't pan out."

"No. I'm saying nobody bothered to look."

That took him aback for a second. Then he said, "Well, hell, what do I know? I wasn't there. Maybe they could tell the doodad they found was years old and had nothing to do with the case. They'd grab and bag it anyway, but…"

"No," I said, cutting him off. "I thought that, too. But read." I handed him some notes taken by the first officer on the scene. As he read over them, I told him what he'd find there. "She was clutching the thing in her hand, Carter. When they found her body, the fucking thing was still in her fist. That's why the paint was still on it."

Carter finished reading the paper and then put it down, saying nothing.

"And nobody followed up. Or if they did, the notes never got saved. Look for yourself—there's no interview notes, no neighborhood canvassing. Nobody contacted body shops or garages. I mean, this is basic, obvious stuff, right? But there's nothing in here dated later than the day of the accident. Nothing."

Carter furrowed his brow and chewed his lip as he looked through the evidence. "Well, it's weird as shit, all right."

"Right? So what do you think? Do investigation notes ever just…not make it into the evidence box, or am I missing something?"

He looked up at me and cocked his head to the side. "You making an accusation?"

"No," I said, surprised. "Hell no. I'm just asking. What do you think the deal is?"

He put the papers down and pushed them back over to me. "This is a good precinct, Jordy. If this is all that's in the box, this is all there ever was. I mean, it's a hit-and-run, for Christ's sake. It ain't Watergate. Nobody's gonna go burning notes or shit."

"No, I know that. But, what is it, then? They just dropped the investigation?"

"I reckon."

"After a *day*?"

Carter sighted and rubbed his eyes. "Yeah, maybe. I don't know. It could happen. You want me to ask around? See who's still here from back then?"

"If you could. I want to be able to tell the father *some*thing."

"Yeah, all right," he said, standing up. "But *you're* buying lunch."

10

Those pictures of Giselle followed me wherever I went, all day— her broken body lying on a cold slab, face smashed, dead eyes staring up at me. The stare was an accusation. The stare said, "Do something!"

And what was I doing? I was still staring at the picture. Everything else had gone back into the box like it was supposed to. But I couldn't let go of that picture of Giselle's face, staring up at me. And I knew why. I *needed* that face to remind me what I was doing, and why it mattered.

So I took it.

Yes, I know—so much for the chain of possession and the integrity of evidence and all the rest of it. I was aware. I didn't care. I was on a mission.

And yet, I didn't want to do *too* much before I heard back from Carter. I didn't want to go flailing around, not knowing what the score really was. So I figured I could pass some time by talking to Giselle's old roommate, Catherine Socolow.

There was only one C. Socolow in the phone book, so I didn't have to engage in any fancy investigative work to leave her a message. But I was impatient, and I hate leaving long voice mail messages, especially with my hopelessly New York accent, so I went online and looked her up to see if I could find an email address. Sure enough, she had multiple mentions, along with a personal blog that included her work email address. I shot her the following message:

```
To: CSocolow@WFBesq.com

From: JGre75@yahoo.com

Subject: Giselle Palmer

Catherine,

I'm an old high school friend of Giselle's,
and I've only just learned about her
accident. I live in Atlanta, but I had no
idea she was even here. I can't believe it.
I'm in shock. I'd really appreciate it if I
could talk with you about what she was doing
here and what happened to her. I always
thought we'd get back in touch someday, and
I can't believe it's too late. I guess you
never know, right? My email address is up
top and my cell phone number is down below.
I'd love to hear from you, whichever way
you're more comfortable with. And thanks.

Jordan Greenblatt
```

I decided not to email her from my work account—not yet, anyway, not till I got to know her a little bit. Some people find the whole private investigator thing creepy. Some people can't believe they exist outside TV shows. And anyway, I *was* an old friend, and I *did* want to know about Giselle, so I wasn't lying. Technically.

I started thinking about heading home, drinking some beer, and playing some music. But every time I closed my eyes, her face was still staring at me, saying, "Do something!" So I looked over my notes and tried to think of something else to do.

The car seemed like a dead end after all these years. There was no way anybody in a body shop or a dealership was going to remember one scratched-up Mercedes from three years ago. The damage wouldn't have been that interesting or memorable, unless the car's owner came in a babbling, sobbing wreck. So what else was there to go on?

Nothing. Give up. Go home.

Which would have made perfect sense—but just as I reached to shut down my computer, this email message came through:

> To: JGre75@yahoo.com
>
> From: CSocolow@WFBesq.com
>
> Subject: Re: Giselle Palmer
>
> Jordan,
>
> Absolutely. Of course. And let's talk in person. It doesn't seem right to do this over email. Too creepy. We can meet today if you want, but my time is tight. I'm heading home in about half an hour for dinner etc., but I have to go back to the office right

after. There's a new coffee shop on North Highland, just above Ponce, at St. Louis or St. Charles--I can never remember which. I'll have my Cursed BlackBerry with me, so email me if you can make it.

Catherine

Jackpot.

11

It was decent of Socolow to meet with me in person, but she was no dummy. She picked a public place, one that was located where several different neighborhoods intersected. If I had been some kind of stalker, it would have been a challenge for me to figure out exactly where she lived. Of course, I *was* sort of a stalker— just not an evil one. Anyway, I already knew where she lived. Well, where she *had* lived, three years ago. It was in the police notes.

The coffee shop Socolow wanted to meet at was close to that old address, in Virginia Highlands, so I wondered whether Socolow was still living in the same place they had shared, or if it was just a favorite hangout. If she was still living there, that was interesting. Virginia Highlands was a yuppie neighborhood, but it tended to skew a little older and more married than a lot of other yuppie enclaves in town. So why would two single women with money have chosen to live among the marrieds-with-children? Had Giselle been living here during her marriage? Had she gotten the house or apartment in her divorce settlement, and needed a roommate to help with the mortgage? An interesting question. Well, interesting to me.

Of course, there was no guarantee Socolow was still living in this neighborhood. She might have moved to the slightly less yuppie developments to the east, on St. Louis or St. Charles Avenues. She might have moved south of Ponce de Leon Avenue, down to Little Five Points or my neighborhood of Candler Park—but I doubted it. Those neighborhoods were a bit artsier and seedier—not slummy, by any means—I mean, *I* lived there—but they had that kind of down-on-its-heels-nobility that lawyers and their ilk tended to avoid…unless they were buying fixer-uppers to gentrify neighborhoods and drive out people like me. And, again, they tended not to do that till they got married.

Just before my prey arrived, it dawned on me that I had, in the space of five minutes, made about a dozen wild and totally unsupported assumptions about not only her, but thousands of people across the city, which is truly terrible behavior for a detective, even a poseur like me. When you're only looking for what you *want* to see, or expect to see, you tend not to see what's really there.

Guess I had some work to do on my technique.

I got myself an overpriced coffee and sat with my back to the wall, watching the customers come and go. It was getting close to dinnertime, so the traffic was pretty light. That—and the business suit—made it easy for me to pick out Catherine Socolow when she arrived. She entered briskly and looked around, scanning the tables left, then right. I raised my cup and she spotted me. She strode over, plopped her briefcase down on the table, introduced herself, and marched over to the counter. There was nothing slow or relaxed about her. She was precise and efficient in everything she did. Clearly, there was no time to waste. I was drinking a small decaf, mostly to pass the time and give me an excuse for being there—but Socolow was ordering an extra-large cappuccino with an extra shot of espresso. This was a woman with a day's worth of work still in front of her.

There's something jagged and prickly about the professional women I've known in this town—especially the ones in their twenties and thirties. They all look the same—hair yanked back into severe buns, never a hair out of place. Sharp suits, sharp noses, thin, sharp, lips. When I worked as a temp, I always dreaded getting assigned to those women. I felt really bad about feeling that way, not wanting to be a sexist or anything, but there it was. I don't know what caused it—maybe the corporate atmosphere was just rigged against women and made them mean and crazy. Maybe they did it to themselves. Maybe the job just attracted people like that. I don't know. But they always had to be more gung-ho, more officious, more unforgiving than their male counterparts, and it was hell on their underlings.

I watched Attorney Socolow terrorize the barista and quietly thanked God for my Susannah, who was probably home by now, lazing on the wooden glider on our front porch with a beer in hand, watching the neighborhood go by. I closed my eyes and could see her there—bare feet on our faded green deck, gently pushing the swing back and forth; long, strawberry hair falling across her shoulders; freckles spreading as her large, warm mouth smiled at the kids biking by or the old men working in their gardens; everyone enjoying the break in the heat now that the summer sun had dipped down below the tree line. I watched her in my mind the same way I'd watched her across a hundred rooms over the years—with love, of course, but also with astonishment—amazement that someone could wear the world as easily as she wears old jeans, as though she belonged wherever she was and enjoyed being part of whatever was going on. That ease she has with people—and with the world—I've never understood it. I've always wanted it, but I've never known how to get it. It seems so alien, sometimes—so strange to me. I gaze upon her with awe.

My guest returned to the table, sat down, and yanked the band out of her hair. She ran her fingers through her loose hair, took a deep breath, and groaned slightly. She looked up at me through her hair with a smile. It made me laugh.

"Sorry," she said. "It takes a while for work to work itself out of my system. I don't think I'm quite there yet."

"Shame you have to go right back," I said.

"Tell me about it." She sipped her cappuccino, twisted her head from side to side as if to work out a sore neck, and then said, "So. You knew Giselle."

"A long time ago. Were you guys close?"

She smiled a thin smile— it was obviously a question she had been asked before. "Not really," she said. "She put up a notice in the break room on our floor, and I was the first person to grab it. I was living with an asshole at the time, and I needed to get out."

"Asshole of the male variety?" I asked, with a smile.

She smiled back. "It's true, one doesn't usually hear the word associated with women, does one?" I was beginning to revise my estimate of Catherine Socolow. She seemed very human, after all.

"Was Giselle in the same position? I mean, I heard she had been married. I wasn't sure what the timeline was."

"She was—that's right. They broke up and he left town. She ended up with the house and started going crazy in it. She didn't need the money as much the company."

"But you weren't close? Even after you moved in?"

"Sometimes it's just nice to hear another person knocking around the house, don't you think?"

"I do."

"So…you know, I can tell you *some* stuff, maybe, probably not everything you want to know. I never really heard the whole story of her breakup. I don't even know how long they were together. She was…she was pretty closed-up. I mean, we got along fine. We did stuff together, hung out sometimes. She was a nice person. But it wasn't like we shared anything deep. We were just roommates. I don't know. Maybe I'm being unfair. Probably it was at least 50% me. But it wasn't more than 50%."

I nodded and sipped my coffee for a minute, waiting to see if she was going to offer up anything else.

"I'm sorry," she said. "Was there anything you really wanted to know about? I mean, in particular? I don't want to yammer on and then run out of time."

"I don't know," I lied. "I guess not. The girl I knew…it was a long, long time ago. I guess I was always curious what kind of person she grew up into. And then…well, I just couldn't believe it when I heard."

"Yeah, it was pretty awful."

"Did they ever figure out what happened?"

"No, just that she got hit by a car. It was early, dark, a little rainy. Who knows? Maybe she skidded out into the street; maybe some guy skidded off. All I know is, the asshole didn't stop."

"You're assuming it was a guy?"

"Yeah, there I go again. That's terrible, isn't it? It could have been anybody. Businessman on his cell phone, drunk teenager coming home from a party, even a mom yelling at her kids in the back seat. I shouldn't presume."

"But you kind of think a mom would have stopped."

"You'd hope so."

We were both quiet for a few moments, slurping our beverages and trying not to look directly at each other.

"She was rollerblading, right?" I offered, wondering if I was pushing it. Here I had said I wanted to know about Giselle, and all I was asking about was the crime.

"Yeah. Stupid day for it, too. It was cold and rainy. I don't know why she did it."

"She wasn't going to work, right? I mean, she had a car."

"Yeah, of course. And I don't think..." She stopped for a minute, scrunched up her brow, and then shook her head. "Well, I don't know anymore. I was going to say, I didn't think she ever bladed to work. I figured she was just for exercise. What time did it happen? I can't remember."

"It was early."

"Yeah. Yeah, that's right. I think she was probably just heading up to the park for exercise."

"Is it something she did when she was really happy? Rollerblading? Or really unhappy? Or worried about something? Or was it just exercise?"

"I don't know. Like I said, she was kind of closed up. Anything I'd say would just be me, guessing. And it was a long time ago."

I nodded and said, "Sure." And we both felt the conversation flutter gently to the floor.

After a moment, I gave it another try. "Did they say…" I started, and then stopped. I tried again. "Did they know if it was…quick?"

"I think it must have been," she said quietly. "She was smashed up pretty bad."

That surprised me. "You saw her?"

"I had to. I was the one they called. To identify the body. I was…you know. I was the only one she had."

I watched her. There was something else she wanted to say. I didn't push. She looked down at her coffee, then over to her left, then down again. Then, softly, she said, "You know, I couldn't drive by that spot for, like, a year after. It was right on my way to work, but for a year—maybe longer—I went the long way around. Even now I hate that fucking intersection."

Silence again —the silence of endings. I tried to think of a way to save it—to put us back on track. I had blown it by focusing on the death, instead of the life. Was it too late now?

"Listen," she said at last. "I hate to do this, but I really do have to get back to work."

"Sure," I said. "I understand." Yep—too late.

"But you've got my email. If there are any other questions, or you want to meet again, or whatever, just, please—let me know. I don't mind at all."

"Thanks," I said, standing up to make her escape easier. "Sorry if I dredged up ugly stuff for you. But you've been really helpful."

She gathered her things, stood up, and said, "Really? I don't...I can't imagine how. But if you think so, then...good. Good." She wavered for a moment. "She was a good person, Giselle. I liked her a lot. She was a little...I don't know. Lost, maybe. But she was good to me. I'm sorry." She shook my hand, grimaced slightly, and left.

12

I felt like I should have been angrier with myself for not pushing things further, but I couldn't work up a good rage. After all, I had established contact. The lines of communication were open. And to be honest, I couldn't think what else I might have asked her. Unless I thought Giselle's death had been some kind of hideous, premeditated murder, there was nothing more to be learned from her life—nothing that pertained to the case, anyway. And I didn't think it was murder. She had been hit by a car coming up behind her, which meant that she had probably drifted or skidded out into the street. The presence of skid marks meant someone had tried to stop or swerve, most likely to avoid her.

I thought about what Catherine had said about the intersection, and then, suddenly, I realized that the scene of the crime was only a couple of miles away from where I was. Stupid of me not to have thought of it before, with all my useless pondering about where Giselle had lived, and where Catherine lived now. This had been the neighborhood—their neighborhood. And the intersection Catherine couldn't bear to drive through was just down the street.

So, while I had a little daylight left, I headed up to Virginia Avenue and drove the long, straight road down to where it ended at Monroe Drive. I pulled into the parking lot at Woody's Cheese Steaks and parked. Virginia Avenue wraps around Woody's as it dead-ends into Monroe—one lane allowing a left turn, to head south, and another lane allowing drivers to turn right and go north. Woody's sits in the middle. It's a ridiculous shack that should have been torn down years ago, but somehow it's managed to hang on while other restaurants have come and gone.

I got out of the car to look around. I'd been through this intersection ten thousand times, just like Catherine, but I had never really studied it before on foot. It struck me as being a strange place for a hit and run—mostly because cars didn't tend to move through very quickly. There were several street lights packed closely together, especially the one at Virginia and the next one, at 10th Street. There couldn't have been more than a couple hundred yards between them. And they were very busy lights. Lots of folks took this route to head up to Piedmont Park, or to the Midtown office buildings above it, or down to the arts center, south of here. Maybe not at dawn, but still.

I walked down to Monroe and tried to pick out the telephone pole that the police report had said she was thrown into. It was just north of the right turn lane that swooped sharply downhill around Woody's—maybe 30 or 40 feet. I turned around and looked back up at the steep drop of Virginia as it met Monroe. It wasn't hard to picture what had happened on that drizzly, February morning—with icy roads and the dim light of not-quite-daylight. She was coming down Virginia on her rollerblades, racing down to make the right turn on Monroe and then the quick left onto 10th to hit the park. Maybe she just hadn't seen the car coming, and flew straight out towards the left-turn lane. Maybe she had skidded on some ice and gotten further out into the street than she had intended. It could have happened to anyone.

But something wasn't sitting right. I looked at the telephone pole, and then back at the intersection. If she had come down the hill here…and gotten hit there…and the impact into the pole had been enough to do the damage I had seen in those photos, then… shit. The guy had to have been *flying*. On this road, at that time of day, in that kind of weather. Craziness. What the hell was he doing?

I didn't have an answer. What the guy had done was way wrong, but it was definitely an accident—a gruesome accident, made worse by the creep's refusal to stay and deal with it. But honestly—really honestly—don't you know at least one person—one regular, not-creepy person who could have done the same thing in the same awful situation? Especially if nobody was looking? After all, we're not heroes. Most of us are just barely decent citizens—and that's on a good day, without rain.

With this cheerful thought in mind, I drove home to my ramshackle house in Candler Park. Susannah was relaxing on the glider with a beer in her hand, exactly as I had imagined her. Sitting next to her was Nurse Melanie, nursing a beer. They waved as I walked up the path, and I waved back. Melanie raised her can in a salute and yelled, "Sam Spade!"

I grabbed a beer from the cooler by the front door and plopped down in a nearby wicker chair. "Just spade-friendly, sister," I said, in my best bad-Bogart.

Melanie laughed and said, "You're bad." Then she threw a pretzel at me.

"Just don't ask him how it went," said Susannah. "He hates it when you ask him how it went."

"Yeah? Why does he hate it when you ask him how it went?"

"Because he thinks he's a phony."

"I already know he's a phony," said Melanie. "Doesn't mean the man can't hold a polite conversation."

"Good point," said Susannah.

"I *am* sitting here, you know," I said.

"True that," said Melanie. "So how'd it go?"

"Terrible. I'm a complete phony."

Susannah stood up and stretched. "Well, now that we got that settled, who wants a shot of tequila?"

I raised my hand. Melanie did the same. Susannah drifted inside, running her fingers through my hair en route.

Susannah is a big fan of tequila. Any gathering of more than two people is an occasion to break it out. When all the other kids in Macon were acquiring a taste for whiskey or rum or Southern Comfort, all mixed with Diet Coke, Susannah decided to strike out on her own and become a connoisseur of tequila.

"Seriously," said Melanie. "How *is* it going? Melvin said you were a mess last night." Melvin was Oticha's secret identity—the given name he had tried to give away. Only Melanie and Oticha's mother still used it. Well, that's not true—*I* used it, from time to time, when I wanted to piss him off.

"He's right," I said. "My head was not in the game."

"Susie said the girl's someone you knew?"

I nodded. "A long time ago."

"That's gotta make it hard."

"That's one of the things, yeah." A pause. Then, "So how's tricks at the hospital?"

"He said, changing the subject."

"Exactly."

"Tricks is fine. You know how it is—every day is different, so every day's kind of the same. Least there's always something interesting going on."

Susannah reappeared bearing a tray with a bottle and some shot glasses. "Dinner is served," she said with a flourish.

"I shouldn't," said Melanie.

Susannah poured out the first shot for her and said, "You always say you shouldn't."

"I know. It's sad. Gimme." She took the glass and knocked down the shot like a pro.

"Something at work you want to forget about?" I asked.

"Always," she said simply. "It's a hospital—you know. Somebody always dying…"

"Somebody always being born," I offered.

"Damn babies," she snorted. "Like that makes it better."

"Very maternal," I said, and drank my own shot.

Melanie sat a little straighter and shot me a Look. "Motherfucker," she informed me, "I birthed three babies of my own. What you ever done?"

I held up my hands in surrender. Susannah laughed and said, "You ever notice Mel's language gets all ghetto, the minute she starts drinking?"

"It's not the drinking," I said. "She just uses it to score points off us. Because all I've got to fight back with is loudmouth Jew."

"Y'all think babies are the answer to life's problems or something," Melanie continued, relaxing back into the glider and wisely ignoring me, "like they're waiting to be found at the end or the rainbow, living with the leprechauns or something."

"*I* never said that," Susannah protested.

"All y'all. All y'all civilians. Well let me tell you something. You have a couple of your own damn kids, then go work in a hospital a couple of years, I tell you what—the bloom be *off* that rose."

"Amen," I said, and we all had another drink.

"Well," said Susannah, after a decent interval, "I'll tell *you* what. I'll take babies over mamas any day. Especially crazy *old* mamas like mine."

"Mm *hm*," said Melanie in sympathy. "That's what I'm saying, girl."

"Lame desk job all day, then go visit with that crazy woman, do all her shopping…"

"Well, just imagine if that crazy woman *was* your job. I get it on both sides, honey. Babies coming, old folks dying, and no one but me in the middle to help."

I made a cartoony kind of coughing noise to insert myself into the conversation, and managed a, "Well, I think…" before getting cut off by a howling Melanie, who said, "You? You want to say something, go get yourself a job."

"Nah," I said, standing up and brushing the pretzel dust off myself. "I'll go watch your husband do *his* job."

And with that, I wandered off into the evening, in search of my friend.

13

"Her mother thinks cottage cheese looks like brains," I said. "And it freaks her out."

"Mm hmm," said Oticha, cleaning up the last of the toys that had been strewn across his living room. "They *do*, you know."

"I know," I said.

"So, if she can't stand cottage cheese—'

"I think it's pretty much all she gets to eat."

"Ah. So it's eat brains or starve? See, *now* you got a problem."

"I guess."

"My daddy just got *nice* to folks when he started to fade. Gave everyone the willies."

"Why?" I asked. "What's wrong with being nice?"

"Nothing *wrong* with it," he said, flopping down on his couch. "It just wasn't nothing the man had ever been before. It was disconcerting."

"I don't know what's bugging her about all this, exactly. She only sees her mom a couple of times a week. But ever since she brought her up here from Macon, the old lady's been driving her crazy."

"Girl needs another hobby. I mean, *another* other hobby—besides taking care of your sorry ass."

"Taking care of her mother isn't a hobby."

"It ain't no recreation, that's for sure," he said. He reached for his horn, but paused with the mouthpiece at his lips for a moment. He shook his head, closed his eyes, and said "Parents," in a wise and meaningful tone of voice.

This is what I both love and hate about Oticha—he can say absolutely regular, stupid shit, and make it sound wise and sagely. I don't know how he does it—if it's his height, or his graying beard, or his totally inauthentic dashiki-and-batik wear, but somehow he gets away with it.

"It's a black thing," he said. Then he caught the look on my face, laughed, and said, "Read you like a book, man. Always could." And with that, he popped the mute into his trumpet and started to play. His kids were asleep, so he played quietly—a gentle, jazzy version of "Father and Son" that I think he was inventing on the spot.

And all of a sudden, something in my tequila-sodden brain finally clicked, and I realized where I could get the help I needed.

14

My parents came down to Atlanta during my tour of duty at Candler College. My father took a teaching job at the law school, and he's been there ever since.

By the way, if you've never heard of Candler College, there's an excellent reason. It doesn't exist. I had to make up a pseudonym, because my father is convinced they're going to sue me for libel, even though I wasn't planning on saying anything nasty about them.

Not yet, anyway.

Anyway. My folks moved down here during my sophomore year, after I had bottomed out of pre-med and been forced to re-align my dreams to aim for the more realistic goal of rock stardom. If I had run away to the South to escape my family (and I had, just a tiny bit), suddenly I was screwed, because there they were—in my back yard, in a house that was too big for the two of them ("We want you to have a room in case, you know—in case the Music Thing doesn't work out"). They enjoyed the expanded buying power that life in Atlanta had afforded them, and they made it clear that they weren't going back. So I was stuck with them.

Of course, if I had ever held out the option of *fleeing* the South and returning home to the bosom of Long Island (such as it was), I was equally screwed, because now there was no place to go back to. If I ended up wanting to move north after college, I was going to have to do so alone.

Which I didn't do. Because Atlanta is a very seductive town. I don't mean that in the way, say, New Orleans or San Francisco or…I don't know, Paris would be seductive. Because Atlanta is not any of those places. There's nothing sexy or enchanting about the place. I mean, it doesn't even have a river worth speaking of. It's hard to work up a sense of Romance without a river or lake or oceanfront you can stroll along. But it's *easy*. It's comfortable. You can get by without working too hard, if you travel in the right orbit. I'm sure not everybody who lives there feels that way. I'm sure the kids I knew at Candler who came to Atlanta from Paducah, Kentucky, or Titusville, Florida, or wherever, found Atlanta to be tense and tough and unfriendly. But I came to Atlanta from New York—and let me tell you, compared to *that* city, Atlanta is a lazy summer day. Especially during the lazy summer days.

Now, years later, my dad was a senior professor at the law school, specializing in evidence and trial practice. He still lived in the same house in midtown, even though my mother had died a few years earlier, leaving him alone in a place that had already been too big for two—a place I should have visited more often than I did.

When I was a kid, I loved helping my father set up evidence displays for his classes—varieties of fake blood stains to fool the grad students, mug shots of my friends to confuse the class when identifying mock perpetrators. And sometimes he read student exam papers aloud to us at night, especially if they were terrible. I was very used to his world—which may be why working as an investigator didn't seem like such a weird stretch for me.

My point being, it was kind of incredible that it had taken me so long to think of going to see him on this, my very first try at solving an actual crime. Which is what I was trying to say about Oticha: one word in his deep, sagely voice, and the Blindingly Obvious gets through my thick skull.

The old man was out when I arrived, so I sat down in his cluttered office and waited for him. His desk was littered with the toys and puzzles that people had given him over the years—from interlocking rings to magnetic ducking birds to those hanging rows of ball bearings that click-clack against each other until you want to scream. The toys always gave his visitors something to do with their hands while waiting for him—or, more accurately—something to do while being grilled and examined by him. My father had a Stern Countenance that tended to scare the hell out of the poor first-year students who were forced to come see him. They tended not to notice the cartoons posted on his door, or the jokey posters taped to the walls between his overstuffed bookshelves. All his poor, terrified puppies could see was his three-piece suit, his steel-grey hair, and his woolly-caterpillar eyebrows. And all they could hear was that gravelly voice saying things like, "*Mister* Beauregard, we are here to learn and love the majesty of the law—*not* to grub for grades." Little did they know that he had learned most of his shtick from watching John Houseman on "The Paper Chase."

I heard him shuffling down the hall and turned around to face the door as he came in. He beamed when he saw me sitting there, which made me feel happy and guilt-ridden at the same time… standard operating procedure for us Children of the Tribe. The fact is, I don't see him very often. I don't like to trawl around the campus; it always makes me feel old and useless, reminding me of all the things I haven't accomplished. More often, we meet him and his girlfriend, Amina, for coffee or dinner somewhere, before they go out to a show or a concert— one of the many Cultural Events they fill their lives with, which we generally can't afford.

I stood up for the obligatory awkward hug, and then we both sat down and got down to business.

"I've been asked to look into a hit-and-run accident, but there's not a hell of a lot of evidence, and I'm not sure what to do with what's there," I said

"Excellent," he said. "Let's see what you've got."

I laid out the story for him and let him sit with the details for a few minutes.

"Not a hell of a lot? You're being generous," he said finally. "There's nothing."

"Well, there's the hood ornament. I mean, it's not much, but— "

"It's crap," he said definitively. "What does it tell you? That a black Mercedes hit that girl that morning? Or that it hit something else a day or week before, and it ended up lying on the ground near where she fell?"

That girl. He didn't recognize the name, and I didn't feel like reminding him. Better to keep him purely objective.

"No, she was holding onto it when they found her. It's connected." I looked to see if there was a reaction, but I saw nothing. "So that's not *nothing*, right? I mean, it's not much, but…" I let it trail off, hoping he'd jump in.

He did. "Three years ago it might have been Not Much. Now I'd have to say it's Nothing." He lifted the Xeroxes I had made and let them sift through his fingers like sand. "Perhaps if it had been lime green paint, you'd have something to play with. But black? Do you have any idea how many black Mercedes there are in Atlanta? Or were, three years ago?"

"Not a clue."

"Nor I, but I wouldn't want to ask. And how many have lost their hood ornaments over the years?

"Not a clue."

"Nor I. And let's not forget that our mystery man knew he had done something terrible. Do you think it likely he took the car straight to the dealership for repair?

"Not likely."

"Not likely, indeed. Which leaves us with the following options: A) He had the car repaired out of state or at some hole-in-the-wall body shop unlikely to be interviewed by detectives. B) He continued driving the car as it was, hoping for the best. Perhaps he repaired it years later. Perhaps he sold it unrepaired—again, years later. Perhaps it's still on the road, as is. C) He hid the car in his garage until the news reports—if there were any—

died down, perhaps using a second car or renting a car. Or perhaps he dumped it in a ravine somewhere. We'll never know. Which leaves you…where?"

I slumped in my seat, defeated.

"I'm sorry, Jordan, but there are usually good reasons why cases like this don't get solved. Evidence that's as common as grains of sand is no evidence at all. I mean, good lord, Judge Harper snapped one of these things off *my* car years ago, in our garage. You could spend your life chasing after hood ornaments."

I sighed. "You know, you'd make this much easier for me if you'd just confess."

He laughed and stood up. "Not even for you, dear boy."

We repeated the awkward hug that had started our conversation, but as we broke away, he grabbed my face in his hands and looked at me intently.

"I remember her name, Jordan," he said seriously. "If it's a job, do the job and let it go. If it's not a job, well…just let it go."

I nodded, and whispered, "It's a job. Her dad found me. Total accident."

"Hmm," he said, never one to believe in accidents. "If you could do everything for him, you'd be doing very little. Just keep that in mind."

"Sure," I said.

He patted my cheek and let me go. "You're coming up for Rosh Hashanah," he said—half a question and half a command.

"Of course. Right after temple."

He rolled his eyes at the idea of me—or him—attending services of any kind. Then he smiled and waved, and I left.

15

Okay, so, let's say the old man was right. There usually *are* good reasons why cases like this don't get solved. So that meant…what? It was just a dumb accident, and the asshole who drove away was just that—an ordinary, scared asshole? Yep, that's probably what it was. It was what I had assumed from day one—maybe what I was hoping for. And if that was the truth, I was done, and it was time to make my call and wrap this up.

But something was bothering me. Was it *really* time to make the call? I mean, what if it *was* a murder? I know, I know, it was a million-to-one shot, but what if? What if someone had followed Giselle from home on that rainy morning, mowed her down, and then covered up his tracks? Wasn't that *possible*? And if it was, didn't I need to at least consider it, if only to rule it out and tie things up correctly?

Of course, if I couldn't rule it out—if something really nasty was going on here, I was going to be in serious shit, because I was going to be in way over my head. But one thing at a time, right?   No sense panicking yet.

So fine, I said to myself. Let's play with the idea and see where it leads. If it was a murder, then Giselle had an enemy. Hard to believe (based on the girl I had known at 17), but…fine. People change. Things happen. And she *was* working in the legal system, where plenty of unsavory characters tend to lurk. I'd seen plenty of lousy television in my time, and God knows, there were plenty of pretty young women who found themselves in possession of Dangerous Information, and so on. It could happen.

I made an appointment to stop by her old firm the next day, up in midtown. The building was one of those shiny, glass-covered temples to money, with lots of covered parking and a couple of restaurants on the ground floor, to make sure the worker bees didn't stray too far from the hive.

The firm of Wilkins, Frewell, Byrd had the three top floors in the building, with secure elevators and a grand, circular staircase at the reception level. I left word with the receptionist for Catherine Socolow, just to be friendly and let her know I was in the building. Then I was led down the hall to the small office of one Teddy Spival. Teddy looked like he was about 15 years old, but he was probably more like 25. He was a paralegal, or an office manager, or something like that—I didn't quite catch it. But he had been dispatched to handle me, so I figured he was probably pretty low on the totem pole.

"So this is about the associate that got run over?" He asked eagerly, motioning for me to sit down.

"Run down," I said. "Yes. Three years go."

"I wasn't here then, but I've heard all about it. I think you can see where it happened from some of the offices here. Or maybe upstairs."

"Mm. I bet you can." I hated this kid already.

"So…they told me you wanted to see Ms. Palmer's case files?"

"That's right," I said. "I'm trying to see if she had any enemies, or if maybe she had angered somebody. Things like that."

"Okay," he said. "But, so, here's the thing. I know it was three years ago and all, but a lot of the stuff she was working on is still ongoing. I mean, they're ongoing clients. So her notes are, like, protected stuff. Attorney-client privilege. So there's not much I'm really allowed to show you."

"Right," I said. "How about just a list of clients or cases? Am I allowed to see *who* she was working for, at least?"

"Yeah," he said. "I can show you that. I printed it up for you."

He passed some stapled sheets of paper over to me, and I glanced down the list of names. There were about 12 major clients listed, all of them local or regional companies. Some large, some small. Under each name, he had listed some of the issues or tasks that Giselle—and, presumably, a small army of other associates—had performed for those companies. They were all very ordinary and boring legal tasks. About three times on the list, though, Spival had written "confidential" instead of a summary.

"Teddy," I asked. "Can you tell me anything about these confidential cases you've got listed here? Even just a hint what they were about?"

"Well, no. Not really. If I could have, I would have. But I don't know if I'd even call them 'cases,' really. I mean, they're just like the other things you see there—writing up contacts, stuff like that. They just involve names I had to leave out, or something because the deal is still open."

"Hm," I said, looking back up and down the list. "Okay. So we can conclude from this list that the life of an associate is incredibly boring."

A short, sharp laugh erupted out of his mouth, and he threw his hands up to cover it, as if to pull the surprising noise back into himself. "Sorry," he said. "But yeah, pretty much. I don't think *any*body around here does anything real controversial. It's a pretty conservative, old firm. But if they did, it'd be the partners that handled it, not the associates. And, I mean, even if the associates were even working on something controversial, they probably wouldn't know what it was about. You know? They're, like, super task-oriented. Not exactly big-picture. But anyway, like I said, they weren't. Working on anything mysterious, I mean. Even the Christmas parties here are boring."

"Got it. So if someone wanted to make a John Grisham movie about this law firm…"

"Oh, God," he said, laughing again. "No. Never happen."

I wasn't sure what I had been hoping for…if "hoping" is really the right word. Maybe some kind of big class action suit, or a pro bono death penalty case or…well, yes, basically a John

Grisham movie. But there was nothing like that here. Unless the contract for setting up a new Chik-Fil-A was something to kill over, I was coming up empty.

I stopped by the reception desk to see if Catherine Socolow had left a message for me. She hadn't. So I headed out, not wanting to spend any more time in those marbled hallways than I had to.

Next stop: my own, less glamorous office, to look up the ex-husband. If it wasn't a work-related murder, then perhaps it was personal. My game-plan: to be as aggressive as possible. Let the guy know it was an investigator calling. Make him sweat. Interrogation is like basketball—or, anyway, it's like the "bunch of out-of-shape guys at the gym" game that I play. You want to get past someone, you've got to push them off their game, throw their usual routines out of whack. Any advantage they might have, you've got to scuttle it fast if you want to have any chance. Because, deep down, you probably don't have any other advantage.

So: hello, Brett Jacobsen. Let's talk about your dead ex-wife. Because maybe I think you killed her, and maybe you ought to be worried about it. Boom. If I rattled him enough, I might learn something interesting.

"Seriously? After all this time?" the voice on the phone was measured, in control, and very professional. It was also very handsome, and not at all nasal. This voice had six-pack abs. I hated him.

"Well, let's just say we've got to keep all possibilities open," I said. "We've got to consider everything." Yeah. Me and my crack staff.

"I thought the police were fairly certain—"

"They were. But now...look, all I can say is that certain parties aren't quite so certain anymore." That was pretty good, I thought—insinuate a ton of things but commit to nothing. After all, I didn't have a clue who this guy was, or who he knew.

"So, if it wouldn't be too much trouble, Mr. Jacobsen, could I ask you a few questions? Five, ten minutes, tops?"

"Of course."

"Did Giselle have any enemies you knew of? Anyone particularly angry with her? Maybe someone who came up in front of her judge, and felt he wasn't treated right?"

"Well, I wouldn't know about that. I mean, there's no one I ever heard of when we were together. But we'd been divorced over a year when this happened."

"Of course. And what was the cause of the divorce, if you don't mind my asking? I mean, was it...amicable?"

He was quiet for a moment. "It was amicable as far as *she* was concerned," he said. "She got what she wanted."

"Meaning...money?"

"No, Mr. Barnes. She didn't want money. She just wanted out."

Hm.

"And you? What did you want?"

"I wanted her to be happy. And if she thought she could be happy… happier…apart, then that's what she needed to do. I tried to get her to go to counseling with me, but…"

"But what?"

"She said to me, 'You go to counseling to save something, don't you? And I don't want to save this.' So…there it was."

I tried to imagine what it must have felt like to hear your wife say that to your face. It must have been a serious kick in the stomach, even for Mr. Six-Pack.

"And *was* she was happier, afterwards?" I asked. "As far as you know? We're trying to determine mental state. At the time of the accident. You know."

"No, she wasn't any happier. She got along all right. She did her job, had her friends, rode her bike, bladed in the park and all that. I mean, she wasn't sitting in a dark room and crying. We had mutual friends, so I heard how she was doing. But Giselle was Giselle. The stuff she wanted to get away from wasn't me. It was her."

Now it was my turn to be silent. I was having a hard time working up the words. "What was it about her, do you think, that kept her from being happy?"

"I don't know," he said simply. "I never knew." We were both quiet for a moment, and then he said, "You were asking about enemies, weren't you? People who might have wanted to hurt Giselle?"

"That's right," I said, happy to get back on track.

"I honestly can't think of anyone. But again, I wasn't part of her life anymore when she was killed. So…I'm sure there's a lot I don't know."

"I totally understand. Maybe I can talk to the judge she clerked for."

"Actually, I think he died last year. He was an old guy. I'm pretty sure I read about it in the paper. Anyway…"

Ah, the accursed "anyway." You can always tell your conversation is on life support when someone throws an "anyway" at you. But I could hardly blame him. The guy wanted to get off the phone and get back to work, and why not? This couldn't have been pleasant for him. But there was something nagging at me. "One more thing, if you don't mind," I said. "Did the police ever interview you, after she was killed? I didn't see any record of it in the file."

"No," he said. "There was a message on my voice mail from some detective. I must have been in a meeting or something. I don't remember. Anyway, by the time I called back, they told me they didn't need me anymore."

There are times when you know you're hearing or seeing something important, and it just hits your nerve endings. You know what I mean? Like you just got plugged in to an electrical outlet. Low voltage, I'm talking about. Not electrocution or anything—just kind of a low hum running through you. A tingle. I had that feeling, right then.

"How much time are you talking about here?" I asked. "I mean, how long did it take you to call back, after the message they left you?"

"I don't know," he said. "Two hours? Three? It was definitely the same day."

I thanked him and we hung up. I didn't want to keep talking when my whole spine was tingling like that. I wanted to think. None of this was making sense. The girl's killed in the morning and by lunchtime the police are ready to give up? I knew there weren't any notes after the first day, but I had assumed the cops had put in a full eight hours on that day. This was insane. You can't know enough to know you're on a dead-end case after just a couple of hours.

I wanted to call Carter and see what he thought about all of this, but as soon as I got out to my car, I found three messages on my cell phone from him, all left within ten minutes of each other. I cursed myself and punched in his number as I pulled out of the parking lot. He wasn't in.

I'm hopeless about my cell phone. I forget to turn it on for days; I leave it in restaurants or in my car; sometimes I forget I even have one. It didn't used to matter—I was either sitting in my little office near a phone, or sitting at home, also near a phone. Or I was on a stakeout, spying on some philandering dickhead, in which case I couldn't take calls anyway. But now I was in a whole different deal. I realized I was going to have to make myself more available.

I decided to head up to Buckhead to see if I could catch up with my friend in person. Three calls in ten minutes from a busy police sergeant—that was something worth paying attention to. I parked by the precinct and walked towards the building, but before I even reached the door, the phone started ringing. It was Carter.

"Jesus," he hissed at me. "Are you fucking insane, coming up here?"

"What's the matter?" I asked.

"Never mind. Just…not on a cell phone. Go back to your car." He hung up and left me standing there. Dutifully, and because I didn't know what else to do, I went back to the parking lot and stood by my car. Two minutes later, I spied him leaving the precinct. I figured it was probably not a good idea to wave at him. He noticed me and did all he could not to show it. He went straight to his own car and drove away—slowly. Okay, I thought—I'm not James Bond, but I get the message. I pulled out and followed him.

Ten minutes later, he pulled into a gas station. I pulled in alongside him in the opposite direction, as I'd seen cops do for years—so that we could talk to each other through our driver's side windows.

"Okay, Starsky," I said. "What's up?"

"What's up is, I shouldn't have shown you that fucking file," he said, clearly upset.

"Why not?"

"I don't know. It's just bad news, that's all, and I'm in a world of shit for showing it to you. Captain saw the damn thing on my desk and chewed me out good. Like it was bad juju the thing was even in our building. Now it's locked up downtown somewhere."

I didn't like the way this was going. "Why would they yell at *you*? It's not your fault—"

"I don't know, man. I didn't think the fucking thing was a big deal, but I guess maybe it is. Or it was. I wasn't around back then— maybe it was just bad publicity and they don't want nobody bringing it back to life. Maybe somebody got fired, or lost a promotion, or something. All I know is, nobody wants to talk about it. And they ain't so crazy about me giving special treatment to some PI they never heard of."

"Special treatment…come on."

He just shrugged.

"Carter…"

He looked away, pretending to study something beyond me.

"Come on—the box had been sitting up there on that shelf for years. In plain sight, you said."

"Don't matter. Whatever the fuck it is, I crossed some line giving it to you. Wish I knew what the line was. But I sure as shit ain't gonna ask about it."

I sat with all of this for a moment, trying to make it make sense. But I couldn't. "Okay, first of all, if somebody got fired for this, they're not going to get *more* fired for it now. Right? They're not even there at the precinct anymore. And if they just got chewed out, embarrassed, I mean…whatever happened, how much more damage could it do to anyone *now*?"

"I don't know and I don't care," my friend said. "Somebody fucking hates this case, that's all I know. It's a miracle the damn box was still in the building. Only reason I can figure is, it got overlooked somehow—pushed outta sight and forgot."

He looked at me for a minute, trying to read my expression.

"So you'll drop it, right? Shut it down? Tell the daddy ain't nothing there?"

I shrugged. "There *is* nothing there."

"That's what I'm saying. So you'll tell him that, and leave it alone?"

I stared at him. "You say leave it alone like there's something else I could do, like there's really something there."

"Jordy…fucking Christ." He paused. "I don't know what there is. Just leave it alone. It ain't worth it."

"What if it is, though?" I offered.

He sighed. "It can't hardly be worth whatever little thing you might end up finding."

"What if it's not a little thing?" I asked. "What if I told you the precinct dropped the case on the same day she was killed. Not even a day after, like I thought. The same day."

He groaned. "Jesus Fuck, Jordy. You think this is *Law and Order* or some shit? You think we got detectives studying on every goddamn cat gets up a tree? She got hit by a car on a rainy day. It ain't rocket science."

I nodded, but didn't say anything.

"Look, it's ancient history, and it ain't yours. Or mine. We got nothing at stake here. So drop it, all right? Forget about it, and go do something productive."

"Yeah, yeah. Sure," I said. "Of course."

He calmed down a bit. "Thanks, buddy," he said. "I'll talk to you later." And he drove off.

16

"You haven't said a word all night," Susannah said to me. It was true.

"I can't get my head out of this thing," I muttered. "It's driving me crazy."

We were outside on the porch glider, as usual, trying to catch any breeze that might be in the neighborhood. She patted her lap and I turned, laying my head down on her and swinging my legs over the side of the swing. She stroked my hair and said, "Tell mama."

"I've got nothing," I said. "Nothing. It's a dead case with no leads and nowhere to go. I mean, I don't know what the fuck I'm doing, but I have a feeling even if I *did*, I'd have nothing. I'm two seconds away from calling the father, telling him Sorry, and sending him back his check. Which is exactly what I should do. Except…"

"Except what?"

"All of a sudden, I'm getting threats to drop the case."

"Threats? Who threatened you?"

"Well, all right, not threats. Warnings. But there's all this fear, all of a sudden, like I'm sitting on a time bomb. But all I've got is the same shit *they've* had for three years."

"They're afraid you're going to find a mistake?"

"Not likely, right? I mean, look at me." I lay there in her lap for a moment and thought about the possibility. "But what if I did? I mean, what if I found some terrible stupid gaffe someone made. Some blatant procedural error in a three-year-old accident investigation. Or they dropped it too soon, gave up on it and didn't give a shit, and now it looks bad. Who gives a shit, right?"

"Yeah."

"I mean, what could I possibly be sitting on that anyone would care so much, they'd scare their own sergeant into warning me off?"

"I don't know, baby."

"It's just a dead girl, you know what I mean? What, did the fucking *mayor* run her down?"

Susannah stopped stroking my hair and sat very still. I sat up and looked at her.

"Jordy…" she whispered.

I didn't say anything.

"Jordy, if that's true…"

"It's not true. That's craziness."

"Yeah. But if it *is*…"

"It's not. The mayor? Come on." I was protesting, but already I was there, believing it.

"Not the mayor, then," she said. "But somebody. Somebody important enough to not want anyone nosing around in the case. That's possible, isn't it?"

Possible? Hell, it was more than possible: it was obvious. If it had been anything else, Carter wouldn't have been so freaked out. He was just a country kid, after all, playing grown-up in the big city. A more sophisticated cop wouldn't have shown his hand, wouldn't have threatened me at all—would have talked me out of the case without ever raising my antenna to trouble. But Carter was scared about something… which meant there was something to be scared about, even if he didn't know what it was.

"You've got to drop this, baby. I mean it. I love you, but this…this is way bigger than you can handle."

I nodded. I agreed with her. I had no illusions about my abilities. None. This *was* bigger than I could handle. I was out of my league. I told her I would drop it, and she calmed down. And we went inside and let Normal Life wash back over us: a nice dinner, some boring television, and some very gratifying sex that I'm not going to tell you about.

But I wasn't back in Normal Life, really, and I didn't know how to get there. Because it wasn't just a dead girl; it was Giselle. That was the part I couldn't talk to Susannah about, and it was the part that wouldn't let me let go. She was staring up at me

from that slab in the morgue—still—saying, "Do something!"
Every time I closed my eyes, she was there, begging me. Asking
for something. Justice, maybe. From whoever had done that
thing to her. And from everyone else who had done things to
her, in all the years before she was killed. All those things that
had left her sad and closed-up and unhappy. Some kind of
justice—some kind of accounting. She was calling out, and no
one was there to hear her anymore. No one but me.

So what did it matter if the asshole who killed her was
important? Giselle was important, too.

17

All right. So, thanks to Carter Wiggins, I had a lead. Well, not a lead—an assumption. But it was a hell of a lot more than I had had before.

The assumption: somebody politically connected in town had committed the hit-and-run, and had leaned on the police to drop the case three years ago. If that was true, then the hood ornament and/or the tire treads might be important. They were in the evidence file, but no one had talked about them or done anything about to follow up on them. I had noticed the omission, but I hadn't thought about it being a deliberate omission until now.

But if this was tampering, where was it coming from? Clearly, it was outside the department. If it had been a cop, the evidence would have disappeared. But the file was complete, and it was sitting there on a shelf—not even shipped downtown to a warehouse. So whatever was scary about the case, it was scary to someone *outside*. To the cops, it meant nothing once they dropped the case. They stuck the box up on a shelf, let the thing wither and die, and went on to other cases.

So it was a chore to them—something they were told to do, and they did it. Either they didn't think it was as threatening or damaging as the perpetrator did, or they didn't think the perpetrator was someone worth protecting all *that* much. Roll your eyes, joke with your colleagues, bury the case—but don't go crazy about it. Forget it; move on.

Now, if the culprit was somebody politically connected in town, the search for a black Mercedes might not be so difficult. There were probably a lot out there—but it might be a much smaller pool to search. Work up a list of the most influential people in city government, business, and so on, from three years ago, and see which of them owned black Mercedes. That should only take…well, all right, it would take forever.

And who was to say my list was going to be correct? How would I know for sure that I had included all the right names? How did I know that I'd be able to come up with all the people that a midtown precinct would have found intimidating? All I had to miss was one name to miss everything.

Well…I wouldn't know. But I'd have to give it a shot. It was all I had.

I went in to the office the next day and got straight to work, energized like I hadn't been in…probably ever. I started with the obvious. On the government side: the mayor, the members of the city council, the district attorney, the local and federal judges. On the business side: partners at the big law firms; old time Atlanta power-brokers and movers; CEOs of the few major corporations that called Atlanta home. I couldn't see anyone at the vice president level or below having enough clout to be able to stop a police investigation, so I focused on the top executive level. Maybe that was a mistake, but I had to draw the line somewhere. The list was already ridiculously long.

Who else? Who else had the kind of gravitational mass that could push cops to stop an investigation? A major civil rights leader with a national presence? We had a couple of those in the city. It was possible, but I couldn't quite believe anyone like that could have pulled this off. In the first place, publicity would have leaked out sooner or later; it would have been too juicy not to talk about. And in the second place, the Midtown cops would have loved nailing any local loudmouth—especially the kind who blames cops for every ill on the planet. Would a political figure like that have even risked asking for such a favor, knowing that his reputation could be ruined by a single redneck cop talking to reporters?

Burying a case was a big deal. Doing it as a favor, or under coercion, was a huge deal. If it had come to light, the whole precinct—maybe the whole city force—would have looked bad. So the question was: who was important enough to make cops risk everything? They didn't have to respect the person, or love him, but they sure as hell had to fear them. And *that* list of names was probably pretty small. I started crossing off some people, and the list began looking a lot more manageable. Now all I had to do was find out how many of them owned a black Mercedes three years ago...and then hope that the actual perpetrator hadn't been driving a borrowed or rented car that night.

I sat back at the end of the day and looked at my final list. Even scaled down from the original, it was grim. Who the hell was *I* to question these people? These were important people—people with weight—people who had accomplished things. How would I even get past their secretaries to talk with any of them? I could just picture it: Jordan Greenblatt? Oh, absolutely, send him right in.

And then it hit me. They *would* say that. Exactly that. Every single one of them. Because they were all friends with my father. Most of them had been to his house. About half of them, I'd met at his parties.

All right, then. They'd talk to me...once. So I had to be ready when I confronted them. First things first, though—which of them drove those nice, shiny, black cars?

18

There were three Mercedes dealerships in Atlanta: one up on Roswell Road in Sandy Springs; one on Piedmont Road, deep in the heart of darkest Buckhead; and one way south, off I-85, below the airport. Obviously there was no guarantee that my killer (I had finally started to think of this person as "the killer") had bought his car here in town, but I had no other brilliant ideas at the moment, so I figured I should push forward any way I could.

I called each of the dealerships and said I worked with an ad agency representing Mercedes-Benz nationally. I made up a name and hoped our local knuckleheads wouldn't know any better. Fortunately, no one called my bluff. I said we were doing a campaign focusing on VIPs who had bought cars in each of our major markets as part of an upcoming TV spot, and were trying to generate a list of possible participants. I figured this would stroke egos and make everyone feel important, without pushing any privacy buttons or make anyone feel suspicious. I was right. At all three dealerships, people were more than happy to give me the names of their most important and influential clients over the past three years. They all wanted me to know that they *had* important and influential clients.

I cross-referenced their lists with the one I had put together, and realized that I had omitted at least a dozen very reasonable suspects on my first pass. I now had a list of 54 Movers and Shakers in the greater Atlanta area who had owned Mercedes cars of one sort or another three years ago. Some had bought them just before the accident; some had bought them years before the accident, and some had bought their cars earlier that same year. The hood ornament being my only clue, I had no idea how old a car I had to look for. But at least I knew, more or less, who had *owned* a Mercedes at the right time.

The color of those cars was left for me to figure out. It didn't seem prudent to ask the dealers for any more information, especially such seemingly irrelevant information.

Well, I said to myself as I added in the new names and expanded my list, you knew you sucked as a detective. But then I thought, No— the guesswork was just guesswork; making the calls was *investigative* work, and you did the job. You got the list you wanted. Give yourself a break.

So I gave myself a break, and went home to play some bass and clear my head. I wasn't ready for making scary phone calls yet. The longer I could fly under the radar and avoid arousing suspicion, the better.

I got home at about three. The weather was typical for September, which meant (at least in my un-air-conditioned neighborhood) you were better off staying outside, where you might catch a breeze. I lugged the bass out onto the porch, cracked open a beer, and started to play. Since I was flying solo, I figured I'd channel Jaco Pastorius for a while. I launched into "Birdland," off the "Heavy Weather" album, closing my eyes and playing Jaco's solo bassline introduction— listening in my head to all those other, lesser-important instruments as they came in. About halfway through the tune, the melody announced itself a little too forcefully for it to be my imagination. I opened my eyes and saw Oticha leaning against the wall, playing along with me. He nodded sagely at me in greeting.

"You lock the kids up in the basement?" I asked.

"Naw," he said, pulling away from his horn for just a second. "Melanie's got the day off. They're at the mall."

We locked eyes and both gave a brief shudder, then smiled and returned to the music. We have this thing about malls. We hate and fear them—especially Phipps Plaza, one of the more upscale and marble-encrusted malls in town, and Melanie's favorite. I go there with Susannah sometimes when there's a movie playing that we can't catch anywhere else, but it always gives me hives. Every time I walk into the place, I feel exposed, like there's a big spotlight shining on me, and a voice on a loudspeaker yelling "Intruder!" Fortunately, Susannah's none too fond of the place either. She's more of a funky boutique kind of girl—just one of the reasons why I love her. Oticha's not so lucky—Melanie is a mall rat and a Serious Shopper, and would happily spend entire days nosing around Saks. And, of course, it's no fun unless she can drag her husband and children along with her.

He claims not to have the same imposter/intruder complex I have when he's strolling the marble corridors of power, but then, he's a former public school teacher, not a Failed Med Student Who Has Disappointed His Entire Family And Will

Never Make Any Money. In fact, in *his* family, reaching the level of college graduate and high school teacher was considered an impressive and respectable accomplishment. Abandoning it all to become a househusband, not so much.

We wrapped up the song and Oticha grabbed a beer from the cooler. "How goes the case, Shylock?"

"Shylock?"

"What do I mean? Shyster?"

"Shyster's a lawyer. You mean Shamus. Or maybe Gumshoe."

"Aha," he said thoughtfully, arranging his long body on a chair and then leaning back in it, pushing it onto its hind legs. "Gumshoe? What's that all about?"

"I honestly have no idea," I said, noodling around on the bass tunelessly. "And the case is going…well, it's *going*, which is a change."

"That's cool."

"Maybe," I said. "Maybe cool. I don't know. Maybe seriously fucked up."

"You get paid either way, right?"

I stopped playing and glared at him. "Yeah, I get paid either way. That's not the point."

"Aight," he said breezily, like one of his former high school charges. "Just axin."

"There's a dead girl. Dead woman, I mean. It's not like I'm serving subpoenas here. This is more than just a paycheck."

"Mm hmm," he said, seeming to agree with me. "She's been dead a long time, though."

"Yes. Yes, she has. Three years. Thank you for the clarification, Professor."

"And a paycheck…you know. A paycheck ain't no small thing." He smiled mischievously, then lifted up his trumpet and blasted a few bars of "St. James Infirmary," which is his way of signaling that he thinks you're feeling sorry for yourself. So I told him to fuck himself. But he was right, and the song was right, so I played him a bass line and we kept the tune going.

> *Let her go, let her go, God bless her*
> *Wherever she may be…*

Yeah, yeah. Maybe tomorrow.

19

I woke up the next morning, still feeling the need to stall. I didn't want to start calling local big shots if I didn't feel strong and confident, but I didn't want to waste the day either. There's just enough of the old Jewish-American, My-Son-the-Doctor work ethic in me to keep me from falling completely into sloth and indolence. I have trouble lying around and doing nothing for more than a day or two at a stretch. I needed to do something productive, without quite taking the next important step and passing some point of no return. For me, productive-but-not-particularly-meaningful equals a trip to the library. And a trip to the library means a visit back to campus.

There are plenty of libraries around town, and some of them, I'm told, are quite good. But I'm spoiled. I spent four years with a wonderful research library on campus, and if my alumni privileges grant me continued access to it, I see no reason to give it up. So I don't, even if it pains me to walk around the damned quad, which it does.

I parked as close to the Coakely Library as I could, which meant off campus, about a half mile away, in a bank parking lot.

I made a beeline for the big, waffle-shaped building, trying as hard as I could not to gaze around at the dreamy and listless undergrads lying on the grass. I got to the library and headed downstairs to the microfilm department. I figured I should finally start doing some of my own research on the accident. I had seen the evidence box and I had read the long-distance accounts of the accident that Palmer had sent me from New York. But I hadn't looked at how the accident had been covered *here*— locally. Was there a reaction to the case being dropped so quickly? Had anyone even noticed?

And I didn't want to rely on Internet archives. First of all, our local paper is crap, and it keeps crap archives online. But more importantly, when they *do* archive stories, they do what everyone else does—they reformat them into a computer-friendly layout. Well, I didn't want that. I wanted to see the paper, the way the paper looked back then. I wanted the articles, sure, but I also wanted the short items, the calendar listings, the classified ads—the whole newsprint enchilada. As a professional snoop, I've found that not everything of importance comes with a byline, or over the fold.

The microfilm department at the Coakely Library was run by an ancient Southern Belle named Aileen, a honey-sweet and charming woman from somewhere in Alabama—one of those Women of a Certain Age whose hair has achieved the supernatural combination of gravity-defying height, permanent, conical shape, and delicate texture that only a weekly visit to the salon can maintain. It's also a shade of orange that only someone in a hair salon could imagine as attractive. She was as much of a throwback as the microfilm she worked with, but she was good at her job, and she had always been good to me. She had two assistants working the room, but they tended to be undergraduates. I try not to get to know the undergraduates, since they come and go like the tides. It's like in those war movies, where the grizzled old veterans refuse to make friends with the reinforcements, since most of them die on their first patrol. Or how starship captains never pall around with the red-shirts in the landing party. You know what I mean.

I told Aileen what I needed, not that I really needed to. The microfilm stacks are open, and I know my way around them. It's just nice to keep the boss involved. You never know when you may need help, and she appreciated being needed. I pulled the appropriate rolls for the Atlanta Constitution and the Atlanta Journal, and sat down at the giant dinosaur of a machine to scroll through and see what I could find. There was one brief article from the day after the accident—more of a sidebar story than an actual article:

Midtown Lawyer Killed in Early Morning Accident

Giselle Palmer, 32, an associate with the Midtown law firm of Wilkins, Frewell, Byrd, was killed yesterday morning in an apparent hit and run on Monroe Drive between Virginia Avenue and 10th Street. The young woman was traveling on in-line skates when she apparently swerved out into the street and was struck by a passing car. The driver of the car may have stopped briefly, but did not linger at the scene of the accident or call the police. Ms. Palmer's body was found shortly afterwards by a bicyclist. There were no witnesses to the accident itself.

And that was all. Nothing provocative or frightening. Nothing that seemed to be pointing in an uncomfortable direction. Definitely not a major story that was refusing to go away. I mean, it looked like the story would have vanished altogether in a day or two without anybody's help, which is exactly what you would have expected. Okay, maybe if an important lawyer or business leader is involved, it gets more play. But even then, how many news cycles is a hit-and-run is worth?

What I found more interesting was this: there was no mention of the hood ornament or the black paint or the tire treads—nothing. Now, did that mean the cops had chosen not to release potentially important evidence for fear of hampering the investigation, like Carter had said? In theory, that sounded fine. But if the cops felt like it was a dead case and worth dropping after a day, why would they withhold information from the press? To what end?

The only thing that made sense to me was that the cops had disappeared these important details right from the start, to stop people from looking to hard at the case—reporters, other cops, or anyone else. Now, if *that* was the case, then someone really *had* leaned on them to kill the case before it even began.

I scrolled on. Nothing on day two, nothing on day three, nothing and nothing, and nothing. Then, five days after the first article, this advertisement appeared:

Information Sought on Hit and Run

Edward Palmer, of Great Neck, New York, requests that anyone with information pertaining to the death of his daughter, Giselle, please contact the Atlanta Police as soon as possible. Giselle Palmer is the young attorney killed last week in an apparent hit-and-run accident on Monroe Drive in Midtown. While bad weather and poor visibility may have been the cause of the accident, leaving the

scene is still considered a crime, and the
family of Ms. Palmer is searching for
information.

So. Five little days after the first story, Palmer is reaching
out in desperation, going around the cops *and* the reporters to
the general public. Five days, and he was feeling like he had to lay
out cash to get anyone to care. Palmer was an impatient man
used to getting what he wanted, but would he really have given
up on the police after only five days?

He might have, if he knew another five days wasn't going to
change anything. Or another fifty. But what would have made
him feel that way? Had someone said something to him? Tipped
him off?

No—if that were true, he would have told me right from
the start. He must have just sensed it from the lack of response
he was getting—from the police *and* the press—after that first
day.

Giselle had been killed early in the morning commute. How
long after that had the Mysterious Stranger asked for his personal
favor? Just a little mess that needs cleaning up—nothing *important*
mind you—just a little nobody who got in the way—you know
how it is—just a nuisance really, but you know how the papers
can manipulate these things.

Who had said that…and what Helpful Friend had he said it
to?

The more I thought about it, the angrier I got. And
remember, friends, I don't get angry. I don't fall into rages of
passion. I don't ride off into town in search of Vengeance, or
Justice. I'm not Clint Eastwood. I'm just the bass player.

But this was bullshit.

And then it occurred to me—I probably wasn't the only person who thought it was bullshit. If someone *had* leaned on the precinct to shut down the investigation, there had to have been at least one cop who was angry about it. Because you don't lean on the foot soldiers; you lean on the captain, and the captain gives the order to his troops. And one of those troops had felt the same way I did…because someone had made damned sure that the evidence box had stayed right where I needed it to be. Carter was right—the box *should* have been put in storage years ago. Maybe somebody made sure it didn't get there. Maybe somebody had tipped off Palmer, somehow, to let him know there was more going on here than met the eye—the same way that Carter had tipped me off without meaning to. Maybe someone in that precinct had been hoping for three years that someday, somebody would give a damn and take a second look.

If I could find that person and talk to him without tipping my hand to his superiors, I might actually be able to make headway in this case and give Giselle's father what he needed.

And maybe it wouldn't be that hard to find him. Maybe his name was already in my notes—the notes I had copied from Carter's evidence box. Because who was a better candidate for Disgruntled Cop than the officer who had actually started working the case—the officer who knew that there were leades to follow—the officer who had to be told to stop, probably with no decent explanation?

I started to realize that maybe I had more than an assumption—more, even, than a lead. Maybe I actually had the beginnings of a *trail* to follow.

Half of me was getting excited. But the other half was quietly wondering how far I would get before I fucked the whole thing up.

20

The investigating officer listed in the case notes was named Wade Burdette. When I called the precinct, I found out he had retired a few years earlier. How few, I asked, as casually as possible. The officer at the front desk couldn't say for sure—he had only been there at the precinct for about two years, himself, and as far as he knew, Burdette had left some months before he got there.

Two years and some months. Could he have taken early retirement as a protest and response to *this?* Or was it just his time? Either way, it would make perfect sense why the man would leave the evidence box in plain sight on his way out.

I asked the officer where Burdette lived, but he very politely told me that he wasn't authorized to give out that information.

This detective work was turning out to be a pain in the ass. When I was following mere fornicators, it was easy. Step 1: follow the asshole. Step 2: wait. Step 3: take pictures. Even when I had to do research, it was usually pretty cut-and-dried. But this—one thing didn't lead to another thing. Every piece of information just led to a new question, and every question was a whole new mystery to figure out. Now I had to track down a guy who could have retired to…well, *any*where. And I didn't even care about him, really—I just wanted to ask him some questions. Find out if I even *wanted* to care about him.

I'm sure the pros have a more sophisticated way of tracking down people, but I was no pro, so I started where anybody else would: with The Google. The entry "Wade Burdette" gave me 15 pages referring to about 12 different people. Some were men, some were women, and some had been dead since the Civil War. Narrowing things down to living males, I had eight Wade Burdettes. A cursory glance at their various pages told me that none of them were the retired cop I was looking for.

Okay, Plan B. On the Atlanta Police Department website, I found a phone listing for the Atlanta Retired Police Reserves. If Burdette had quit in protest, he probably wouldn't be on that list, but it was worth a try. I gave them a call.

Sorry, no information about that individual.

Plan C? There was a phone number online for the police training academy. Would they have records going back as far as when Officer Burdette was Cadet Burdette? It seemed like a long-shot, but what the hell. I gave them a call and said I was trying to deliver something special from the estate of my grandfather, who had been saved from Some Horrible Fate by Officer Burdette many years ago. I had heard the officer had retired to his boyhood home, but I didn't know where that was. Might their records indicate his original home address?

Now this was ridiculous on a number of fronts. In the first place, no, of course they weren't going to have his original home address on file from god-knows-how-many-years ago. And even if they did, who said he had retired back *there*? Most of the cops I knew in the city came from godawful little towns in the South Georgia swamplands or the North Georgia mountains—poor, hard, nasty places they had no intention of even visiting again, let along relocating to at retirement to hunt and fish and…I don't know…whittle things for their grandchildren. No—the cops I knew all retired to Florida.

But guess what? The man on the other end of the line was proud to inform me that after a massive effort to update their files and put everything on a single computer system, they actually *did* have Wade Burdette's original application to the force, and that he had come to Atlanta from Dahlonega—the old gold-mining town up in the north mountains.

The next step was easy: call 411 and find out if there was a Wade Burdette currently listed in Dahlonega, Georgia. I made the call, closed my eyes, and crossed my fingers.

And believe it or not, that's exactly where my missing officer was living.

I ran home, packed a suitcase, and was waiting for Susannah on the porch when she came home from work.

"Going somewhere?" she asked.

I smiled as sweetly as I could. "What would you say to a weekend in the country?"

"I'd say, what gives? We haven't had a weekend in the anywhere since forever."

"It's for work," I admitted. "But that means all expenses paid."

"So I'm tagging along with you on a case? Does that make me the wisecracking but eternally unmarried girl sidekick?"

"Except for the unmarried part. Maybe we can be Nick and Nora Charles. Without the dog."

"I wouldn't mind a dog."

"One thing at a time. First we have to crack this case wide open."

"Then a dog?"

"Then we'll see."

"All right. Sign me up."

21

To be fair, Dahlonega is none of the things I just said about little towns in Georgia. Maybe it *was*, back when Wade Burdette was growing up. I have no idea. But these days, it's a gentrified, lovely tourist destination up in the north Georgia mountains. It's a great escape from the heat and humidity of the city, and it's probably attractive in the winter as well, for people looking for a little snow (I'm assuming they get snow). It has lots of boutiques and restaurants, and quite a few bed-and-breakfasts and country inns. It's also close to a state park with a lovely waterfall. Susannah and I hit all of these charming spots and had a lovely weekend away from the concrete jungle. Good sightseeing, good food, and some of that good sex I'm not going to tell you about. All in all, a four-star vacation for the young Greenblatt family of Atlanta.

So there, Chamber of Commerce. You can throw away those nasty letters you were about to write. Dahlonega, Georgia, is okay by me.

I had Mr. Wade Burdette's phone number with me, but I chose not to call him before setting out from Atlanta for two reasons. Reason #1: I hadn't figured out exactly how to approach him. Reason #2: I didn't want to spoil the chance of spending a couple of expense-account days with Susannah in the country, just in case he said No before we left. This was probably very bad business ethics, but I'm all about honesty and openness here, so…there it is.

I waited until our final morning, after a massive, southern-style breakfast of Everything In The World Plus Biscuits, and then made the call. A vigorous-sounding man answered right away.

"Is this Wade Burdette?" I asked.

"Yeah, this is Wade."

"Mr. Burdette," I asked, "were you a police officer in Atlanta until about three years ago?" As you can see, I had decided on the direct approach. Very businesslike, very New York, very wrong for this particular subject, who instantly became quiet and guarded. I plunged on quickly. "Sir, my name is Billy Barnes. I'm a private investigator looking into the hit-and-run accident that killed a young woman named Giselle Palmer. Do you recall the case?"

"Yes sir," he said heavily. "I do recall it."

"Is it something you might feel comfortable talking about? In private? I happen to be in Dahlonega on vacation with my wife, and thought maybe we could get together for a coffee or something."

There was a pause. He wasn't buying it. Fortunately, Susannah was standing right by me. I kicked her in the shins and she yelped loudly. I pulled my face away from the phone and called out, "Oh, sorry, honey—I must have dropped the suitcase." I gave her a plaintive look, and she rolled her eyes. I returned to the phone. "Sorry about that, Mr. Burdette. As I was saying…"

"Before you broke your poor wife's toes," he said.

"Right."

"Listen, why don't y'all come on up to the house. There's things I could tell you, I reckon." He paused. "I'm not saying I *will* tell you nothing. Just…you come on up to the house and we'll see. I'll put up some sweet tea for you, let your wife get off her feet."

I thanked him, hung up, and turned to Susannah. "Thanks, Dollface," I said, tipping an imaginary hat. "I owe you one."

22

When we got up to Burdette's house, he was sitting in his TV room with a beer in hand, watching "Down by Law" on some cable channel. A tray with a pitcher of tea and some glasses stood by, waiting for us.

"Sorry," I said. "I didn't know you were in the middle of something. We could have come later."

He shut off the TV and waved us in. "Don't matter," he said. "I can't make no sense of the damn thing, anyway."

"Yeah, it's a little out there," I said. "But it's got a great soundtrack."

I could see immediately that I had started off on the wrongest possible foot, so I introduced Susannah. She turned on her native Southern charm and shook his hand while I backed away. He asked her where she was from and where her people were from, and she gave him her whole Macon family history. And I knew we were in.

Here's the thing about the South. There's Atlanta, which is a concrete island ringed by highways, and is in no way is a part of the Real South to real southerners. To me, of course, a Yankee Jew from Long Island, it's Way South, Deep South, sometimes even Scary South. But to someone like, say, Wade Burdette, Atlanta is basically New York City with better weather. You drive an hour outside Atlanta in any direction, though, and, boy, *then* you're in the South. And in that South—the real South—they ask you where your people are from. Because it matters. You know who asks me where my people are from? No one, that's who. Because my people are from some nameless, burnt-out shtetl somewhere in Eastern Europe, and even *they* didn't want to remember anything about it. They ran as soon as they had the chance, and they never looked back. That's not *people*—that's not *connection*. Here in the South, they want to know where you went to prep school, or cotillion, or whatever. They want to know if your people are the right people, and whether any of their people might know any of your people. You say, "Macon," when they ask you where your people are from, and they suddenly *know* something about you. I have no idea *what* they know, but they know something. They know where to put you, where to plug you in, what to think of you.

Give me credit for this—bringing Susannah along was genius. Within five minutes we were old friends and everything was sweetness and light. I hated to break it all up with the Business at Hand, but, you know, I just had to. I was charging the trip to my client, after all (see? Ethics).

"Do you mind if we talk a little about Giselle Palmer?" I asked, as gently as I could.

"Sure, sure. It's what you come up for. I ain't no fool." He smiled at me a little carnivorously.

"Once a detective, always a detective," I said with what I hoped was a nicer smile.

"If everyone's intentions was as obvious as yours is right now, woulda been a much easier job."

"That's true. So, I was looking into the case— "

He interrupted me. "They let you? They was okay with that?"

"Well, I don't think they realized what it was, at first. New people at the precinct. They gave me the evidence box right away."

He grinned.

"You're grinning," I said—master of the obvious.

"You have any trouble locating that there box?" he asked mischievously.

"No, sir." I said innocently. "Now that you mention it, I did not."

He laughed "You know where that damn box shoulda been?"

"I'm guessing some warehouse downtown?" I asked.

"Some hole underground, more like." He leaned back in his chair with a happy, shit-eating grin. "I told them I took it down to the warehouse, like they asked. Then I shoved it up on the shelf, all properly tagged and labeled, case somebody decided, someday, to give a shit."

I took a deep breath. "Officer Burdette," I said carefully, "can you tell me who told you to bury this case?"

He looked at me equally carefully, and for a long time. Then he sighed, and shook his head, and leaned back in his chair. "Nobody told me nothing, son," he said. "It wasn't like that. It just kinda happened." He stopped for a moment. "These things—murder cases and such—they don't move forward on their own. You gotta push them and push them. Every day, you come in to work, you pick it up where you left it the day before and you push it a little bit further down the road. And if you don't push it, it don't move. You get me? Yeah, you know what I'm saying—you're in the same line of work."

I nodded.

"So when they don't want you nosing around a case no more, they don't say nothing *outright*. They just pull you away from it for a day—send you out to do something else. And then the next day it's something else again. And something else. And sooner or later, you get the message—leave it lay there, wherever it is. And sooner or later, someone comes along and boxes it all up, and you never talk about it again."

"So this happened a *lot*?"

"Different reasons, sure. Usually it's just bigger stuff coming along, you gotta drop the small stuff. Ain't nothing sinister about it. Just never enough people to do all the work. You know you *ought* to keep at it, but you just can't, and you feel bad, so you just don't mention it no more. Too bad, so sad."

"But not this time."

"No sir, not this time. This time was different. One day on the case, Captain starts pulling me off it. And every time I try to go back on it, he gets angrier and angrier. Finally he says, Christ, Burdette, can't you take a *hint?*"

"Why do you think they pulled you off the case?"

"You'd have to ask my Captain about that."

"All right. How about this one: why didn't they want anyone investigating the hood ornament? It was the only decent evidence you had, and no one did a thing with it."

"You right there, nobody did. But you tell *me*, son. You're the P.I. What do *you* think it means?"

"I think it means the owner of that Mercedes made some phone calls and told your boss to shut things down."

Burdette smiled again—but a thin grimace of a smile this time. "That's what I figured, too. And I said so. Yes sir, I said so. More than once. And that right there was the end of my career." He lifted his beer in a toast and drank the rest of it down.

"You were fired?"

"Aw, hell no. Just…waddyacallit? Eased out the door."

"And it wasn't for knowing something you shouldn't have known? It was just for asking?"

"Well, now, asking…asking is the beginning of knowing, ain't it? Anyone in law enforcement can tell you that. Asking the right questions, knowing *who* to ask …hell, that's half the game, right there. Maybe more'n half."

"I reckon you're right," I said, trying to sound southern.

"Course I'm right," he said, leaning forward. "And like I says, anyone in law enforcement would know that, wouldn't they?"

And he winked at me.

23

"He did not."

"He *did*."

"Jordan—"

"He totally winked at me. I'm telling you."

"You're an idiot."

"Well, maybe so, but he still winked at me."

We drove in silence.

"All right, *why*?" she said, unable to let it go. "Why would a grown man—a grown redneck—cop—wink? At *you*?"

"I don't know," I said humbly, "Maybe he thought I was cute."

She reached into the back seat for her purse and said, "That's it. Stop the car. I'm walking home."

I laughed. "All right. Seriously—I think he was just trying to tell me something he couldn't say out loud."

"What, does he think his house is bugged or something?"

"I think he's just trying to be careful. If he's been sitting on something for three years and hasn't said a word to anyone in all that time...you know, the guy's going to be careful. So he gave me a hint. If I make something of it, it's all on me; he didn't cross any lines. If I don't, no big deal. Either way, he hasn't said anything he shouldn't have. He's covered."

"All right, so what did he say, exactly, before he winked? I don't even remember what was going on."

"He said *asking is the beginning of knowing*—like if you start asking the right questions, you're going to find out things somebody doesn't want you to know, so you'd better not ask any questions. Or you'd better be sure you want to know. And then he kept repeating how anyone in law enforcement would know that."

"And then he winked?"

"Right. So he's telling me...what? That his captain clamped down hard on him because he knew there were real clues to be followed, and he knew who they led to?"

"Or that the guy you're looking for is in law enforcement—like another cop or something."

"Oh. I hadn't thought of that."

"Or the chief of police."

"Shit."

"I mean, if he had to fucking *wink* about it…"

"No, no, you might be right. Jesus, that's all I need."

"I told you to drop this, didn't I? Didn't I *beg* you to drop it? This whole stupid thing is getting dangerous."

"It's not *dangerous*. I mean, come on."

"It could *get* dangerous."

"What—do you think I'm going to end up at some abandoned warehouse or something, pinned down in a withering crossfire?"

"*I* don't know."

"Well, I'm not, okay? I'm not Spiderman, for God's sake."

"Well, all right. I'm just saying. If I'm going to be the girl sidekick, I've gotta say all the sidekicky don't-go-in-there-it's-dangerous stuff."

"Fair enough."

"Plus, you know, I love you and shit. So I'd rather not see you get killed."

"Well, I'm not going to get killed. I'm just going to see if I can put some of the pieces together, and if they lead to a name, then great—I send the name to the father and collect my final check. That's all I was asked to do, so…that's all I'm doing. He can take it from there if he wants to." I stopped and glanced over at her. "Okay?"

"Okay," she said softly. I slid my hand across the seat and patted her leg. She grabbed my hand and held it tight.

"Seriously," I said, turning to look at her. "There's nothing to worry about."

She turned away and looked out her window. She didn't believe a word I was saying. I wasn't sure I did, either.

24

The next day, in my little hole of an office, I pulled out my list of 54 possible suspects and wondered whether I should cross off anyone who wasn't involved in law enforcement. It was a risky move, based on my interpretation of a complete stranger's wink. On the other hand, every decision I had made in this case had been based on whim, guesswork, or a wild hunch, so what did I have to lose? Plus, anything to cross some names off seemed like a good idea.

So fine, I said to myself—cross 'em off. See what happens.

I worked my way down the list, axing CEOs, politicos, and other local VIPs. I kept judges, law firm partners, district attorneys, and, God help me, the chief of police. I ended up with nine names. Nine. That didn't mean there were only nine important movers and shakers in Atlanta law enforcement—just nine who had owned a Mercedes when the accident happened. Well…nine I had *uncovered* who had owned a Mercedes. I'm sure there were more.

I looked at my nine names—my nine model citizens—and I tried to imagine each of them driving recklessly on a rainy winter morning. That was easy—they were all busy, over-stressed, important people. Every one of them probably drove too fast while talking—or yelling—on a cell phone. Then I tried to imagine each of them fleeing the scene of a terrible accident he had caused. That was harder to imagine, but not impossible. They were all public figures with reputations to protect. But they were also moral and ethical people—or, at least, they presented themselves that way to the general public. Could they really have done that? Could they really have been so frightened about the public fallout that they could have left a dead woman by the side of a rainy road? And if so…if so, which of them would have had the clout…and the balls…to compound the crime by manipulating and halting a police investigation?

It's tricky, doing this kind of imagining. On the one hand, I've seen enough bad behavior in my job, committed by allegedly upstanding citizens, to know that appearances are nothing if not misleading. Anyone is capable of anything. On the other hand, well, I just have trouble making that fact make sense in my brain.

Oticha says this is because I am a hopelessly naïve white boy from the suburbs who has not received an appropriately radical and progressive education in racial politics and modern economics, though God knows he's tried to fill the gap over the years.

Pete, our keyboard player, has a slightly darker vision. He's convinced that what's lacking in me is not political perspective, but *personal* perspective. As far as he's concerned, anyone *is* capable of anything, me included—and just because I haven't heaved a loved one's body into a canal somewhere, doesn't mean

I don't *want* to, deep down—or that I'm not capable of doing so, if properly motivated. "You don't know who you really are until you're *tested*, Dude," he likes to say. "What percentage of your potential do you think your life has really brought to the surface? Fifteen? Twenty-five? We live soft lives, man. We don't know who we *are*."

Pete reads a lot of graphic novels about swords and honor and shit, in case you couldn't tell.

When he goes off like this, I like to tell him that I have examined every inch of my soul and have determined that the shallow, unmotivated, barely interesting loser he sees before him really *is* all I've got to offer the world. He shakes his head sadly, amazed at the extent of my self-delusion, and says, with deep meaning, "Dude."

Susannah, of course, knows me better than anyone—better than my dad, better than my friends. And late at night, when I lie awake thinking of the Evil That Men Do, she understands some of what's rattling around in my head. She gets that I have trouble making it all make sense. I look at the things I have to look at, whether it's a philandering dickhead in bed with a waitress or Giselle's broken face staring up at me, and I say, "How could someone *do* that?"

Susannah strokes my hair, and sidles up next to me, and says, "Because they want to, baby. And because they can. And for some people, that's all it takes."

And I know she's right. I know it better than she realizes. And not just because I've seen plenty of shitty behavior, though I *have* seen plenty of it—and not just through my camera lens. When I was with Fuck Guitars, back in our glory days, I had my groupie moments—I know how intoxicating it can be to have the world offered up to you, free of charge—or, if not the world, at least someone's hot body. And I said *Yes Please* more often than *No Thank You*—of course I did. And I saw how other guys in the group took more than was offered. Because when so much is given, how you do draw the line when someone pulls back and says, "No"?

"Fortunately for the rest of us," says Susannah, "there are men out there like you."

She doesn't know what she's saying, and I'm not going to tell her.

Look, I'm no better than anyone else, but I've tried not to use people just because they make it easy to be used. I've tried to be a good person. Even when I was playing with the band, I never acted like I had some divine right to eat the world. I always knew, deep down, that I was just me, and I was lucky to be up there, playing my music and having a good time. And I knew the guys made fun of me for that: always the bass player; always hanging back; always playing it cool.

I've known guys like that my whole life. They never think there might be reasons for things—reasons they should take some time to understand. They just think things *are*, and so they laugh about it. It's easy. An easy, ignorant laugh. They always go straight to the easy, whether it's laughing at some kid who stutters, or fucking some drunk, teenage girl who doesn't know any better. They question nothing.

Not that asking the question separates the dreamers from the do-ers. I mean, just because you have a conscience doesn't mean you obey it all the time. As Pete says, you don't know what you're capable of until the moment when you find yourself doing it. So why do some people take that fateful step, and other people don't?

"I don't know," my wife says, kissing me on the cheek. "It's the mystery of the human heart. I'm just happy you're you and not them. Happy and very lucky." And she goes to sleep—instantly and effortlessly.

And I lie there, awake, staring at the ceiling and thinking, *the lies, the lies, the lies.*

25

Nine names. Nine. That ought to be handle-able, even for a novice like me. Nine men, nine cars. Of course, I could be missing a name, if someone had bought their car outside of Atlanta or many years ago. On the other hand, I could be looking at fewer than nine, too. Which of you gentlemen owned a *black* Mercedes three years ago? Raise those hands.

Hmm… maybe I *could* get them to raise their hands. In a way. I called Susannah at her office and asked her how busy she was.

"Ooh, I like the way you think," she said. "What are you wearing?"

"That's not what I mean, Suse," I sighed. "Sorry. I just need to know if you've got a few minutes to do some layout work for me."

Susannah is a graphic artist and…whatever they call it…layout person…for some local bank's main office here. She knows absolutely nothing about money, or banks, but she's great at what she does. She treats her job with absolute scorn and derision, but she does it very well and is adored by the people in her office.

"Yeah, I've got time. It's slow as shit today. Email me what you need."

"Excellent. I owe you one." I rang off before she could say anything else provocative and went straight to my computer, banging out the text of a survey in about five minutes. I sent it along to Susannah with a note about what it should look like, and then tracked down office addresses for my Nine. I sent those to her as well, so that I could have pre-printed envelopes to go with the survey. Within two hours, I had this waiting in my Inbox, beautifully and colorfully laid out, and stamped everywhere with the Mercedes logo:

> Dear Valued Customer,
>
> Car and Driver Magazine is considering a story on the resilience of our cars and the loyalty and satisfaction of our owners. As a valued customer of long standing and a pillar of your community, we would love to have you featured in this story. Obviously we have no control over how the magazine will write the story or which owners they will feature, but we would like to offer up some of our more important customers for their consideration. If you are interested in the possibility of being profiled in this article, please provide us with a little information about yourself and your Mercedes automobile.
>
> Your friends at Mercedes-Benz, USA

Below the letter was a short questionnaire asking when the customer had purchased the car, from which local dealer he had bought it, the make, the color, and whatever other random information I could think of to hide my true purpose.

It looked stupid and corporate and entirely innocent—to me. I hoped it would look the same to my Nine, and that they wouldn't think twice about the Atlanta post-office box to which the surveys were supposed to be returned—a box I had rented a couple of years earlier to receive less-than-savory case materials.

I emailed Susannah with thanks and asked her to bring the printed envelopes home with her. I could send them out the next morning and then sit back and see what happened. Maybe I could even take a break from thinking about all this and get ready for our band's upcoming gig—something I'd been ignoring for weeks.

Unfortunately, when I got home that afternoon, eager to practice and have a few beers, my friend Carter Wiggins was waiting for me on my porch. He did not look happy.

"You're damn right I'm not happy," he said as he accepted a beer from me. "You been nosing around this fuckin hit-and-run—after I asked you special to drop the thing."

I tried to keep calm and channel my inner Sam Spade, but I wasn't used to being called out on a lie by a police sergeant, and my heart was thumping a mile a minute. I kept my nose in my beer can and said, "I don't know what you're talking about."

Carter slapped the can out of my hand. It thwacked onto the floor of the porch, rolling down the steps onto the lawn. The beer seeped down between the cracks of the wood slats. I watched all this, unable to meet my friend's eyes.

"Don't fuck around with me, Jordy," he said angrily. "I know what you been doing. I know you been up to see this

Wade Burdette asshole. I don't know what the hell he coulda told you about anything, but I know you been up there."

"He didn't give me a lot," I said. "He was pretty cryptic."

"Cryptic. What the fuck's that supposed to mean?"

"It means he was hinting around about a lot of stuff, but I couldn't make any sense out of it."

"Well, that's probably because he's a crazy drunk, what folks tell me about him." He started pacing around the porch — agitated, unsure what to do with his hands. "Jordy, God *damn* it. I told you there's bullshit piled all over this thing that you got nothing to do with and I got nothing to do with. But I'm under strict orders to leave the pile where it is. You understand?"

"I understand. But I've got a dead girl's father who's paying me to shovel the shit *off* the pile. What do you want me to do?"

"I want you to *listen* to someone who's trying to keep your ass out of trouble. Give the man back his money and tell him there ain't nothing more he can do. Cause there ain't."

"Look…listen, Carter…I know there's somebody powerful behind all this, someone who made the case go away back when it happened —"

He sighed and sat down hard. "You don't know shit," he said.

"I must know *some*thing, or your captain wouldn't be riding your ass like this," I said, sitting down near him. "Tell me I'm wrong."

"If you knew shit about anything," he said, fixing my eyes with his, "you'd know the more folks got to lose, the harder they fight not to lose it."

I laughed. "Now *you're* being cryptic," I said.

"No, see, you think there's all this mystery going on, like people's keeping shit from you. But the fact is, I don't know a fucking thing about what happened here. I seriously don't. I don't want to. The way my captain looks at me when he tells me to shut you down, I can tell this is coming from someone with shit to lose—a *lot* of shit to lose. And I don't care who that someone is, cause it ain't got shit to do with me. I just know some old mole wants to stay in his hole. And far as I'm concerned, that's all you and me need to know."

"Even if the mole did something bad? Something really bad? Come on, Wiggins. Don't you care about justice? Or is covering your ass the whole job description these days?"

That hurt—I could see it. He paused for a minute, then grunted, "Shit didn't happen on my watch. Not mine and not my cap's, either."

"It's happening right now, Carter. It's happening still. You act or you ignore it—that's *now*, Carter. On your watch."

Nothing.

"So…what? You're saying this somebody with something to lose is having me followed? I go up to Dahlonega, he's got someone trailing me to Burdette's house, calling his boss and whispering where I'm going and what I'm doing?"

Carter sighed and rubbed his tired eyes. "Boy, you are so far off the fucking deep end it ain't even funny," he said. "Nobody's following you, or tapping your phones, or any shit else. All right?"

"But you know I went up to talk to Burdette."

"Yeah, cause the crazy shitbird called my captain and *told* him you'd been up there. Crowed at him like the cat ate the fucking canary. Ha, ha, ha, Cap'n—shit's all gonna hit the fan now. Too bad for you."

"And your captain didn't like that."

"You're fucking A right he didn't like it." He stood up and started pacing. "Look, Jordy, I got no idea what this is all about. And if I knew, I'd think twice about telling you. I swear to God, I ain't nothing but the messenger boy here. Really and truly. Maybe I got stripes now. But that don't mean I call the shots. We got a chain of command, and I don't do shit unless command says. So I'm just the messenger. But you better *get* the message. Lay off it. All right? Leave the mole in his hole. I don't want nothing to happen to you."

He noticed the surprised look on my face. "Yeah, that's right, asshole. I actually give a shit about you. In fact, I give more of a shit about what happens to you tomorrow than I do about what happened to some dead girl three years ago. Go figure."

I wasn't expecting that, and it hit hard. I nodded, and after a moment, I said, "What could happen to me?" I asked. "I'm a peaceful, law-abiding citizen."

Wiggins stopped pacing and drained his beer. "You're a God-damn pain in the ass sonofabitch, is what you are," he said, tossing the beer in the recycling bin by the door. "Just lay off it, okay? Go back to spying on fornicators." He punched me in the arm and sauntered, in that southern, good-old-boy way of his, back to his car.

26

Before I could clear my mind of that little encounter, Oticha and Ray and Pete descended on my porch to rehearse. We had a gig coming up in Little Five Points, and we hadn't had enough time to work up the two sets were supposed to play. We don't play in public very often. We don't even have a name for our group. One of my neighbors just happened to own a club in Little Five Points, and he heard us practicing one evening as he drove by my house. Thus, a gig was born. And here my band mates were, expecting me to focus on them.

Everything we do is pretty much built around Oticha. As the horn player, he's the star. I may dream of Pastorius and Mingus, but I'm just Greenblatt, so my bass plays a supporting role. Pete can do some amazing electronic things with his keyboard, but most of what we do is straight jazz, so he has to stick to sounding like a piano. Which is fine—he's a great player and doesn't have to hide behind technology. But there's other stuff he'd love to be able to do. He and Oticha get into it sometimes and argue for hours. But like I said —Oticha is the star. So we build around him.

And of course there's the drummer. There's just never the *same* drummer. Ray was playing with us again that night as a favor, but he wasn't going to be able to sit in the following weekend. I can't remember if we had anyone else lined up for the gig at that point, but it never seemed to worry anyone —a drummer could always be…drummed up. You could always find one; you just couldn't ever *keep* one.

We warmed up for a few minutes, joked around, and then started working through some songs we'd been practicing, to see which were close enough to decent to play for paying customers. I kept quiet through most of it, just playing my bass line. I was still pretty shaky from getting yelled at by Carter. We were about halfway through "Do You Know What It Means to Miss New Orleans?" and, as usual, Oticha's phrasing made me hear the words that no one was singing:

> *The moonlight on the bayou…….a Creole tune…. that fills the air I dream… about magnolias in bloom……and I'm wishin' I was there*

Suddenly, Oticha pulled the horn from his lips, leaned towards me with a smile, and said, "Take it, Jordy G." And everything stopped. Ray brushed the drums in time to the missing solo he was expecting, and Pete and Oticha just looked at me. And I, acting like a clown in an old movie, looked behind myself, as though my friends were looking past me at something important.

Oticha laughed and shook his head. "Don't you *never* want to take a solo, man?"

"Leave him alone," said Ray. "We don't have time to fuck around. Let's just stick with what we've been rehearsing."

"Yeah, let's," I said, my face burning.

Oticha took up the horn again and went back to being Louis Armstrong. And I went back to trying to be invisible.

> *Do you know what it means to miss New Orleans*
> *When that's where you left your heart?*

Pete and Ray fell in line and started playing, eyes glued to the trumpeter. Oticha kept his eyes shut in a jazz reverie. But it didn't help. I felt watched and exposed, and I wished they would just go home.

27

I lie awake, staring at the ceiling and thinking, *the lies, the lies, the lies.* Because they *are* lies, and I know they're lies. What separates me from other people? Nothing. I know what I am, what I've done, what I'm capable of. And yet I let Susannah blather on about what a Good Man I am, and I pretend to agree with her, my stomach churning but my mouth glued shut.

You lie awake and you go over it all, a hundred times, and you wonder: How do the bad things happen? Where did they come from, when you never meant them to happen? Did they just erupt out of nowhere when the moment presented itself? Or were they brewing there your whole life, just waiting to be revealed? You don't know. So you walk your life backwards, step by step, to see if you can understand where you came from. You take an event and you look for the clues that preceded it. And maybe you find real clues, and maybe you just create clues, finding causation where there was nothing but chronology. And when you do that, your whole life starts to feel like an indictment.

Either way, when I walk it all backwards, I stop at age 12. I was at a summer camp up in Massachusetts—my first time going to a sleep-away camp. All the summers before then, I had just hung around at home, or gone to local day camps when we could afford them. After my father became a full professor and my mother went back to work, we had a little more money to spend, and I got to do more of the things that my friends and neighbors were doing. So I began my camp experience about five years after everyone else I knew. That was a great thing, of course, because boys are *very* tolerant and forgiving of newcomers who don't know their way around a place.

In this particular camp, which was an all-boy's camp, we slept in three-sided lean-to's—shacks, really—that were humid and moldy and smelly. Always smelly, even with one wall open to the air. There were three sets of bunk beds against the three walls, and six boys per cabin. One kid in our cabin was a huge pain in the ass. He complained all the time. He was spoiled. When we went on a hike and someone got hurt and needed a bandage, he refused to give up the bandana he was ostentatiously wearing around his neck— because it was expensive and he didn't want it to be ruined. We all hated him.

And was I, the new kid, relieved that we all hated *him*—that *he* got to be the goat instead of me? You bet your ass I was.

One lazy afternoon we were all sitting around the cabin— all of us except the Goat. And it occurred to us, in the way terrible ideas seem to drift in on the breeze and take over everything like a strong smell, that it would be seriously fun to cut holes in the Goat's underwear. Why this idea occurred to us, I have no idea. He had underwear; we had Swiss Army Knives. Apparently that was all that was necessary. So we opened up his trunk, took out all his briefs, and cut big holes in all the crotches. We laughed and laughed. Then we cut his soap in half. That was also pretty funny. Then we cut up his letters from home. Then we threw his transistor radio in the woods. Then we ruined his tennis racket. Then...

Well, you get the idea. When we finally looked up and caught our breaths, we had destroyed everything the kid had brought from home. Hundreds of dollars of stuff. And no one could exactly remember having *decided* to do all that. We *had* decided to embarrass him with some holes in his shorts. And then we just got... carried away.

Obviously, we did the only thing that honorable pre-teens could do—we lied like hell and told our counselors we had seen some Strange Adult lurking around the cabin. I don't think it occurred to any of us how stupid the story sounded, since only one boy's possessions had been touched in the whole cabin. But, you know, we were stupid.

The counselors made it clear the police would have to be called if our story was true. They interviewed us separately and worked each of us over until we broke. One of our counselors was a Brit who loved James Bond movies. He took the lead in the interrogation, thinking he was pretty suave. In fact, his true ace in the hole wasn't his withering line of questioning, but the fact that his elbows were double-jointed, which allowed him, while looming over the table in front of us, to flex his arms in horrible, inhuman ways that freaked the shit out of us. I don't know about the other kids, but after ten minutes of that treatment, I wanted out.

In the end, we all gave each other up —within fifteen minutes of each other, if I remember right. Amazingly, we didn't get kicked out of camp. We just had to pay to replace the Goat's things.

But who cares, right? It was summer camp. Why dwell on old shit like that? It's not like it launched me into a career of crime and mayhem. In fact, it did completely the opposite. And we're talking about murder and corruption in this Giselle case. You can't compare things like that to a little summer camp vandalism.

And that's valid. You can't compare them. But I'm just saying…I get it. I don't wreck things or like to see things wrecked. I'm a creator, after all—a musician. I'm a law-abiding citizen. But we've all had our moments, haven't we? There have definitely been moments where we've gone too far —each of us—crazily too far. And the nasty little secret is that those moments feel *great*. Not in retrospect, when your brain kicks back in, but right then, in the moment. Maybe you don't plan those moments, or ask for them to happen, but once you open the door to them, well…party on.

I hid from that fact for a long time—pretended I had never felt that thrill you feel from lashing out and just…*doing*… regardless of the cost. Because, to be honest, the feeling scares the hell out of me. I don't like the fact that I ever felt it, and I don't like the fact that I liked it, even for a second.

So yeah, maybe I've hung back too much and watched the parade go by. Maybe I haven't taken solos when I should have, or made demands and said "I want," or attracted attention to myself in other ways. Maybe that's just my character flaw—I've stayed in the shadows too much and observed. So sue me. But you know what? Maybe that's why I ended up doing what I'm doing for a living. Because to be a good investigator, you can't be a grandstander or a rock star or a showoff. You need stealth and silence.

There's a third thing, but I can't remember it right now.

28

I waited a week before I went down to the post office to check on my secret rental box. Then I checked every day to see if any questionnaires had been returned. Nothing. At the end of the second week, I started checking the box every *other* day. Still nothing, Either all nine of my Nine had tossed the thing in the garbage or all of their secretaries had done it for them. So…great idea in theory; lousy in practice. Kind of like my career as a musician.

And then, miraculously, three weeks after the survey had gone out in the mail, the responses began to trickle in. Little by little, they all came home to me.

See? Patience. That's the third thing I always forget. Patience.

They were all nicely filled out—all my stupid little questions answered with typical, Atlanta boosterism. No surprises in the whole bunch. With each returned survey, I learned whether or not someone had once owned a black Mercedes, and I could cross names off my list.

Until the very last one came in. This one was different. It had been crumpled up and then smoothed out, as though someone had thrown it in the garbage and then retrieved it. And instead of answers to my questions, someone had scrawled over it, in red marker, "LEAVE ME ALONE!"

Like hell.

Now, here's something I forgot to mention earlier. My brilliant wife did more than lay out one cover letter and survey to be copied; she actually created nine different letters, each with its own little identifier—a tiny little heart here, a circle there, a triangle—each one tagged in an Excel chart to a particular name, so that I could keep track of who was sending back what, just in case one of my big shots forgot to include his name. So I checked for the code markings, compared them to my master list, and within two minutes, I had my suspect.

That's right. Just like that. No Maltese falcon. No ancient curse. No hiding out in parking garages to meet Deep Throat. Just an Excel spreadsheet.

I told you—this work is *dull*.

29

Bobby Dokum was the kind of man who liked having his name on things. He liked having his name on a law firm—not the first name, but right up there in the number two position before the age of 40. He liked having his name on lists of angels and benefactors at the High Museum and the Woodruff Arts Center, two places he scrupulously avoided going to, except for fund-raisers. And he liked having his name in the newspaper...although probably not for running down junior associates at rival law firms.

He wasn't part of my father's circle, so I hadn't ever met him in person. But I knew his reputation. I knew all about him from my starving artist friends from college. Dokum was well known in their world for his financial generosity to—and his personal contempt for—the arts. He was the kind of guy who gave tons of money to an organization while badmouthing it and mocking it in public. He didn't care. He knew the money would buy him the prestige he wanted. And once he figured that out, I guess the public mockery and insult just made the purchased prestige that much more satisfying, as if he was saying, "you *have* to like me now, even if it kills you." And it really stung our local artists. They wanted to be loved. I mean, I know most artists want to be loved, but in a small city like Atlanta, it really upsets people when they're hated, because they know exactly *who* hates them, and it's their neighbors—the people they see every day.

Atlanta can be very strange like that. It's a city of four million people, depending where you draw the lines, but it feels like a small town. Maybe that's just my New York bias showing through, but I've lived here for a long time, now, and it's still pretty weird to me. I remember once, back in college, a local radio station ran a promotion or contest or something, where the winners got to go on a cruise with other people from Atlanta. That was the selling point—the chance to go on vacation with a bunch of random people who lived in your city. Come on down! Party with your fellow Hotlantans! Again, maybe it's just me, but I remember my reaction being, "why would I want to do *that?*"

Maybe it's a southern thing—that sense of place, or community, or family. I always find myself running into that and finding it strange. Whatever it is, it can make the city feel small. When you break up with someone in Atlanta, you actually have to parcel out which bars and restaurants each of you is going to get in the breakup, so that you don't have to cross paths and be embarrassed.

Anyway…where was I?

Bobby Dokum.

My point was: unlike in some other cities, you can't just write a check in Atlanta and be considered an angel. They expect you to show up, schmooze at intermission, be their *friend.* And when you don't do that—when you flaunt your beneficence and act like a pig because of it, word gets around fast. And so,

Lawyer Dokum, who liked to put his name on things, had also put his name on a big, ugly reputation—a reputation that had nothing to do with his ferocity as a litigator. They said he was a mean drunk, and a loudmouth, and a *nouveau riche* asshole with garish taste in cars, houses, and women.

Now, this is Atlanta, Georgia we're talking about, where they practically invented the concept of *nouveau riche*. This city is ground zero for tacky and ostentatious displays of wealth. And even in *this* environment, Dokum had outdone himself. He had a fleet of fancy cars, and a mansion to make Atlanta's standard mini-mansions look like chicken shacks. I mean, this house was so big it had elevators. Okay—*one* elevator. But still.

This was one of my Mercedes Men, and this was the author of the red, scrawled, "LEAVE ME ALONE!" And I have to admit, it pleased me greatly to think that this crass egomaniac was the man I was going to hand over, on a silver platter, to Ted Palmer.

I placed a call to Manhattan, to Palmer's office, happy for once to have some good news to report.

"I have a name for you," I said, trying not to sound too excited.

"Really?" he asked. "That's….that's great work, Jordan. I'm impressed."

He didn't sound impressed. He sounded amazed, and maybe a little suspicious. But I let it pass.

"Yes, sir," I said, super politely. "It turns out there were some real leads to pursue. The police just didn't pursue them."

"Are you certain? That sounds very—"

"I know it does, Mr. Palmer, But you'll understand why in a minute. Our guy is a lawyer here in town. A pretty well-known one, actually. Powerful. The cops had reasons for not pursuing this case."

"What do you mean, they had reasons?"

"Well, I don't know for sure, Mr. Palmer, but I'm pretty sure they knew who killed Giselle. The cops did. Either they decided not to go after the guy or he convinced them not to go after him. But they knew."

I could hear him take a deep, stay-in-control breath. "That's a pretty serious accusation, Jordan."

"I know it. So the question is: what do you want to do now?"

"Hmmm." He pondered on this for a while.

"If you give the police the name," I prompted, "they'll probably have to do something with it. Especially since it's a whole new crew now, at the midtown precinct."

"Yes…" he said slowly and carefully. "Perhaps. But something might not be everything."

"Do you really think they'd bury the investigation a second time?" I asked.

"I'm not saying they'd bury it. But they're down there, and I'm up there."

"That's true, but I can keep an eye on them for you, if you want. Make sure they stay on it."

"Yes…" he said again, slowly and carefully. Clearly he didn't love that idea.

"Okay, here's another idea," I said. "You could leak the name to the newspapers and let them stir up some trouble for you. That would keep your name out of it, but it would make the thing public enough that the police couldn't weasel out of investigating it."

"The papers. Interesting," he said. "The papers didn't care a hell of a lot about this story three years ago."

"Oh, they'd care now, Mr. Palmer. If they heard this name, they'd care."

"And what is that name?" he asked.

"Dokum. Bobby Dokum. He's an attorney here in town."

"Dokum? With a k?"

"That's right." I could hear him scribbling down the name.

He snuffled a little. "I've never heard of a lawyer with a name like Bobby before."

"It's the South, Mr. Palmer," I said. "It could have been Bubba just as easily."

He didn't seem to find it funny.

"And you say he's an important man?" he asked.

"Oh, yeah," I said. "A lot of exposure. A lot of money."

"All right," he said. "That's good. Thank you, Jordan. I'll take it from here."

The brush off caught me by surprise. "Well, hold on," I said. "I think before you do anything, we ought to investigate a little bit more, just to be certain. I want to make sure—"

"Yes, yes. I understand. But I think we should settle up accounts now. Invoice me and I'll put your last check in the mail."

"Sir, if we could just—"

"I'm perfectly capable of calling a newspaper, Jordan. If that's what's required. Thank you."

This was weird.

"Yes, sir. Of course. I know you are. I'm just saying—"

It didn't matter what I was saying. I tried to find another opening, but we were done. He was making that painfully clear. I had served my purpose.

Listen, I wasn't expecting accolades or anything, but a thank-you might have been nice. A "let's work together to finish this," would have been nice. But I guess it was stupid of me to expect anything from him. He wanted to be rid of me as quickly as possible. I had to remember that it was a miracle he had hired me in the first place.

I hung up the phone and felt the silence of my dreary office close in around me. I didn't want to be there anymore. I didn't feel victorious, or vindicated, or even relieved. I felt nothing—just a kind of echo inside, where I knew something else should be. So I closed up shop, forwarded my phone, and headed home.

30

The house was quiet except for Eliot the cat whistling past furniture and curtains. Susannah wouldn't be home for another hour or two. Oticha was probably at home with the kids, but I didn't much feel like going over there. I wasn't in the mood for quiet, but I wasn't in the mood for conversation either. I stuck a speaker in the window, cranked up WCLK, the jazz station out of Clark College, and sat out on the porch with a beer, to watch my corner of the world go by and let some good tunes drift past my ears. Some Miles, maybe. Some Monk.

But no such luck. The music was so god-awfully bad I had to turn it off after ten minutes.

I'm not a snob, I don't think, but half the shit they were playing sounded like the soundtrack from a movie you'd never want to see, and the other half sounded like someone trying to be Spyrogyra and failing (not that succeeding would have sounded much better).

All right, so maybe I *am* a snob. But the radio had barely been on for five minutes when a jazz interpretation of "Love Shack" came on. I mean, seriously, people. "Love Shack?" Just because someone is stupid enough to record a track like that doesn't mean you're obligated to play it. Have a little respect for the form, will you?

I turned off the radio and sat, watching traffic, but there were too many voices in my head, too much of that empty echo in my chest, and the whole point had been to *avoid* that. So I grabbed my IPod, set it to play the loud headbanger music of my childhood, and went for a long run.

And that's pretty much how the next few days went by. I had a couple of other cases waiting for me at the office, but they weren't urgent, and I wasn't feeling real motivated. Which was strange, because they were exactly the kinds of cases I had been handling before all of this Giselle mess had happened: an angry, alcoholic daughter wanting a bigger chunk of her late father's estate and looking for leverage; a high school principal concerned that his school was harboring a cheating ring, but not wanting to call the cops; and three very ordinary background checks. They were my bread and butter.

Every morning, I put in my handful of hours at the office, then came home to exercise, or play the bass, or read. It was the same slacker routine I had been living for years, but all of a sudden, my heart wasn't in it. Or maybe my heart *was* in it for the first time, and I had just discovered how stupid and meaningless my days had been. All of a sudden, my usual cases felt empty. And the case I had just closed felt unresolved.

That was the problem. What I needed was resolution. Ordinarily, I don't care what happens to my clients. I take a picture of some married dipshit in a hotel room with a cheerleader, and I collect my check. I don't need to know what happens when the wife confronts the dipshit. I don't care if they end up in counseling, divorce court, or a threesome with the cheerleader. I don't *want* to know.

But this was different. Not knowing was killing me. Had Palmer made a call? Had anyone taken the bait? Were the police finally doing their job? Why wasn't I hearing anything about it on the news?

That's what I was asking. And for my sins, I got my answer.

It was about two weeks after Palmer had brushed me off. The fall weather had turned foul just as I had started an afternoon run around Candler Park. I raced home, soaked to the bone, and decided to call it a day. I dried myself off and decided to plop down in front of some bad daytime television until Susannah came home. I found one of those Judge Judy clone shows. Idiot A suing Idiot B because B borrowed A's car and got it all dented up. It was perfect.

I must have nodded off, because the next thing I knew, the phone was ringing, a different show was on TV, and the room was dark. I grabbed the phone groggily and answered before I was even sure where I was.

"Is this Jordan Greenblatt?" a sharp voice snapped at me.

I mumbled something in the affirmative, rubbing the sleep out of my eyes.

"Name's Marshall Micton. I'm an attorney with Anderson, McIntosh, Lamarr."

"Okay," I said, noncommittally. I knew the firm, but not the guy. I had done some work for them over the years. They were ambulance chasers. Not that I cared. A job was a job.

"Mr. Greenblatt, you've been named in a civil suit being brought against an Atlanta attorney named Robert Dokum. Are you familiar with this gentleman?"

That woke me up. "What do you mean, named?"

"As a witness for the plaintiff, Mr. Theodore Palmer of Great Neck, NY. We're representing Mr. Palmer in this action."

What?

"I'm sorry," I said. "You said this was a civil suit? What kind of civil suit? I mean, what's the…what's he suing for?"

"Wrongful death, Mr. Greenblatt."

I scrambled for something to say, but nothing came out of my mouth.

"Hello? Mr. Greenblatt?"

"Yes, I'm here," I said, finally.

"I'm scheduling depositions for next week, and I wanted to check your availability."

"Yeah, okay," I fumbled. "I'm…I'm pretty flexible."

We set up a time and I hung up. I was still dazed. But it wasn't from sleepiness; it was from the news. I didn't know how to process it. I wasn't even sure where to start.

A lawsuit? Really? Where the hell had that come from? When Palmer had hung up on me, we were talking about going to the newspapers, or getting the guy arrested, whatever. Getting some serious justice, after all this time. But a *lawsuit*?

Second, why was Palmer using Atlanta locals instead of whatever hot-shit Manhattan firm he probably kept on retainer? That didn't make any sense either. You bring suit against another attorney, you bring your big guns, don't you? What was the play here, going local, using people Dokum probably knew and despised? I mean, of all the local firms, why *these guys*? These guys were hacks. I mean, I hate to bite the hand that feeds, and all that, but…you know…it is what it is. They're hacks.

Finally—and most importantly—*wrongful death*? What the fuck was *that* all about? That's what they hit OJ Simpson with., when they couldn't pin murder on him. It's a desperation play.

I hadn't really thought about what might happen once I gave Palmer the name. As usual. But if I *had* thought about it, I definitely wouldn't have expected *this*. A newspaper or TV investigation is where I thought we were going. A prod to get the local police to re-open the case. I mean, he was looking for *justice*, wasn't he?— someone to get perp-walked into a police car and hauled off to jail, finally? Giselle's name and story resurrected and discussed in the light of day? Someone to speak for his dead little girl? Isn't that what he wanted—someone to *pay* for his little girl?

Whoa.

Well.

Maybe "pay" was the right word here—because that's all he was going to see out of a civil suit. He'd get Dokum to admit negligence and responsibility, or a jury would admit it for him—and the loudmouth little bastard would have to pay some kind of restitution in cash. And then he'd go home. That's what wrongful death gets you. An admission and a payout. Maybe just the payout, along with an agreement that everyone keeps their mouth shut.

Suddenly, I had a sinking, horrible feeling in the pit of my stomach. When Palmer had first called me, he had mentioned something about not being able to fly down to meet me. I had wondered, back then, whether he had fallen on hard times. Is *that* what this was about? Had he resurrected this case, three years later, just to make some *money* off of it?

I sat down at my computer and started doing what I had been tempted to do right after he first called me—what I probably *should* have done. I started snooping on my client.

It was an easy snoop. He was plastered all over the Internet. Bad investments, suspect investments, businesses closing, wealth collapsing like a house of cards. There were stories stretching back over a year. I didn't understand half of them, but the general gist was pretty clear. Palmer was in trouble.

I didn't spend a whole lot of time with Palmer types, growing up, but I knew the kinds of things they dressed their lives up with. Country clubs, golf games, summer trips to Europe, houses in the Berkshires. All of that, plus a few Ivy League tuitions thrown in for good measure. It couldn't have been an easy ship to keep afloat. When the money dries up, what do you cut out first? What do you decide you can do without, if your whole personality and status is built on doing with?

Or do you decide you *can't* do without?

So maybe he *was* after the cash, and justice be damned. Find out if the killer has deep pockets, then frighten the guy into a quick payoff. That was the only scenario that made sense to me. He had pumped me for information and then hung up on me to spring into action. He must have been salivating when I told him who Dokum was. It must have sounded like a dream come true. He was probably praying, every night, that the killer didn't turn out to be some house painter or fraternity jock.

Now it all made sense. Why the local hacks? For the same reason he hired me instead of one of the better known firms in town. Get the job done cheap. Cheap and fast, without a lot of questions. And maybe he figured we'd be hungry enough not to care too much about the ethics of what we were doing, happy to cash his checks and call it a day.

So that's why he hadn't hung up on me, back in August. What he thought I was…all the worst things he thought I was— that was exactly what he wanted. I was a dream come true.

I didn't have a lot of time to process these thoughts. The phone rang and my sinking feeling turned to nausea as I saw from the caller ID that it was Palmer. I had no idea what to say to him, or whether I'd have the nerve to say it. I flirted with the idea of letting it go to voice mail, but I gave in at the last second and picked it up. Before I could even get a "hello" out of my mouth, he was yelling at me.

"Are you watching the news?"

"What news?"

"The news. The goddamned news. What do you mean? He's on the fucking television right now."

The TV was still on in my darkening living room, with the volume down low. I turned it up and surfed through the channels till I found a local station showing its early evening news program. There was Bobby Dokum, holding forth in front of a forest of microphones. He looked happier than a pig in shit, as they say down here. He always looked happy when he had the attention of the press. I turned up the volume and caught him in mid-rant.

"…And this is exactly how these lawyers get the reputation they have—these TV-advertising, strip-mall office, so-called attorneys…" he pontificated. I had no idea what he was talking about.

"This is on in New York?" I asked the phone, amazed.

"He's on CNN, for Christ's sake!" Palmer yelled. "What's the matter with you?"

Why was he so angry? What had Dokum been saying? I couldn't figure it out. He was going on and on about his noble profession and the ethics of the law, clearly enjoying his moment in the spotlight. I slowly began to put the pieces together. Palmer's idiot lawyers must have opened *all* the floodgates today. And their mark wasn't reacting the way they had hoped.

"Are you watching now?" Palmer yelled at me. "Are you listening to this shit?"

"Mr. Palmer." I said his name over and over, trying to get his attention and calm him down. "Mr. Palmer, please…when did all of this happen? Why did you—"

"Did you *hear* him? Did you hear him talk about his alibi?"

"No. No, I didn't. What's—"

"He wasn't *there*. He wasn't in town. He has evidence, witnesses, you name it. It's blatantly fucking obvious. And he's going to *counter*-sue, for fuck's sake."

"Oh. I didn't—"

"Didn't what? Didn't check? Didn't bother to find out before handing his name over to me? What the fuck kind of operation are you running down there? You've screwed up *everything*!"

My cheeks were burning, and I could feel a line of sweat breaking out along my forehead. No, I hadn't checked his alibi. I hadn't checked anything. Was I supposed to? I had just...what *had* I done? I guess I had figured someone else would do all that, down the road. My job was just to give him the name. Wasn't it?

"LEAVE ME ALONE!" Dokum had written on the response form. Had that been a sign of a guilty conscience, or just an act of self-righteous pissiness from a loudmouth egomaniac? Which answer made sense? Which was a stretch of imagination?

Fuck. How had I gotten here? I hadn't even been looking for this. I hadn't been expecting anything except some basic information from the car owners. All I wanted to know was the color of the cars. But then he *did* respond the way he did, and I must have assumed...well, I *did* assume. I thought his scrawling was in response to... that it was making him remember the accident. And then somehow, I must have assumed that he had assumed that the survey was from someone looking into the accident…

Shit. This was bad. That was way too many "assumes," and none of them made any sense. Why the fuck had I called Palmer so soon? Why hadn't I waited until I really knew something?

Why? Because I was lazy, that's why. I didn't think about what was in front of me. I didn't question it. I didn't *doubt*. I just grabbed it and ran.

Dokum kept yapping and yammering about how he was going to protest this and stop that, introduce legislation to bar something or other. Palmer kept yelling about my incompetence, and his humiliation, and what this was going to look like for him in tomorrow's papers. But I couldn't hear either of them anymore. All I could hear was the roaring in my ears. And it didn't matter if Palmer was a cheap shithead who wanted to cash in on his daughter's death. It didn't matter what his motives had been. All that mattered was that I had fucked up.

31

There are three things you need if you want to be a good investigator: stealth, silence, and patience. Stealth so people don't notice you when you don't want to be noticed; silence so you can hear things that other people miss; and patience to get through the times when people scream at you on the telephone, call you a loser and a failure, blame you for embarrassing them, and tell you never to call them again.

You need a lot of patience.

It was late October—the time, in Atlanta, when the weather finally begins to cool down, and the leaves, if they're going to turn color at all, start to turn. I had been working on this case since mid-August. Now it was over. I had been fired—loudly, angrily, and unequivocally. I was to pack up all the articles and photos that Ted Palmer had sent me and ship them back to him as soon as possible. And I was never—ever—to contact him or his family again.

If he hadn't shut me out when I first told him about
Dokum, I could have told him he was moving too fast. I could
have told him that I didn't have all the facts. I tried to tell him.
Just maybe not hard enough. And granted, I shouldn't have
called him at all until I had all the facts. Point taken. But he *had*
moved too soon. And he had made a fool of himself…on my say
so. Can you blame the guy for blowing up at me?

I couldn't. I don't, even now. I fucked up. And I got what I
deserved.

Susannah got home about twenty minutes after I hung up
with Palmer, and she could tell instantly what kind of a day I'd
been having. It wasn't just an "oh, poor dear" look on her face.
When I looked at her, I could see something crushed in my own
face, reflected in hers.

There's nothing worse than seeing that look on the face of
someone you love. You get it for just a second, before they
change their expression to something like sympathy and worry.
It's a look of fear, and you can tell it's you who's causing the fear.
And for a second—one of those long, strung-out seconds—you
have this whole monologue with yourself. Did I do that? Did I
do something to cause you to have that look in your eyes? Don't
be *afraid*. It's just me. You know me. You don't need to be scared
of me. Or are you scared *for* me? But you shouldn't be scared at
all. It's just me.

It's only a second—and then the look is gone, and your
monologue is gone, and the scene changes into something else.

Susannah didn't say a word. She just took my hand, led me
to the door, and walked me down the street to Fellini's Pizza.
She didn't say a word until we were sitting with a pitcher of beer

and a platter of pizza warming up the table. And then all she said was, "What happened?"

So I gave her whole, ugly story, in three part harmony—theme, variation, and resolution. When I finished, we ate our pizza in silence for a while.

"So what now?" she finally said. "You go back to medical school?" Which gave me the first smile of my day.

"Too late for that," I said. "I guess I go back to work. I've got a bunch of cases waiting."

"Anything exciting?"

"No," I said simply.

She nodded, then reached out to take my hand.

"Good," she said.

32

"Blues for Mingus" on the office stereo. Me at my desk, studying photos of Mr. Darshi Patel's asshole—or, rather, the raw meat left behind by a series of clumsy surgeries on Mr. Darshi Patel's asshole. Was his hemorrhoid surgery botched? This is what he wanted to know.

Blues for Anus.

Outside my grimy window, the one tree I could see amidst the concrete had lost its leaves. Halloween had come and gone. Thanksgiving was fast approaching. The Palmer nightmare was receding in the rear-view mirror. Life and work had gotten back to normal.

Of course, normal for me is a little bit strange. I mean, it's unsettling to look at medical records and x-rays and photographs of people you don't know, especially if you're not their doctor. There's something creepily intimate about the whole thing. Maybe if I had made it all the way through med school…or even *to* med school…it wouldn't seem like such a big deal. I don't know. It's a very small part of my work, so when I sit there, having to study it, it feels weird. And the fact that it feels weird is, itself, kind of weird, right? I mean, remember, you're talking to a guy who spies through a telephoto lens on total strangers having sex in motel rooms, so...creepily intimate is something I should be used to. But there's something about looking at people's insides, I guess—seeing their medical secrets, understanding before they do when they're doomed—stuff like that gets under my skin (so to speak). I don't like it.

But here's this nice man, Mr. Patel, and he's in pain, and he's embarrassed, and he doesn't know who he can trust. He thinks he's been screwed, and he thinks he's being ignored. No one at the hospital wants to talk to him about his surgery. They're treating him like a problem now, not a patient—to the point where he's convinced his surgeon has called all his doctor-buddies to make sure no one gives Patel a reliable second opinion, or even a return phone call. Not that he can afford to go trotting around town, paying for doctor visit after doctor visit. His insurance does not look kindly on such expenses. He's lucky they covered the surgery in the first place. So what's he supposed to do?

He comes to see me, that's what. Someone tells him there's a PI in town who has a little medical training—maybe just enough to tell him if he has a case, to tell him if it's worth investing in the lawyers. Either way, the PI's office visit is cheaper than a doctor's. So he comes to see me, large manila envelope in hand. And I say I'll look at his pictures and let him know if I see anything that looks strange.

Now, like I said, I dropped out of pre-med in college, so calling what I have "a little medical training" is misleading. But I can do research. And I can usually tell what I'm looking at—more than my competition, anyway.

So I studied the photos, and I compared them to pictures I had in some of my old textbooks, and some other gruesome photos online, and then I called the man back with my verdict: yes, it looks like they butchered you. Call the lawyers. Hire the experts. For me: case closed. Check's in the mail. Grateful client.

This is how it's supposed to be done. No angst. No worries. No emotional connection or baggage. It's a job—like everyone else has a job. You go to work, you do your assignment, you get your paycheck. Whatever the assignment is, you do it. Solve a problem, write a report, clean up a mess—whatever. It's just *work*. And if you do it well, you can feel good about yourself.

So why didn't I feel good about myself today?

Never mind. On to the next: standard issue divorce case—a wife who thought her soon-to-be-ex was hiding some assets from her, and wanted them accounted for before the Big Split was formalized by the lawyers. Very common, very ordinary, very boring.

Unfortunately, after my morning smorgasbord of organs and viscera, I wasn't in any shape to plunge into a new case. And I definitely wasn't in any shape to face lunch. So I took a walk to get some fresh air, then drove down to Underground Atlanta to do a little Christmas and Chanukah shopping, since my marital situation requires covering both bets. The Chanukah part is easy, since it's just me and my dad. But the Christmas part is pretty hardcore. Susannah has sisters and nieces and nephews and cousins with children and on and on and on. Family planning is, like, Item #17 in the long list of ways that her family and mine are from different planets.

When I got back to the office, the lack of any free space where I could giftwrap my packages inspired me to clean up a little. I put Mr. Patel's photos back in their envelope, addressed it, and left it on top of another box waiting by the door. Then I grabbed the garbage can and began the Great Purge.

Usually, when it's time to get out of the office for the day, I don't stick around to clean up. It's small, it's airless, and it's lonely. No one ever sees it but me. If I thought I could get any work done at home, I'd never leave home. But I'm not super-productive at home. Not when the bass is leaning against the wall, waiting for me, all day, and Susannah is leaning against the wall in a strangely similar pose at night.

Anyway, my point is: my office is a mess, and it stays that way for months. So when I say "Great Purge," I'm not kidding. When I finally get around to cleaning, I'm not real picky. Everything goes—everything that hasn't been filed or stowed somewhere. So, on this particular November day, there was a flurry of burger wrappers, newspapers, notes that once meant something, notes that had never meant anything, obscene doodles, and a pile of those old Mercedes surveys that had gotten shoved into a corner but never thrown away. All of it went into the can as I tornadoed around the room.

And then I stopped. Something was tickling at the corner of my brain. I looked down into the can and saw, sitting at the top of the papers, the checklist I had made to keep track of the Mercedes surveys —names, addresses, date mailed, date received, and so on—the same piece of paper where I had excitedly and idiotically circled Bobby Dokum's name. I looked at the incriminating evidence and wondered, for a moment, if I ought to keep it as a memento—a reminder of my haste and a warning to take time (patience!) and go through all the necessary steps. Let other people frame their diplomas or the first dollar they ever earned—at the Billy Barnes office, we'd frame failure.

I pulled the paper back out of the garbage can and sat down at my desk to ponder on it, as they say here in the South. And suddenly, for the first time, I noticed something. Right there in the middle of the list—just two names below the big, red circle around Dokum's name—was a name without a check mark.

Was that possible? Had I really missed that? Out of all my so-called suspects, had one—and only one—sent nothing back?

I remembered what Carter had said: the mole wants to stay in his hole. The mole doesn't want to bring attention to himself. I had gotten all excited about Dokum, thinking he had given himself away, when that was the *last* thing the real culprit would have done. If there really was a missing survey, could it have been the mole himself, speaking loud and clear in spite of himself? It didn't have to mean that he knew why I was sending the survey—all it had to mean was that he had some reason for not wanting to think or talk about his old car.

Could I have really been that lucky without realizing it? And that stupid?

I went back to the garbage can and dumped the contents on the floor. So much for the cleaning tornado. I sat down next to the pile and raked through the papers to rescue the original surveys I had just thrown away. I cross-checked them with the list of names on my checklist. It was true—they were all present and accounted for...all but one: Judge James Harper.

Did I grimace when I saw that familiar name? Did I pause when I realized how close to home this whole thing could hit, and how dangerous it was going to be to take up the chase again?

I did not.

Did I stop for even a second to think to myself, "this is way out of your league—you were right to let it go"?

No.

Not at all. I was too pleased with myself. I was energized again. Yeah, yeah, it's a job. It's an assignment. I know what I said. But you know what? That's all bullshit. When you get the scent of blood up in your nose, you can't help it—you strain against the leash and you want to *move*—you want to get out there and find the bastard. When you realize, "this asshole *is* cheating on his wife," you *want* to get out there with the camera and catch him, even if you couldn't care less about the wife. Because it's wrong, what he's doing, and maybe you're the only one who knows it. And that means it's your job to do something about it.

So instead of worrying about my next step—instead of worrying about my family—instead of worrying about my*self*— I leaned back in my chair, plopped Billy Barnes' old fedora on my head, and said: *Gotcha.*

33

"This is impossible," my father said.

"Because you want it to be," I countered. "You saw what I sent out. He was the only one who didn't respond."

"Which means exactly nothing," he said, trying to maintain his professorial voice, but clearly angry with me. "At best, you can prove that he hates junk mail. Or that someone in his office hates junk mail. Or that it was lost. This is every bit as irresponsible as what you did with that idiot, Dokum."

"Come on," I said, getting up and starting to pace. "This was a total vanity play, and every guy I mailed it to sent it back. Every single one of them. So you're saying he—just him—just the judge, alone—has no ego?"

"No," he said quietly. "If I said that, it would be an assumption. Just as your preposterous decision that he's a murderer is an assumption." He stared at me coldly. "Not a fact. Nothing like a fact."

"But still—"

"But nothing, Jordy. You're basing a very damning conclusion on an assumption of how people—in general—should behave. People in general do X. This person—if it *was* that person and not a secretary, which you don't know, and if it *was* a willful action and not an oversight, which you also don't know—did Y. Therefore this person is suspicious—not because he did anything wrong; but because he did something unusual...according to *your* definition of the usual. Which could be completely wrong. You don't have a clue. And I mean that literally."

"It *is* a clue. It's not a good one, maybe, but it's something."

He snorted, and looked back down at the work he had been doing before I interrupted him. I could tell I was starting to sound petty, so I retreated a bit. "Anyway, he's *your* friend. You know him better than I do. Would he really turn down a chance to have his picture in a magazine?"

He sighed, lifted his hands to his face, and kneaded his caterpillar eyebrows, as if to drive away a headache. "Probably not, Jordy. Probably not. But there are a hundred reasons why he might not have responded to your little game. A hundred, minimum. And murder is the least likely of them. I know the man, Jordy. *You* know the man. He's my friend."

He removed his hands from his eyes, leaving his face red and tired-looking. He tilted his head to one side, studying me. "The girl's dead, Jordy. She's been dead a long time. Why keep jumping the gun like this? Why rush to judgment?"

"Who's rushing?" I said unhappily.

"You are. Where's your proof? Where's your evidence? Do you realize what would happen if—"

"I'm not one of your students, Dad. I don't need *proof*. I mean, it's not like I'm trying a court case. I'm just the guy who digs up the dirt, as you always remind me."

"And you're happy about that, are you? Satisfied to be settling for dirt, rather than proof?"

"All I have to do is give her father a name. He wants to make trouble with it, that's his business. He wants to sue the judge and go for a payout, he can hire people to do the legwork, like he should have done with Dokum. He can hire some other PI. I don't care. Or if he really cares about justice, he can harass the cops to go find proof, like they should have done in the first place. But either way, I'll have done the job he paid me for, and that actually does matter to me."

My father stared at me with a look of stunned disappointment I knew too well. He didn't say anything. He didn't have to. I knew his moral compass; I knew what he was thinking.

"All right, all right," I said, plopping back down in the chair. "I know Palmer is an asshole. I wouldn't ruin the judge's career on a hunch. That's not what I meant. But it's a start, isn't it? At least now I can focus on one name, instead of a hundred. And if it *does* turn out to be credible, then I can give Palmer the name."

"Always the short cut," he sighed. "Always looking for the easy way out."

"That's not fair," I said softly, knowing it was more fair than I could admit.

See, this was always my problem. My dad was always the smartest grown-up I knew—my whole life. In high school, I wanted to be a teenage rebel, like everyone else, but it was impossible to disagree with him. He was right. He was always right. And being a lawyer, he loved forcing you to concede the point. Even at the dinner table, just talking about whatever. Politics. Music. He loved to provoke an argument, test your logic, hear your opinion. But God forbid if you couldn't back up what you were saying. God fucking forbid. You think the Stones are better than the Beatles? Why, Jordy. Based on what? And what does better mean, anyway? Better at *what*, exactly? I'm sorry? What was that? They rock? "They rock" is not an answer. Not that he disagreed, mind you. No, no, no—in fact, you might find out, after the fact, that he preferred the Stones, too. But *he* had reasons. And if you didn't have reasons—logical, supportable reasons—he'd tear you to shreds. Even if he agreed with you. Just for the blood sport of it.

And if he turned that laser beam on *you*—your clothes, or your haircut, or your schoolwork, or your choice of friends— well, God help you then, for real. If you couldn't support and defend whatever was being dissected—stand by it and fight for it—you might as well just abandon it. You want to be a rebel, Jordy? That's fine—the world needs rebels and dissenters. Just explain to me what you're rebelling *against*. What is it you're trying to accomplish?

Accomplish. I was a fucking teenager. I wasn't trying to accomplish anything.

Which, in his eyes, was precisely the problem. No drive. No goals. No stick-to-it-iveness, he called it.

And it was true. He challenged; I folded. Over and over again.

And now here he was, for the ten thousandth time, staring at me with those prosecutor's eyes. Weighing the evidence before him and finding me guilty on all counts.

"You say I'm not being fair," he said quietly. "Because...what? You're working at your full potential here? Trying your hardest? Fulfilling your destiny? Living the life you want?"

I groaned.

"All right, you want to muck around as a private eye. Fine. But do a decent job at if, can't you? An ethical job? At least?"

"I said I wasn't going to turn over his name yet."

"Even so, Jordy. Do you really think this...postcard you sent out represents top-flight investigative work? You were so certain it was Dokum, and look what happened there."

"I know." I said—shrinking in the chair. "It's just a place to start, I said. I know I have to do my homework. I just wanted to...see what you thought about it. About him."

"What do I think? I think this is a federal judge you're talking about. You can't go stalking him like your usual prey, taking pictures of him with his girlfriends. The man—his position—they deserve respect and circumspection. That's what I think. The man can sue you for defamation just as easily as look at you. The man can have you arrested. Think about who his friends are. Think about what you're doing."

"I am."

"I don't think so, son. Not clearly enough. You're about to put yourself in a very dangerous and untenable position. You've sat in on my classes. You've seen how difficult it can be to build a case. How painstaking and slow. But you take the time, and you do it right, because if you cut corners, you lose the case. Or you never get to make the case, because it gets thrown out of court. You have to be sure, Jordy—you have to be so terribly sure before you really shine the light on this thing and let other people see it. If you haven't considered every angle, examined every assumption, the whole thing will blow up in your face."

I said nothing. There was nothing left to say.

"And he's my friend, Jordy," he added. "On top of everything else. He's my friend. You come here, you say you just want to see what I think, but you know....you *know* who he is. His friends are my friends. His circle is my circle. He's a good man."

He started to say something else, then thought better of it. Maybe he figured it wasn't worth it. He nodded to himself—a little sadly—as if to confirm that he had said enough, and then he looked back down at some student papers on his desk and shuffled them a little. I got up from his guest chair and waved a hopeless goodbye. He nodded, smiled weakly, and stared back down at his pile of papers. I stumbled out, as though I were a teenager again, unused to my growing body.

Well, it was my own, stupid fault. I had come to gloat, show the old man I knew what I was doing. And I had gotten exactly what I deserved. Did I really think a little thing like this was going to change our whole relationship? The whole embarrassing dance he and I had been doing since I was eighteen? No, actually: twelve. This had been going on since I was twelve—ever since my sixth-grade class had taken a field trip to watch his law students put on a mock trial. We had had to leave before the end, but my dad had taped the whole thing for us. I took the video in to school the next week, so we could watch the ending and find out how the jury had ruled. We watched the last witness or two, and then all of a sudden, my dad's face came on the screen, and he started talking—on and on—about evidence. About trials. He was *teaching*, for Christ's sake! I was totally embarrassed. He had spliced himself in, right before the ending, to make the whole thing about *him*. Everyone in class started to grumble and whine. Some of them laughed. So I fast-forwarded past him so we could see the jury's verdict. But—surprise! There *was* no verdict. The old man talked and talked, zooming by in fast-motion, and then the screen went dead. The whole class started yelling and griping, and they all blamed me. A whole day's field trip, and then all this time in class, and now we don't even get to see the end? What kind of stupid rip-off was this?

So I went home in righteous, twelve-year-old rage and confronted him. And, of course, as it turned out, I had misunderstood everything. He had left the verdict out on purpose, so that we could act as our own jury. Because the point of the whole thing was supposed to be that we weren't watching some movie, but participating in a real-life event that had no foregone conclusion. *We* had the power to determine the conclusion. In fact, there *was* no conclusion without us. Which I would have known if I had just allowed the tape to play and let the class hear him speak. He had spent two hours writing up instructions for us, like a judge would give to a jury, but written specifically for a kid audience, telling us how important our job was, how exciting and scary it was to sit in judgment of one's peers. He had had a student come in and tape him, and he had fussed over it until it was just right. It was a gift to me—to my classmates. It was a big fucking deal. And I had zoomed right through it, too embarrassed to let him speak—too stupid to understand what I had been given.

And it's been like that between us ever since.

I could tell you the whole scene that followed my first misguided confrontation with him—how sad and embarrassed my dad looked as he explained what he had tried to do for me and my friends— the terrible, wish-I-could-crawl-off-and-die feeling I had, deep in my chest, standing there and learning what a shitty son I was.

But fuck it. I don't have the stomach for it.

34

Porkchop let out a profound, resonant belch and pushed his plate of nachos back towards the center of the table. He leaned back, folded his hands over his belly, and smiled at me.

"Does this mean the meter is running?" I asked.

"Jordy boy," he said in a reedy voice that in no way matched his bulk, "If I had a meter on you, it would have started the minute you walked in the door. Now, what's the problem?"

Porkchop is my attorney. Actually, he's a friend who just happens to be an attorney. I've never had to use his legal services, though I'm told he's quite good. I just like to refer to him as my attorney for the gonzo-ish joke of it. I can't even imagine him in a courtroom. Whenever I try to picture him, he's still wearing the grass skirt I first saw him in, at a rugby party, when he was trying to talk a freshman girl into bed by drinking a glass of soy sauce on a dare.

Porkchop no longer wears an actual pork bone on a string around his neck like he used to, but the name has stuck in certain circles. For a lawyer, he looks reasonably respectable and grown-up. For a Viking, though, which he swears is his genetic heritage, he isn't much to look at. Short and round and bald, he's gone soft everywhere but in his eyes, which have remained sharp and dangerous long after the rest of him has turned to mush. At the moment, those eyes were trained on me.

"It's like this," I started. "I have a client...well, I *sort of* have a client, who wants me to tail a prominent guy in the community. And...first of all, it's not about anything this guy is currently doing; it's about something he may have done in the past, so it's not like I can really *tail* him to catch him in the act. But like I said, he's a prominent guy, so I'm not sure I could get away with that even if I wanted to. The problem is, I'm not sure what I *can* do. I mean legally, to...you know...get the mole out of his hole."

Porkchop cleared his throat and gave a little laugh. "Well, to begin with, I like your assumption that the *non*-prominent among us are legally open and available to your harassment—and when I say 'like,' I mean, of course, that I'm appalled and horrified."

"Yeah, yeah..."

"I'm guessing you don't have anything that we in the legal business would call evidence."

"Not as such, no."

"Excellent. But you have a hunch."

"More than a hunch."

"More than a hunch, but less than an indictment."

175

"Exactly."

He paused for a moment, then brightened up. "You could beat the shit out of him."

"Thanks. Is that your legal counsel?"

"Legal counsel? Jordy boy, whatever you're doing, no lawyer should be connected with it in any way beyond gossip."

"So, simply as a friend and a former rugby player, you advocate violence."

"Whenever possible."

"There's got to be another way."

"You liberal Yankees always say that, but then you never manage to come up with anything practical."

"Yankee? What the hell does that make you? You're from Minnesota."

"True, but the South long ago welcomed me into her fragrant and voluminous bosom."

"I'm happy for you."

Porkchop polished off his beer and waved to the waitress for a refill. "Okay," he said, getting down to business. "You've got a mole in the hole, as you say, and you need to get him to come out and show his face."

"Just so."

"Okay. Basically, you've got two ways to pull someone out of the shadows. He comes out to *get* something or he comes out to get *away* from something."

"I'm with you."

"How secure is your man where he is? How safe is his mole hole?"

"Pretty damned safe."

"You said he was..."

"A prominent member of the community."

"And you're using that ridiculous euphemism because..."

"It's better if you don't know who he is."

"Outstanding."

The waitress cruised by and dumped a new beer in front of my attorney, splashing foam everywhere. "By God, I love this place," Porkchop yelled, either to embarrass or reward the waitress for her truculence. It's hard to know which. Either way, she didn't care. Manuel's Tavern is well accustomed to its clientele of blowhards, loudmouths, politicians, actors, and other egomaniacs.

"All right," I said. "So—to get something or to get away from something. But what the hell do I have that he would want? I can't bribe the guy or anything. I'm trying to nail him."

"No, no, quite right...a bribe is for getting someone to *do* something. You need him to *reveal* something. Reveal something you can't find by yourself. And he has no reason to do so, as

177

things stand. So. Hm. You've got to drive him out of his comfort zone, somehow—pull him out of hiding to get *away* from you. Make him say what he'd rather *not* say, or show what he'd rather keep hidden, if only to escape."

"That's tough. If I'm right, he's been careful to avoid anything that even reminds him of that night."

"Does he know that you know about him?"

"No. But it's possible he might think *some*one knows."

"Okay. But he wouldn't know how much or how little that person knew."

"No."

"HA!" He said, slamming the table and making his beer jump. "Then you're in a better position than you think. You just have to convince him you know *everything*."

He looked triumphant, but I was confused. "I'm not following you," I said.

"THINK!" he bellowed, reaching across the table and thwacking me on the forehead with the heel of his hand.

"Still not following you," I said.

"All right," he said. "You make your man think that you know more than you're saying. That you've got the goods on him. That you're ready to tell the world. That should be enough to make him come out of hiding—to shut you up, if nothing else."

"So you're talking about…what, extortion?"

"Never," he said resentfully. "Okay, maybe. Call it pretend extortion. It's all just an act. You act like you already know what you want him to reveal, and that you're after money, or favors, or whatever. This gets him engaged in a conversation on the very topic he doesn't want to talk about. It forces him to talk about it, if only to stop you. But you turn up the heat a little bit at a time. Taunt him. Play with him. Drive him a little nuts. He's focused on the threat now, not protecting his little secret." He paused for a moment, then added, "It's best if he's not thinking too clearly."

"I get it. And if he thinks I already know everything, then he doesn't think he's giving anything away when he talks about it."

"If you play him right. But you've got to be careful. If you give him a chance to reason things through, he may be able to figure out that you couldn't possible know everything you're claiming to know. Plus, anything that feels overt or threatening to him could send him straight to the police, regardless of the risk. He might decide he doesn't care anymore. Also, if he's as prominent as you say, he'll have plenty of friends willing to protect him." He paused again, weighed something in his head, then said, "Of course, it goes without saying, actually threatening a public figure is...ah...what's the word we use for it?"

"A felony?"

"There you go. Try to stop short of that, will you?"

He drained his beer, stood up from the table, and stretched his stubby arms to the ceiling.

"Where, exactly, do you come by all of this detailed knowledge of skullduggery, counselor?" I asked him.

"You read *Rolling Stone;* I read depositions," he said absentmindedly. He patted his growing stomach twice, belched loudly, and, before leaving, executed a small and a humble bow for anyone who might be watching.

35

Taunt him. Fine, but with what? Lure him out of his hole—but how, without revealing who I was? Which I really didn't feel like doing—especially since the guy knew me from years of parties at my father's house.

I went back to my office and sat at my desk, thinking. Nothing came. Then I spied the box I had been meaning to send back to Ted Palmer. It was still sitting on the floor by my office door, starting to gather dust. I grabbed it, ripped it open again, and dumped the contents across my desk, hoping for inspiration. But as usual, all I could see was Giselle's face—that face from the autopsy photo, staring up at me and saying "Do something." Everything else was just paper.

Yeah, I had put her autopsy photo in the box for her father. I was an asshole. I had wanted it haunt him like it had been haunting me.

Which suddenly gave me an idea. If her broken face could freak me out so much, what was it liable to do to the man who had killed her? If I was right, and he had gotten nervous about a harmless, little car survey, her smashed-up face arriving anonymously in the mail would really rattle him…especially if he got it once a day, every day, for a week.

I made copies of the grisly picture, drove across town, and mailed the first copy to the judge.

Merry Christmas.

The next day, I drove to another post office and mailed the second copy.

The third day, I mailed it from another location.

On and on, for a week. And the result? Nothing. Maybe he was sweating bullets, maybe he wasn't. The problem was, there was no way for me to know.

"So what happens now, Charlie Chan?" Susannah asked, as sweetly as she could manage, while handing me a beer.

"That's Chanowitz, sweetheart," I said out of the corner of my mouth.

She laughed and lay down across my lap on the porch swing. Summer had long since passed, but here in the South, we still had some nights that were warm enough for the porch.

"What's next, my young friend," I said with great calm and cool, "is to catch the conscience of the king."

No response.

"It's a line from *Hamlet*," I said.

"Big whoop."

"Philistine."

She reached up behind her and thumped me on the arm. "I asked you a question. You just gonna keep sending murder porn to this guy?"

"Yes," I said. "Every day. Right up until next Saturday. And then we'll see what we can see."

"I don't like the sound of this *we*."

"Well, you'll be there anyway, so you might as well make yourself useful."

"I'll be where, exactly?"

"My father's party."

She sat up and looked at me.

"What party?"

"His holiday party—the one he has every year."

"I hate that party."

"So I do. So what? We always go. And I have it on good authority that our friend, the judge, will be there."

"Yeah, what authority is that?"

"Well, he goes every year, same as us."

"That's what I thought."

"Anyway, he'll be there, we'll be there—it's a perfect set up. We'll get to see what kind of shape he's in, without me having to spy on him at home. Plus, it'll give us something to do at the damn party, for once."

She leaned up and gave me a kiss that a better writer would call languid or sensual. And she whispered, "Clever boy."

Yes, very clever indeed. And just to make sure I had him properly rattled, I added something to the mix on the night before I was going to see him. In the middle of the night, when all of the high-class folks in his sleepy, high-class neighborhood were asleep, I spray-painted this message on the street in front of his house:

I KNOW WHAT YOU DID.

36

I had known Judge Harper for almost as long as I had lived in Atlanta. He had helped recruit my father to Candler, back in the day, and the two had been good friends for years. Any time my father had a party, the judge and his wife were there. The couples shared season tickets to the symphony and the Braves. So I knew the man, kind of. I mean, we exchanged polite small talk whenever we saw each other, but it wasn't like he was real interested in who I was and what I was doing, and the feeling was definitely mutual.

Now, though, I needed to know him. I needed to understand who he was. Because my father was right—I needed a hell of a lot more than a missing survey if I was going to call Ted Palmer again, or take it to the police. If it was true that the judge was my man, I needed to know why? Why *him*—a federal judge who had been on the bench forever—a dignified and respected member of the community, as they say. Why was he on that road that morning, driving that fast? And why didn't he stop? What the hell could he have been so afraid of, that he sped off and then covered it up?

I started to do a little background research, and the more I learned, the less sense the whole thing made. He had been on the bench in Atlanta for 12 years. Excellent record. Beloved by all. Before that, he had been the district attorney in Mobile. Not beloved by all, but that comes with the job. There were pictures of him all over the Internet, shaking hands with national figures like Jimmy Carter and Bill Clinton, and with local heroes like Maynard Jackson and Andy Young. People had been pushing him to enter politics for years, to run for mayor or senator or maybe even Governor. He had never taken the bait—but everyone thought he could have, which is the important thing.

And he played the part well. He had that thing people always talk about in politics—that thing you need if you're going to convince people to pay more taxes or send their kids off to war. Gravitas.

James Harper was Mister Gravitas. He was maybe an inch shy of six feet, solidly built, with a moustache that was fully gray and a fringe of hair that was on its way. He had a soothing baritone voice that always made people feel at ease—a great asset when managing a court in a murder case, but also pretty useful for just holding court at a cocktail party. He had a calm and easy manner about him that matched his voice. I always thought he and my father made a strange pair: the tall, Black judge and the short, Jewish professor—one calm and centered, the other intense and pacing. One born and bred in the South; the other a diehard Yankee (and Yankees fan—that was the one issue they disagreed on). But they were both powerfully smart. I think that's what attracted them to each other when they first met. God knows, my father didn't suffer fools well. I had a feeling the judge wasn't any more charitable.

Now, if a man like that *had* been running for office, maybe I could see him covering up a hit-and-run. Stupid decision, sure—but in the heat of the moment, who knows? Smart people do stupid things. Even famously calm and centered smart people. That's the thing about a crisis—you never really know how you're going to react until you're in the middle of one.

But he *hadn't* been running for office. Not even close. I tried to find any news items about him from three years ago, and there was nothing. Not a word. The man was just doing his job, trying his cases, living his life. No scandals. No divorces, drug problems, locked up teenaged children—nothing. So…what happened? Did he really think a traffic accident would destroy him if word got out? It totally wouldn't have. So what was it? The hit and run? That made a little more sense, at least. But I didn't get why he *would* have run. Him, of all people. And then, having done one stupid thing, why would he compound it by pushing the cops to cover it up? It was craziness.

There was only one thing I could think of that might make even a little sense, but it didn't feel right to me. So I consulted my local authority.

"Oticha," I said, during a break in that evening's practice session on my front porch. "You're a proud African American."

"So they say," he said, leaning over a garbage can to let the spit roll out of his trumpet.

"And you've been here how long? In Atlanta?"

He sat up, pushing the can away with his foot. "I don't know. Twenty years. Longer than your cracker ass."

"Seriously, Melvin," I said, leaning the bass against the wall, "I've got to ask you something." Out of the corner of my eye, I could see Pete and this week's drummer roll their eyes and get up to fetch another beer. I didn't care. I was focused on the horn player. And he was focused on me.

"I've got a guy—a possible suspect in this hit and run thing. I think he probably did it, but I can't think of a single reason *why*."

"I thought it was an accident," he said.

"Not that part—the cover up, later. This is a very distinguished guy—a very important guy, actually. So this major player in the city hits a girl on a rainy street—no fault of his own—and then not only does he drive like hell to get away from it, but he convinces the police to drop the case and say nothing."

"Sounds like he's scared of something."

"Okay, but what's he got to be scared of? Everybody loves this guy. He's friends with the mayor—hell, he's friends with the last *three* mayors."

"I don't know, Jordy G. Why the hell you asking me? You think I got some special Jazz wisdom on this shit?"

I took a deep breath. "Okay, look. Let's say, for argument's sake, that this guy is not just a distinguished, important, well-respected member of the Atlanta elite, but also a distinguished, important, well-respected Black man."

Oticha sat back a little in his chair and scrunched up his mouth a little. This was not a topic of conversation he liked. Behind him, I could see Melanie's head lift up, as though she had caught the last shred of what I had said, and wanted to make sure everything was all right.

That's race, as I know and live it at my end of the social spectrum in Atlanta, GA. Everybody wants to make sure everyone's all right. It's important to be all right. It's important that we're *all* all right. Because this is Atlanta, the city too busy to hate, as they say—and we all just want to get along. So we agree not to talk about certain things. Ever. Except for some performance artists I know, who can't shut up about it—but nobody pays too much attention to them.

Meanwhile, back on my front porch, Oticha studied his horn for a minute or two, trying to figure out what to say. He shook his head a little, kind of like he was arguing with himself. Then he looked up at me.

"You're asking if that changes things? Course it changes things. I get stopped by the police, I don't know what I'm gonna get. Dumbass cracker from Tifton who wants to arrest me for Driving While Black? Could be. Sympathetic brother who lets me off with a warning? Could be that, too."

Mel had left her usual perch on the porch swing to join in the conversation and was standing behind her husband. "Could go the other way round, though—decent white boy trying to show he's not a racist shithead versus hard core black man showing nobody no mercy."

"So fine. That's what I'm saying," Oticha continued. "But that's me. That's Mel. That's most people. We get what we get. Now your man—you say he's an important cat."

"Pretty important, yeah."

"So a bad thing goes down, he's alone with it out on the street, maybe he's thinking to himself: do I want to be somebody's boy again, sitting here, waiting for some punk beat cop to saunter over like he's John Fucking Wayne? Or do I want to walk into the precinct like a man with friends?"

"Okay, I get that," I said. "I totally get that. But then why not just pick up your cell phone before the cops even get there and call one of those friends? Hey, this shitty thing just happened to me, and I don't want a lot of press about it, so I need some help. Right?"

"Which is maybe exactly what he did."

"But why force a cover-up, then? Why take an accident and turn it into a crime? He could have walked away from this, easy. Keep the press away from it. Or even if he can't, it's two, three days, more sad than bad. Shit happens on an icy morning—you know it, we all know it. And then it's done. They bury the girl, they bury the story, and everyone goes home."

Oticha nodded. He looked over his shoulder at Mel. She shrugged and went back to the swing to keep an eye on her kids, who were playing on the front lawn in the dying daylight. "I don't know, man," he said. "I don't know the cat—I don't know his life—the things that set him off during the day, make him stare at the ceiling all night. I don't walk around in his skin. You know what I'm saying?"

"Yeah," I said. "I do. That's exactly my problem. Inside his skin, what he did must make some sense. From where I sit, though, it sure as hell doesn't."

Susanna walked by and handed me a beer. "Maybe that's because it *doesn't*—inside or out. Maybe you're just wrong."

And, of course, I knew that. I had been thinking it. The whole story was already starting to sound suspicious. Maybe I was barking up the wrong tree. Again.

Well, all right. Maybe I was and maybe I wasn't. I wasn't going to get into a funk about it tonight. I could wait until my father's party. I had been stealthy and I had been silent—now I just needed to be patient and see what walked through his door. An innocent man might bitch to his friends about the creepy asshole who was sending him weird pictures in the mail, or he might not give a shit about it, either way.

And a guilty man? Well, I wasn't sure how a guilty man might respond. But it had to be different.

Right?

37

You probably know enough about me now to guess that I hate going to parties at my dad's house. And you'd be right. Whatever the occasion, the crowd is always a combination of university types and high-end lawyers, and I'm not super crazy about either population. I'm comfortable out on my little edge of normal, living in the dignifiedly seedy, surrounded by the interestingly funky. I don't like having to put on a tie and answer questions like, "*What* is it you do, again?"

I'm tempted to say that Susannah is more tolerant of these occasions than I am, but as you know, she likes to slip in here and read what I've written, so I have to be honest. The truth is, she hates going to his place more than I do. It's the southern tomboy in her, I think. If Susannah could arrange life so that she could go barefoot all day, she'd be a happy girl. She doesn't mind dressing up fancy if we're going out to do something fun—a nice dinner, maybe, or going out dancing (we *did* do that once). But stuffy cocktail parties among people she doesn't know or care about? No thank you.

Every so often, we come up with some excuse and beg off these parties, but not for the holiday party. That one is mandatory. And this year, I was just fine with the mandate. I needed to see how Judge Harper was composing himself after my barrage of death photos. And Susannah needed to be there for moral support. Or immoral support. Whatever the occasion required.

I wanted to come early to catch the judge's entrance, but there were already a lot of cars parked along the street by the time we got there. We hustled inside and checked in with my dad. He was happily swaddled in his double-breasted blue blazer—the captain on the bridge—with Amina on his arm. He looked panicked at the sight of us.

"Oh, don't worry," I said, "I'm not gonna talk to him."

"We're just here for the food," said Susannah.

My father grimaced, ever the curmudgeon. Amina laughed, ever the generous hostess. She gave us each a hug and a very non-American double-cheek kiss. We walked away to find the bar, and to find a good place to stake out the front door.

"I sure wish I liked her more," Susannah said, with a sigh.

"Yeah, me too," I said.

When my father had parties like this back on Long Island, they were totally law school and lawyer parties, which is to say, deadly dull. Of course, I was in high school, so any adult party seemed like torture to me. But I'm pretty sure, looking back with absolute objectivity, that they were shitty, boring parties. When we moved down to Atlanta, though, he got more involved in the life of the university, and now he has friends from the music department, the classics department, you name it. In fact, his girlfriend, or consort, or whatever she is, is a political science professor (I'm not trying to be mean—she's just way too interesting and exotic to be anyone's "girlfriend"). So his parties have a little more variety and spice to them than they used to. If I were a more enlightened being, I'd probably enjoy them. And I'd probably like my dad's whatever-she-is more, too, because she's lovely, and I know I should just get over it, already.

Susannah and I found a loveseat perfectly positioned across from the front door, and hunkered down with our beers to watch the spicy variety of guests arrive. We got to see the tall and skinny defense attorney who always wore bow ties and did magic tricks; the fat, Irish DA who had done something dramatic against the Mob and had written a book about it; a philosophy professor I remembered taking a class from once, whose comb-over was even less defensible now than it was when I was an undergraduate; and a few people I didn't recognize, who had to be Amina's friends from the Poli Sci department. Susannah and I traded whispered, snarky commentary as each guest entered, occasionally taking breaks to run up to the food table for some hors d'oeuvres (she was only half-kidding about coming for the food).

About twenty minutes into our stakeout, the judge and his wife entered. I nudged Susannah—hard enough to knock a mini spinach pie out of her hands and into her lap.

"Thanks a lot," she said.

"That's him," I whispered.

"I know it's him," she said. "I've met him like a hundred times."

"Well, what do you think? Do you think he looks different?"

She brushed the crumbs off her skirt and looked up at him. "I think he looks tired," she said.

I watched him circulate around the living room, shaking hands and slapping backs. He looked no different than any other time I had seen him. Except…except he *did* look tired. And it wasn't just a sleepy tired. You could see it in those moments after he had said hello to someone and had moved on—those in-between moments, when he thought no one was looking at him. The façade slipped just a little, and his whole face kind of fell—just for a second. Then he pulled himself together as the next friend stepped up to greet him.

"I'll tell you what's interesting," Susannah whispered. "The wife is interesting."

"Why?"

"Look at her. Watch her."

I watched. I didn't get it. "What am I watching?"

She snorted. "Honestly. Maybe *I* should be the private eye. You can be the cute sidekick."

"All right, all right. What is it?"

"Look," she said. "See how she never leaves him? I don't think she's actually let go of his arm since they walked in."

"So?"

"So that's pretty clingy for a nice, Southern lady. And I don't think I've ever seen her do that before. Usually she's off working the room, just like him, beaming out that South Georgia charm in every direction."

"You're saying you actually remember how Connie Harper schmoozes at parties?"

"That's right, honey," she said, condescendingly. "Because I'm the girl. If you give me some time, I might even remember what she wore last year."

"Holy crap," I said. "You're a force to be reckoned with."

"That's what I keep telling you."

I watched the Harpers move from guest to guest, and Susannah was right—there *was* something strange going on. Mrs. Harper held his arm as though she had to push him forward, hold him up, keep him going. It was very subtle, but it was there. And Susannah was right about the judge, too—he was weary and wary. He did not want to be there. Something was bothering him. Something big.

But that didn't prove anything. An innocent Judge Harper could just as easily be losing sleep over the barrage of horrible pictures as a guilty Judge Harper. Who is sending me these awful pictures? What do they want? What is it going to lead to? Is someone going to hurt me or my wife?

Or it could have been something totally different. He was a judge, after all. He carried a fair amount of weight on his gravitas-y shoulders.

Fortunately, I had a backup plan. I snuck into the bedroom where everyone had tossed their jackets, and I slipped yet another photograph into the judge's pocket. Then I went back to Susannah and told her we were off duty till the end of the party.

"Thank God," she said. "I can finally sit in a corner, have a drink, and make nasty comments about your dad's friends."

I nodded and said, "Live it up." And I went off to fulfill my filial responsibility of saying hello to my dad's colleagues and friends, and having all of them say, "*What* is it you do, again?"

It was only about an hour later when Susannah found me, tugged on my sleeve, and said, "They're getting ready to leave."

"Really? So early?"

She shrugged. I gently pushed my way through the crowd and positioned myself so that I could see the judge approach the door and pull on his jacket. I prayed for him to find the picture before he exited, so that I could see his reaction.

"What are we looking for?" Susannah whispered.

"A reaction," I said. "Annoyed or confused is innocent; scared is guilty."

"You're sure?"

"No."

The judge, courtly gentleman that he was, helped his wife on with her jacket first, and then pulled on his own windbreaker. He stepped toward the door and then stopped. He could feel it. He could tell there was something there—something he hadn't put there. I could tell from the look on his face that he knew what it was. He touched his wife's shoulder and motioned for her to wait for him outside. Then he reached in and pulled out the picture, keeping it very close to his body so that only he could see it. And I watched him.

It was as bad as spying on adultery, somehow. There was something truly awful about watching this moment of discovery and trying to read the emotions passing over the man's face. An invasion of privacy, even in this crowded room.

He held the picture carefully, like he couldn't quite believe it was in his hands. Then he crumpled it quickly and shoved it back into his pocket, glancing around the room in a panic. Had anyone seen him? Was anyone watching him? I stepped back a few inches, hoping I was invisible. He didn't seem to see me.

"Give me one word to describe him," I said in a whisper.

"Hunted?" she offered.

I nodded. Hunted was good. Caught was also good. Someone in this house had been sending him the pictures. Someone here! Among his friends! Who would do such a thing?

But was there a "why?" on his face? The innocent man would ask why. The guilty man would know. Tough call. Can you really spot the "why?" amid all the panic and confusion? Or the absence of it?

The judge hustled out of the house, and Susannah and I left a few minutes later. We were silent for a few minutes.

"That was about the worst thing I've ever seen," she said, finally, as we drove home.

I nodded. "It's up there," I said.

"You're gonna give that man a nervous breakdown..."

"But?"

"But what?"

"The way you said it. Sounded like there was more."

She shrugged, then looked out her window for a moment. "I don't know," she said. "I was going to say he deserves it, but I'm not sure why."

"Just a feeling?"

She nodded.

After a few seconds, she turned back to me. "You know what it is?" she said. "He looked hunted, like I said. He looked scared. But he didn't look...I don't know how to say it. He didn't look like he didn't know why someone would have done it to him. You know what I mean? Like he hated it and he was scared by it, but not...confused by it. Does that make any sense?"

I breathed a deep breath, and relaxed for the first time all night. "Yeah, Suse," I said. "It makes a lot of sense."

"So he's the one?" she asked.

"He's the one." I said. "Probably. More probably than yesterday, anyway. Not that I can do anything about it yet. But it's a step in the right direction."

"Not bad, Chanowitz," she said, leaning against me and wrapping her arms around my arm. We drove in silence for a few minutes. I felt pretty good about myself, until she looked up at me, worried, and said, "How long before he figures out it's you?"

My hands tightened on the wheel.

Shit.

He knew it was someone in the house now. I hadn't thought that part through.

Obviously, he was going to run through the list of everyone he had seen there. And one by one, he would check them off. One by one, until he came to me.

"*What* is it you do, again?"

38

We stopped at the Majestic Diner on Ponce de Leon, one of the few places where you can hang out in the middle of the night, as long as you're not too particular about the food you order. It wasn't really late enough to *require* the Majestic—there were plenty of other places still open—but there was something comforting about the skuzzy old diner—and I was feeling the need for comfort. I had fond memories of sitting in those booths with Porkchop and other college friends deep into the night, eating chicken livers (well, watching Porkchop eat them) and talking through the heartbreaks and woes that seemed so important back then. Right now, all of that seemed pretty tame.

"So…what happens when he *does* figure out it's you?" Susannah asked, having held back from asking me in the car.

I just shook my head. I had no answers.

"He can't really do anything, right? If he's guilty?"

I nodded. "If he's guilty. But I'll never get within a mile of him now."

"I guess it's your best test, though, isn't it? If he's guilty, he keeps away from you; if he's innocent, he has you arrested for harassment."

"True," I said. "Unless he's ballsy enough to be guilty and still have me arrested."

We sat there in silence, pushing bad food around on our plates as though something interesting was eventually going to happen.

*

"I remember that," Susannah says to me, standing behind me late at night as I type these words, her warm hands on my shoulders. "That was a hard night."

I nod, and pull my hands off the keyboard, not sure what to write next.

"You were wrong about me, though," she says.

"When?"

"Back a bit. When you were writing about your dad."

"During the party?"

"Yeah—I was reading it last night."

"Why? What did I say?"

"You said I hate going to your dad's house because I don't like formal parties."

"I meant it nicely."

She ruffles my hair. "I know you did. But you were wrong." She bends down, resting her chin on the top of my head. "It's because of your mom. It just never feels right being in that house without her."

I nod, pushing her head up and down along with mine.

"Stupid, right? I mean, if it doesn't bother him, it shouldn't bother me."

"Who says it doesn't bother him?" I say.

She straightens up, drumming her hands on my shoulders. "Then why doesn't he get a new place?"

"I don't know. Because he's my dad. Because he's stubborn, and he hates change. Or not. I don't know. I don't know why he does what he does, any more than he knows why I do what I do."

"That's sad," she says. "It's sad she's gone and there's still this hole between you two."

"Yeah," I say. "It's sad." There's nothing else to say.

Some people leave holes you never fill.

39

A week passed and nothing happened. No angry phone call from my father, accusing me of harassing the judge. No warrant for my arrest. Just silence.

Further proof of guilt? *I* thought so—but who the hell cared what I thought? I mean, if I were the judge, and I were innocent, and I thought my good friend's son was fucking with me, I'd say something, right? Unless he hadn't put two and two together and ID'd me, which I had trouble believing, given how smart the guy was. No, the only thing that made sense to me was the he really *was* my frightened old mole, hiding in his hole and afraid to stick his head out, even to ask for help from an old friend.

The week dribbled uneventfully to an end, and I found myself eating broccoli casserole and creamed corn at the Our Way Café with Porkchop, who was overindulging on an entrée-plus-three plate. I was in no mood to eat *or* socialize, but when I tried to cancel on him, I couldn't get through to his office or his cell phone. So I watched him stuff his face, which was enough to put anyone off food.

"You know," I said, "you're feeding a lawyer's body a rugby player's diet."

He nodded. "Habit," he said.

I never played rugby back on Long Island. I'm not sure I even knew what it was. I discovered the game and the players in college, when I stumbled across a table of them in the cafeteria—a whole squad of big, thick-bodied guys shoveling food into their mouths, all talking a mile a minute about some play the theatre department had just put on, and whether the stage picture created by the director had supported or contradicted the word imagery supplied by the playwright. I decided, right then, that I needed to know these guys.

I had never met anyone like them. They were fiercely intelligent, where the smart kids I had grown up with were just suck-ups and grinds. But at the same time, they were totally physical beings—tough, competitive, with huge appetites for everything in life. Now don't get me wrong, there were tough kids in my home town, too. Plenty of them. But they were just thugs and losers. Before Porkchop and his friends, I didn't know you could live so completely in your body *and* in your head— both things at the same time, all the time, full out, with no apologies. For someone who lives most of his life in his head, it was a revelation.

"How's your mole?" he asked, between bites, shaking me out of my reverie. "You coax him out of hiding yet?"

"A little," I said. "I definitely got a reaction out of him. The problem is, it's just a reaction, not a piece of evidence. And I'm not sure what to do next."

"Hm," he said, thoughtfully, bouncing a chicken leg off his lower lip. "Sounds like you stopped halfway."

"I did, kind of." I admitted. "I think he knows who I am, though. I mean, he's always known who I am, but…I think he knows it was me, taunting him. So now I'm laying low. So far, he hasn't done anything."

"So he's being cautious. Or he's scared."

"I think it all points to his guilt, but, you know, so what? My word isn't worth shit to anyone. I need something concrete."

"I would think so," he said, resolving finally to eat the chicken leg.

"You're a big help," I said.

"Never claimed to be," he said, with a mouthful of poultry.

I laughed and said nothing. He held up his hand, as if to hold me there at the table, and swallowed the bite he had in his mouth.

"I did suggest, I think, that you needed to do more than freak him out, to get him to show his hand."

"I know. You did."

"You've got some momentum going, J. Don't let it slip away. You've got to follow up on what you did—push him further out of his hole. If he goes back to feeling safe, he's not going to make the mistake you need him to make."

"Yeah, but... if he knows who I am, isn't that kind of dangerous?"

"Totally," he said, wiping his chin on the tablecloth. "That's why I'm not going to have lunch with you anymore." He grinned at me. "Could be bad for business."

His cell phone started to buzz, and he took the call. Something was blowing up with one of his clients, and his presence was needed back at the office. He rolled his eyes, excused himself, and ran out the door. By the time I got my leftovers boxed up for Susannah, he was long gone.

I walked out to the small, gravelly parking lot behind the restaurant and found two guys sitting on the hood of my car. Two big guys weighing down my poor old Volkswagen. I stood there, leftovers in one hand and car keys in the other, heart pounding.

"Hey," I said, trying to be nonchalant. I wasn't used to having enormous strangers perched on my car, waiting for me to finish lunch. One of them lifted himself up off the hood; the other slid off. They were both so big that the car heaved a sigh of relief.

"What's up?" I said, trying to remain calm.

The bigger of the two guys walked over to me—slowly but not dramatically. No overt threat. That didn't stop my heart from trying to shatter my ribcage. He didn't say a word. Just walked up to me, took the Styrofoam box out of my hands, and placed it gently down on the ground next to me. Then he straightened up and looked at me. The other guy stayed further back—maybe as a lookout? This wasn't good.

"Who's that guy you were with?" the mountain asked—calmly, conversationally. It didn't matter. He scared the hell out of me.

"He's…he's a friend of mine." My mouth was bone dry.

"A lawyer?"

"Yeah."

"Personal injury?"

"I…guess. Maybe. I don't really know."

He put a hand on my shoulder. "Listen, man. Don't be talking to no lawyers. I don't care who they are. Don't be talking to lawyers. You understand what I'm saying to you?"

"I think so. But I'm telling you—"

Before I could get the words out, the hand on my shoulder tightened and the other hand came whipping out of nowhere, straight at my face like a freight train. I felt my nose and cheekbones explode, a wave of blood washing into my mouth. I reeled back, coughing out blood and spluttering, my legs like Jello, but the hand on my shoulder kept me in place. I felt dizzy and faint, but I couldn't do anything—not even fall down. I lifted my hands to my face, as though there was something they could do to help. All they could do was get soaked with blood.

"Don't tell *me*. I came here to tell you. Stay away from lawyers and keep your mouth shut."

I nodded as best I could. He pulled away from me a bit, and I thought he was about to let go of me. But he wasn't. He was only rearing back to punch me in the stomach. If I hadn't had my head in my hands, I might have seen it coming. Not that it would have done me any good. He hit me hard enough to lift me off my feet for a second. Every molecule of air was squeezed out of me like a bellows. I felt like as solid as an old newspaper, crumpled and drifting on the wind. The pain shot out from my stomach in every direction—up my arms, down my legs, and crashing into my head.

He let me go and I fell like a sandbag, which was what I really wanted right then—just to be on the ground, and to curl up like a hedgehog. I didn't care that I was in the middle of a filthy parking lot, in the middle of the day. I didn't care where I was. I just wanted to disappear.

But I didn't disappear. And they didn't leave. I could feel them both, now, towering over me.

"You think you know something, motherfucker?" the second guy yelled at me, his reedy voice full of anger. "You think you know something important?"

I shook my head. It was all I could do.

"That's right," he said. "That's right. You don't know shit. You fucking with shit you don't know nothing about."

The other one spoke again—without a trace of menace or threat, which somehow made it worse. "Listen. This friend of ours asked us to give you a message if we saw you messing around with the wrong kind of people. And that's what you just did, so that's what we just did. Now…can I tell our friend you understand the message? Or do we need to explain it better?"

"I understand it," I said in a tiny, whispery voice.

"All right, then. Let's not see each other again."

He walked away, but I could feel his friend—the angry one—still standing over me, deciding what to do. "Come on," the first guy called back to him. The angry one took a step or two away, but then came back and kicked me hard, twice, in the kidneys. I screamed in pain and tried to roll over, burning with pain from back to front and top to bottom. There was no comfortable position—no fetal ball I could curl up in and feel safe. My mouth was open, gasping for air, blood and saliva dripping out of me onto the ground. I rolled back and forth, trying to reach the parts that hurt. All I accomplished was a mouthful of gravel.

And there was no fade to black, or helping hand on my shoulder, or even anyone coming out of the restaurant to find me. I was just alone on the ground, with the air getting colder and the pain throbbing through every part of me. It went on and on. And I didn't know what to do.

40

"*I* should kick you in the fucking kidneys," said Carter Wiggins, staring down at me, beer in hand. Susannah pushed him away and shot him a dirty look. Carter just sighed and continued the pacing he had been doing since he walked in the door. "What the hell were you thinking?"

"I thought I was having lunch," I mumbled. My face looked like an eggplant that had fallen off the back of a pickup doing 90. Everything hurt. I was sprawled out on the couch so I could spend my days watching TV and sleeping. My swollen nose and shattered cheekbone made eating, or even talking, painful. Everything else made everything else hurt. Susannah had built a fortress of drinks and mushy junk food around me, making our living room look dangerously like the starship bridge that our keyboardist, Pete, had built for himself.

I still don't remember exactly how I made it home that day. I know it was late. The sun had started to set, and I was shivering with cold and pain. Susannah says she never got a call from me, but I don't know why I didn't call. I had my cell phone, and it hadn't gotten broken in the fight.

I know—"fight" is overly generous.

Anyway, I don't know how long I lay there on the ground, or why I didn't call for help. If someone came out of the restaurant and helped me, it's vanished from my head. All I know is, I eventually managed to make it home, in my own car, on my own steam. Susannah was on the porch, in a heavy sweater, waiting and worried. And when she saw me stumble out of the car, unable to get to my feet, she raced down off the porch to me.

For all the things I can't remember, *that* image is firmly and forever in my head: my wife racing toward me—terrified and confused—coming to my rescue. And whenever I think about it, I remember what it felt like to sit there on the curb, paralyzed. I don't remember the pain, but I remember the feeling inside my chest—that horrible, tightening feeling—one part grateful but ten parts ashamed. Needing help but not being able to accept it, not feeling like I deserved it.

Always, wherever I go, I can't escape it. She throws me a birthday party, she cooks me a special dinner—it doesn't matter. There's always this feeling grabbing my chest and giving it a sharp twist, this feeling that she shouldn't, that it's wrong, that I don't deserve it, that I'm not worthy of it, that if I let myself enjoy it, or appreciate it, it'll all disappear.

So when she said she'd take a day off work and stay home to take care of me, I told her not to. And when she brought me blankets, or ran out to get to a smoothie or some ice cream, I pushed her away. "Oh, for God's sake, will you cut the macho shit!" she yelled at me. But that's not what it was.

So there you go. I said I'd write it all, so I'm writing it all. Thankfully, none of it is a surprise to her. Anymore.

"Seriously, Jordy," Carter said, sitting on the edge of the sofa and looking down at me. "Didn't I tell you to drop this motherfucker? Didn't I beg you?"

"Yeah, yeah, you begged me," I said. "Meanwhile, what do you make of it?"

"What do I make of what? Your face?"

"No," I groaned, annoyed at having to spell it out for him again—it hurt too much. "What I told you. How they kept harping on lawyers, not cops. Like they didn't care if I was talking to the police."

"What do they care if you talk to the police? Your guy knows that dog ain't gonna hunt. He took care of that three years ago, whoever the fuck he is."

"So you believe me?"

He smacked his forehead like one of the Little Rascals and got up to start pacing again. "Jesus H. Christacles, Jordy."

"Well, you keep saying I'm crazy."

"You *are* crazy, sure as shit, but that don't make you wrong." He paced back and forth again. "Naw, I figured a while ago you had to be on to something. But with my captain watching my ass, there wasn't a damn thing I could do about it. And your man, whoever he is, I reckon he knows it."

"So why would he care about a lawyer?"

"Well, a lawyer ain't part of my precinct, is he? A lawyer don't answer to whoever this guy once talked to. A lawyer could sue your man's ass and then we'd *have* to re-open the case. And your guy can't lean on every single ambulance chaser in town—I don't care *how* scared he is. You do something like he did, you pick your target careful. You pick someone you can trust. Someone who owes you something."

I nodded.

"You think you know who this fucker is?" he asked.

I nodded again.

"You got any evidence?"

I shook my head.

"Course not."

He left me, went into the kitchen to get Susannah, and dragged her back into the room with him. "All right, now," he said, "I'm telling you this in front of your wife, and God, and everybody. Whoever this old boy is, he's powerful enough to shut down a police investigation just by asking for it, and he's scared enough to send two punks to beat the shit out of you. You poke this fucker with a stick one more time, you're gonna wind up dead somewhere. You hear what I'm saying?"

"Yeah," I muttered. "I hear you."

"If he didn't have goddamned kryptonite around him, I'd go after him for you, whoever the fuck he is. I swear to God I would. But this is one well-protected bubba."

"Jordy," Susannah started, but I waved her to stop.

"You wanna give me his name, I'll see what I can do," he said, hopelessly. "You know I can't promise nothing, but..."

I shook my head. "You can't do anything," I said. "If I thought you could, I would have given it to you a long time ago."

He threw his hands up in the air and walked away from me.

"It's Judge Harper," Susannah said. "James Harper." She looked at me, but before I could get a word out, she said, "Shut up."

Carter looked at her, and then at me. And he deflated—really—he sagged, like all the air had gone out of him. He sat in the nearest chair, put down his beer, and rubbed his eyes with both hands. When he was done, he stayed there, hands on his forehead, for a long moment. He was silent. He looked old.

Susannah reached down and took my hand.

"That's great, Jordy," he said softly. "That's just the second most important Black man in the whole goddamn city, that's all. Maybe the first."

I didn't say anything. He was right.

"Listen, now," he said. "Let's talk like grown-ups here for a second, huh?"

I nodded.

"All right. Say you're right. Say it's him. Say Judge James Harper, close personal friend of God, did some damn fool thing like run down a girl and then ask the police to cover it up. I don't know—it could happen. The thing is…" He leaned forward towards me. "The thing is, Jordy, there ain't a goddamn thing you or me is ever gonna be able to do to bring it justice. There just ain't. It's too long ago, and he's too dug in. Even if you had something on him—and you don't—it wouldn't never see the light of day. He's got too many friends. And if it did, by some crazy-ass miracle—if it did see the light of day, the whole damn city would just call it a racist witch-hunt and set him free."

"Then why is he so scared?" I asked. "He could have threatened me himself. He's a big judge, I'm a little nobody. He could have told me to lay off or suffer the consequences. He could have gone to my dad and told him I was looking at getting arrested if I kept up my shit. But he did this instead. Why?"

Carter sighed, shrugged, and leaned back. "Hell, I don't know," he said. "It don't seem like a smart play to me, either, but I don't know the man. I reckon even a big shot judge got a right to be scared of ghosts, though, right?"

"I guess."

He rose, gave Susannah a kiss on the cheek, and patted me on my foot—one of the few safe places to touch me. "Leave it be, Jordy," he said. "You solved the riddle and you made him nervous, but that's all you're ever gonna get out of this. Leave it be now."

And with that, he left.

41

By the end of the week, I was back on my feet and back at work, doing some easy personal-records snooping to bring in a little money. I didn't think it was a good time to see new clients, with my face being all swollen and purple, but at least I could finish up some work that was sitting on my desk and take on a couple of quickie email-contract jobs where I didn't have to meet anybody face to face.. And I needed to get out of the house.

The box of Giselle pictures and clippings was still in my office, taped up again and ready to go to the post office, as it had been for weeks. Palmer had left more than a few angry messages about it on my voice mail, always in the middle of the night when I was sure not to be answering. And he was right—it should have gone back to him by now. The man had fired me. He deserved his property back. The question was: should I include a note? Should I call him to let him know the box was on its way? And, oh, just incidentally, I have the killer's name for you?

I was tempted, even though the man had made it clear he never wanted to hear from me again. I was tempted, even though I had a feeling he wouldn't do anything about it. But I had the right name now, and that's what he had hired me for. I know I claim to be a disinterested slacker, but I do have a little professional pride. I said I would do the job, and I didn't like leaving it half-done.

So I didn't have proof. So what? I had been hired to find a name, not bring an indictment. And my bruises told me the name I had come up with was legit. All right—so Palmer had expected me to hand him over, signed, sealed, and delivered. And I had failed him. But I could explain to him what was possible, and what the next steps were going to have to be, to pry this mole out of his hole. Someone else was going to have to take those next steps. I needed heavier artillery.

And anyway, didn't he deserve to know? Shouldn't I just man up and make the phone call?

Yes, I should.

I placed the call. Listened to it ring. Considered hanging up the moment he picked up, like some lovelorn undergrad calling the girl who had dumped him. But when he picked up, I stayed on and introduced myself.

Silence.

"Mr. Palmer," I said, pushing past the thick nothingness on the other end of the line, "I just wanted to let you know that your box is on its way back to you, as of this afternoon."

"All right," he said evenly.

"And also…well, I thought you might want to know that after that false start we had, I actually have a good idea who was responsible for the accident that killed Giselle."

Silence. Then: "What are you doing? Why are you still working on this? I thought I told you we were done."

"Yes—yes, you did, Mr. Palmer. You absolutely did. It's just that when I was packing up the box, I found something I hadn't noticed before, and—"

"Jordan, I specifically asked you *not* to look into this any further, and I meant what I said."

"Yes, sir, I understand that. Only—"

"Only nothing. I meant what I said. I'm not in the mood to be publically embarrassed by you or your nonsense any more. This whole thing was a mistake, right from the start."

"I understand, Mr. Palmer, and by the way, this isn't about the money—"

"I don't care what it's about!" he yelled. "Stay away from it, and stay away from me." He paused, caught his breath. "Haven't you caused us enough pain already?"

Now it was my turn for silence.

"Listen to me, you dumb little shit. You do not represent us, and you do not work for us. I don't want my name connected to anything you are doing. Do I make myself clear?"

"Yes, sir," I said, trying to control my voice. I was really getting tired of being yelled at by this asshole. "I got to tell you, though," I said evenly, "you're really missing the boat if you were hoping to cash in. I mean, this guy is loaded."

He yelled something at me—probably motherfucker or something like that—it was too distorted to really hear—and then slammed down the phone.

I sat there in the silence of my stale office, with nothing to distract me from the echo of Ted Palmer's anger. I could have put some music on, but for some reason, I didn't want to. The angry silence felt right, somehow. Like I had pissed him off for the right reason, this time.

I got up and went down the hall to the men's room to throw some cold water on my face. Reaching for a paper towel, I caught sight of my smashed face in the mirror, and stood there for a moment, just looking at myself. And I said, "now what?"

Nobody wanted me to keep going with this thing. Nobody. Not Giselle's father, not my father, not Carter, not Susannah, and certainly not the judge. Nobody thought I could pull it off— and even if they did, nobody wanted me to try. There was nothing to be gained. Even if I could prove the judge was responsible, all I would get is angry attacks in the paper—Carter was right about that. No one would be pleased about the revelation or feel satisfied. Nobody would shake my hand and say, "Justice has been served." Nobody would even care.

I went back to my office and sat down at my desk. A new email message was blinking at me on my computer screen. It was from the Georgia Board of Private Detective and Security Agencies, my professional licensing board. They regretted to inform me that my license had been suspended because of accusations of gross misconduct, pending an investigation.

Because of whistleblower laws, they could not tell me who had made the accusations against me, but I should rest assured that a fair and just process would be followed in the investigation. And they thanked me for my patience,

I read through the email three times, just to make sure I wasn't imagining things. Then I closed the message and turned my chair around, away from my desk.

Well, that was that. Now I didn't even have a job. Now I was totally exposed. No way to make a living, no way to make a move against the judge with any credibility or legal standing. Anything I did, he could have me arrested—and not just for harassment. A more effective one-two punch, I couldn't imagine.

The man knew how to get things done.

I got up and paced, the way Carter had done in my living room, but I got nothing out of it. Finally, staring at the bookshelf that I never used, I grabbed Billy Barnes' old copy of *The Simple Art of Murder*, and sat down with it. As soon as I put the book down on my desk, it fell open to a page that Billy had obviously returned to again and again over the years. He had underlined Chandler's famous line: "But down these mean streets a man must go who is not himself mean, who is neither tarnished nor afraid."

Classic. Neither tarnished nor afraid. A knight in shining seersucker.

"Fuck you, Chandler," I said, slamming the book closed. "And you too, Billy. Easy for you to say." The sound of my voice, out loud in the silence, was jarring.

I got up and started pacing again, feeling bad about cursing the spirit of my old mentor. Maybe it *hadn't* been easy for him—I didn't know. He had been a quiet, man, private, and he was already near the end of his run when I first met him. If he felt like he had accomplished something important in his life—or if he felt like he'd been a useless loser—I never knew. He just came in to work every day in his shirt and tie and fedora, and he did what he knew how to do. And he helped people. Maybe it wasn't big help, all the time, but he helped people. That was his job.

Who had I been helping? Nobody. Not even myself.

Neither tarnished nor afraid. I said the words to myself, and shook my head. That was just too much, man. Too much. Who the hell gets through life without some scars and nightmares? I mean, even just a regular life, not the fucked-up kind of cowboys-and-Indians game I was playing? I thought about the face that had stared back at me in the mirror, and it seemed pretty goddamned tarnished to me. And getting more afraid by the hour.

So why couldn't I let it go? Why couldn't I just say, "You win, asshole," and move on with my life? It's not like this was the first time Life had told me to quit. Far from it.

But it was a stupid question. I knew why I couldn't let it go. It was Giselle. The one person who wasn't here anymore. She wouldn't let me go, and I couldn't let it go.

And it was the principle of the thing. What he was doing was wrong. It just was. I didn't care that he was a judge, or rich, or powerful. It was wrong for anyone. And the more I thought about it, the angrier I got. Sending two punk kids to beat someone up? Making false accusations to make someone lose their license? It was just like the shit he had pulled after Giselle. Gravitas, my ass. He was nothing but a bully. Him, Palmer, all of them. Throwing their weight around and making people flinch, like playground bullies. I was so sick of them.

So I put the book back on the shelf, and I sat back at my desk, and I said No. No, you can't just walk away from the wreckage you make. You have to be held accountable. You have to pay. That's how we keep living together. That's the rules. And if nobody gave a shit anymore, so what? I still gave a shit.

I poked around on the computer until I found a picture of the Great Man, and I stared at it for a long time—long enough to really see him. And I pointed my finger at his little head, and I said, "I'm coming for you."

42

Back to basics. Investigation 101. Take out the personal, emotional shit, stop shooting from the hip, and *look* at the thing for once. Straight on, carefully, like a detective. Play the game for real, one time—even if the buzzer's already sounded.

So all right. What have we got? The suspect was headed north on Monroe Drive, pre-dawn. He hit the victim just above the intersection with Virginia Avenue, as the victim was turning north onto Monroe. Likely she skidded on a patch of ice and drifted out into the street, and he was going too fast to stop. But why was he going too fast? Why was he even there? Was it his usual route to work? Could I place him there, at that time of day, every day?

Well. Now we're talking about your basic snooping mission, your basic stake-out with camera. Now we're talking about what I *do*. The only thing different between this and my usual fornication work was that the suspect knew who I was, and was probably looking over his shoulder. So I needed to be careful.

Stealthy, you might say. Extra stealthy, now that I was operating without any cover.

I was betting the judge's "messengers" weren't watching me closely anymore, after my beat-down. I figured they had me pegged as the kind of guy who knew how to take a fall. But they did know my car, so I figured I should use something different to tail the Great Man, just to be safe. Fortunately, my hemorrhoid client had paid his bill, so I had enough money to rent a car. I picked something as non-descript as possible, rented it in the evening, and set my alarm for much earlier than I liked to get up.

The next morning, while Susannah was still asleep, I snuck out of the house and headed north through the winter fog to the judge's house up on West Paces Ferry—the same street where I had written my nasty message before my father's party. On that earlier trip, nothing interesting or shocking had occurred to me, dimwit that I am. But this time, not ten minutes into the trip, the clouds of idiocy parted, and the light of intelligence finally shined down upon me.

If you don't live in Atlanta, you won't understand my epiphany, so let me explain: I was heading north from my house in Candler Park up to West Paces Ferry. The judge worked downtown, in the Russell building on Spring Street. Imagine a right triangle, with his office and his house at the two ends of a straight line, south to north, along I-75, and his office and my house at the two ends of the west to east line. Right now, I was driving northwest from my house to his house along the hypotenuse.

And the accident site? It wasn't anywhere along that triangle. It wasn't anywhere *inside* that triangle. It was directly

225

north of *my* house. In other words, there was no logical pathway leading from his house through that intersection to his office. So either he wasn't going to work that morning, or…

Or he wasn't coming from home.

That was my *aha* moment, as they say. My head-slapping, "d'oh!" moment. Of course! All this time, I had been wondering why the judge would go to such lengths to hide a simple accident. But maybe the accident wasn't the point at all. Maybe there was something much worse that the judge was trying to hide, like why he was even on that road so early in the morning.

It takes a while, but eventually I get there.

43

I had never tailed someone at dawn before. Usually my suspects were sneaking around for nooners, or "I have to work late" indiscretions. But I figured, if anything, an early morning mark would be easier to stalk than my usual prey—and let me tell you, my usual morons were pretty easy to follow. There isn't much of an art to tailing the average, clueless Joe. You find him; you follow him; you take your picture. The horndogs I usually concerned myself with could barely focus on the road in front of them, much less the array of cars in their rear-view mirror. But that's just my personal experience. I'm sure other investigators have marks who suspect their wives have called a PI, and are always looking over their shoulders. But I don't hang out with them; I don't know their stories. In my world, ninety-nine times out of a hundred, it ain't James Bond.

I waited just up the street from the judge's house. It was a crisp, see-your-breath kind of morning (we do get those in the South), so I kept the car running to keep myself warm, and I listened to NPR. A little after seven, Himself finally emerged, with his devoted wife behind him, still in a bathrobe. She gave him a kiss and sent him on his way. He climbed into a black Lexus and glided down the street. I counted to five and pulled out behind him.

Lexus. All right. But had he owned it forever? I wished I knew more about cars so I could tell if his car was a newer model—say, less than three years old. But looking at the judge's impeccably tailored clothes and his beautifully manicured house and garden, I didn't take him for the type to keep a car long enough for it to start looking old. I snickered to myself and wondered if it made his wife nervous when she looked in the mirror.

And that was my second *aha* moment of the morning: she probably *was* nervous, looking in the mirror. She probably did wonder if his eye was straying, looking for someone younger of years and tighter of skin. She probably wondered if he was looking for a trade-in.

And what if he was? In fact, what if he had already found one—maybe one who lived downtown somewhere? One from whose house he could have been driving, early one winter morning.

It was becoming clear, really quickly, that there might not be any reason for me to follow Judge Harper to work. If my new *aha* was right, it was later in the day that I'd need to focus on. Where did he go for lunch? Did he stop off somewhere on the way home? High profile philanderers have to be creative with their time, so I'd have to stick pretty close to him to catch him in the act. All day. Every day.

See, you were thinking, all this time, that the freedom and flexibility of being an investigator sounded cool, right? You kind of liked the idea of being in control of your time—nowhere you have to be, no timecard to punch. And you're right: it's great— except when you're on a case like this. Because when the circumstances call for you to sit in a car all day, every day, watching some idiot go about his business and hoping to catch him doing something unusual, well…that's what you have to do. That's what the freedom and flexibility are for: so you can sit in silence, patiently waiting for something to happen. The something could happen at any time—but all that really means is, most of the time, it *isn't* happening. So you sit, and you wait, and you watch…for hours. Sometimes for days. You watch someone else living his life, while you put your life on hold.

Have you ever done that? Eavesdropped with total focus and intent for a long period of time? It's worse than reading someone's diary. There are no cuts, no fades to black, no editing at all. It's just every boring moment followed by every other boring moment. You spy through a window and watch a woman washing the dishes. You watch it all, every detail, every dish. There's no escape. You watch the washing, the rinsing, the drying. Maybe you watch her face to see if you can read any emotions on it. But it's a veil; whatever she's thinking, she's off in some private place. She's barely even there in the room. The repetitive motions are like a trance, letting her slip away from her body and wander somewhere, free. But you're not out there with her; you're stuck in the kitchen with the body she left behind: washing, rinsing, repeating. You can feel the loneliness and desperation of every life you spy on—because they *all* seem lonely and desperate from the outside. And they all seem the *same* from the outside. You see them trying to fill up the silences and empty spaces with stupid TV, or stupid drugs, or stupid sex. But the moments are fleeting, and when they end, you're left watching their silences and empty spaces. Except after sex— because for me, sex means I can get my picture and get the hell out.

Well, I could have opted out right then, at least for the morning, but I didn't want to lose track of the judge at lunch time. To pick him up at lunch, it would be easier if I knew where he parked. So I followed him down I-75 to Spring Street and I watched him park his fancy car. And I watched him walk inside the building, so that I'd know which entrance he used. I debated going home for a while, but it didn't seem professional. I didn't know his routine yet, and I should. I spotted a coffee shop across the street from the Russell Building, so I parked nearby, bought a newspaper, and camped out with my eye on his door.

Nothing happened all morning, of course. I burned through the paper within half an hour, the Atlanta Constitution being what it is. Usually I have a book or two with me on a stakeout, but since I wasn't in my own car, I had forgotten to load up the rental with supplies. So I just stared out the window, eyes trained on the Russell Building's front door. And like the woman washing dishes, I let my mind wander.

44

The last day of SAT prep was more like a party than a class. Halloween was that night, and the test was just a week away. After that, it felt like the rest of senior year was just going to dribble away: college applications, holidays, one last, meaningless semester, then prom, then out. We were all champing at the bit to get it over with and get on with life…and at the same time, it felt like time was running out. We all knew that nothing was going to be real after our fall grades were submitted. As long as we didn't kill anyone during second semester, we could get away with pretty much anything.

We were cocky as hell about college and cocky as hell about the test. We had been well trained and well drilled, like all good, suburban kids are supposed to be. We were ready. And if the class as a whole was cocky, that made me (the class clown) a complete asshole. But Giselle smiled, so I kept it up.

We retreated to our usual bar after class for one final round of kamikaze pitchers. And Giselle was mine all night. She kept me at her side the whole time, laughing and drinking and leaning on my shoulder when she got sleepy.

I felt glorious, the whole ride home. Everything felt magical and perfect. We listened to Bon Jovi, singing at the tops of our lungs with the windows rolled down, and we were happy. But the closer we got to her house, the more nervous I felt. Because this was it—the last time I was ever going to see her. For weeks I had been wanting to tell her how I felt about her. For weeks I had been wanting to get her alone like this—but not with the car running. Not with anything running. Just her, and me, and the quiet of the night.

We pulled in to her driveway and instead of just putting the car into park, I shut it off. She turned to me and gave me a mock pout. "I guess this is it," she said.

"I guess so," I said. "I'm going to miss you."

She laughed and leaned against my shoulder again. "Oh, my poor little Jordan," she said. "What am I going to do with you?"

"What am I going to do without you?"

And just like I hoped, just like I had been imagining it, she turned her head up from where it lay on my shoulder, looking straight up at me. And I leaned down and kissed her. She closed her eyes and sighed into my kiss, and I closed my own eyes and reached up to touch her cheek.

Suddenly there was a rapping at the car window. My eyes shot open and I saw Giselle's father standing at the passenger side door, glaring down at us. Giselle jumped, bumping into my head as she tried to right herself. Her father opened the car door and said, "Very nice, Giselle. Very nice. Your mother and I have been waiting up for you for hours."

"Sorry!" she yelled, extricating herself from the seatbelt and grabbing her backpack.

"You know how worried we get on Halloween."

"Sorry, sorry, sorry!" she said, jumping out of the car. She stopped, looked back at me, and gave me a little "oh, well" shrug. Her father grabbed her by the arm and pulled her away from the car towards the house.

And that was it—my one chance, shot to shit. The front door closed on Giselle, and the front lights went out. I slammed my hand on the steering wheel and cursed. Then I started the car and got out of there, not wanting her father to come back outside to lecture me.

It was a long drive back to West Hempstead. The cold fall air we had enjoyed on the drive up was suddenly too cold, so I rolled up the windows and put on the heat. I turned the music on, then shut it off, then turned it on again to stop the angry monologue in my head. I had waited too long—I should have made a move weeks ago. I should have taken her somewhere else on the ride home. I had blown it. Fucked it up. Even if I got the nerve to call her now—and what were the odds of that?—we'd never have another night like this one. Everything had been perfect. Magical. Everything had been *right*. And I had let it slip away. Idiot. Dumb shit. Can't you do anything *right*?

On and on like that, all the way home. Even the loudest music couldn't drown it out.

45

The judge exited the Russell building at about 12:30 with three other men and walked a block away to a restaurant. I could see both buildings from where I sat, so I stayed put and ordered another coffee. He came back an hour later and went back into his building, where he stayed until 4:30. As he rounded the corner to where his car was parked, I paid my bill and got into my rental, ready to follow him. But he went straight home.

The next day, exactly the same thing happened. Except I remembered to bring a book and my IPod, and I used my own car. After all, I didn't have a job anymore—I had to be careful with my resources. And I hadn't noticed anyone keeping an eye on me while I had been keeping an eye on the judge.

The next day, exactly the same thing happened.

The next day, exactly the same thing happened.

The next day, he stopped at a drug store on the way home. Excitement.

The next day, we were back to the old routine.

This was idiotic. Even if the judge *had* been having an affair with someone three years ago, the accident could have put the Big Fear on him and made him call it off. Or some other event could have done it. Three years is a long time. I could follow this guy for the rest of my life and learn nothing more about him than the fact that he had boring lunch habits.

Unfortunately, it was all I had. So my choices were: (a) follow the guy for the rest of my life; or (b) give him a little push. There were risks involved in choosing (b), obviously. I could get my face bashed in again. I could get arrested for stalking or harassment. I was way out on a limb. But I didn't know what else to do, so I chose (b).

It was a Monday in mid-January. The holidays were behind us. The weather was doing that thing it does in Atlanta in the wintertime—up one day, down the next—like it's trying to figure out whether it's ready to commit to winter. I was at my regular station at the coffee shop. The judge had been safely ensconced in the courthouse for an hour and wouldn't be out again until lunch. I waved over my regular waitress, Billie, and asked her if she'd do me a huge favor. I gave her a typewritten note and asked her if she wouldn't mind copying it out by hand. She took a quick look at it and her painted eyebrows shot up into her hair.

"I know," I said, "it's a little weird. I'll make it worth your while."

She shrugged, cracked her gum, and copied it out carefully, making it look just the way I wanted it to: girly.

"One more thing?" I asked. She shrugged again.

"Could you walk the note across the street to the Russell building and leave it with whoever's at the front desk—and make sure he knows to give it to Judge Harper?"

"Jud who?"

"Judge. Harper."

"This ain't illegal, is it?"

"No, Billie. Not hardly. But you know what? I'll tip you like it's murder."

"Sounds good to me."

She grabbed the note back out of my hand and sauntered out.

This was the love letter she delivered:

> *Hey, stranger. I've been thinking about you a lot, but thinking isn't nearly good enough. I thought I'd be daring and meet you at your favorite lunch place. If it's safe to sit with me, I'll be in the back corner. If not, just pretend you don't know me and I'll be okay. I just want to see you…in the flesh. All my love…me.*

It was a gamble, but I had written it carefully to cover a few different possible realities. If he was actively involved with someone, it would make sense. If the affair was long over, the "thinking about you" still might make sense. Of course, if I was just dead wrong about him, it would simply be mystifying. Either way, I wanted to see how he reacted.

For a twenty dollar donation, the kitchen staff at the judge's favorite lunch place let me stand just inside the swinging doors and peek out. That gave me a perfect view of the judge when he walked into the restaurant with his usual companions. His friends didn't seem to notice anything, but I could tell he was glancing around furtively, trying to get a look at the faces in the back booths of the restaurant. It wasn't easy; this was one of those places with high-backed benches in the booths. Great for privacy; lousy for snooping. The judge's friends made it worse by taking a table by the front window, denying him the chance to cruise most of the floor.

It looked to me like he was annoyed. And sure enough, within two minutes he was on his feet, excusing himself to go to the rest room. I watched him walk the length of the restaurant, looking left and right for a familiar face. Obviously there was none. At the back of the restaurant, just inches from where I was hiding, he turned around and looked back at the restaurant floor. Then he gave up and went to the rest room.

I know what you're probably thinking: of course he was looking for someone; no doubt about that. But was he looking for an old flame, a current lover, or some weird stalker? No way to tell. He had a nervous and apprehensive look on his face, but so would any of us in that situation. So you're right—my little stunt hadn't proved anything definitively. But I hadn't intended it to. It was just meant to be a little push.

Now, if there really *was* a woman out there in his past or present, and the judge thought she had left him a note and then vanished, what was he likely to do when he got back to the office? Call her, of course. And I didn't care whether it was a "how dare you send me a note at work" call or a "darling, I've missed you" call. It would be contact. And my hope—my real gamble here—was that a phone call might break the judge's pattern and lead to a meeting.

And my gamble paid off that very evening. As usual, the judge left his office at 4:30 PM. As usual, I waited discretely and then pulled out behind him once he left the parking lot. But this time, he didn't head onto the I-75 ramp. He passed it by, went up to North Avenue, and made a right. We approached Boulevard Drive. If you're not from Atlanta, that name won't mean anything to you. If you're a native, though, you know that Boulevard Drive changes its name to Monroe Drive just a block to the north of where I was. And Monroe Drive, a bit further north, is where Giselle was killed.

Atlanta streets are famous for changing their names at key north/south intersections. For years, I thought it was just Atlanta's wacky inefficiency and strangeness. But there was actually a reason for it. There's always a reason if you're willing to dig. The streets changed their names when they crossed certain east-west streets because, once upon a time, White folks didn't want to live on the same street that Black folks lived on. So they drew a line, they changed the name, and they stayed on the north side of the line.

We were approaching Monroe Drive on North Avenue. Turn north and you're at the accident site in ten minutes. Maybe less, if you're speeding. But the judge didn't turn north today; he went south, just a few blocks, and then turned left onto Morgan Street.

Morgan Street was wide and open, with some trees set back around the houses, but not much along the road. Some of the houses were private homes, but most of them looked like they'd been cut up into apartments. As we moved away from the main drag, the apartments thinned out and the private homes increased. The buildings had the same kind of dignified seediness as my neighborhood. The houses looked lived in and well loved, but the paint tended to be a little old and cracking, and the porches were a little warped and saggy.

The judge stopped in front of a red brick building with a scraggly lawn pockmarked by stray flagstones that didn't seem to form any path or pattern. The lawn led most of the way up to the house, then took a shallow dive as it approached the house, leaving more of the first floor exposed at the rear of the building than was visible from the street. A large wooden staircase led from the lawn up to a second story entrance, right at the point where the lawn began to glide down. At the top of the stairs, lining the front face of the house, was a wooden porch that matched the stairs. There seemed to be an entrance below the stairs, down the little hill. It looked to me like apartments.

I passed the judge's car, then made a discrete U-turn and parked on the opposite side of the street. The judge was already out of his car and was walking beneath the stairway to the first-floor entrance. He knocked. Someone answered. He entered. I couldn't see a thing.

But that didn't bother me. There were windows aplenty all around the first floor, and the gentle downhill grade meant that passers-by on the street would be less likely to notice a peeping tom, especially once the sun went down, which it was just starting to do.

I checked the sidewalks and the nearby windows for neighbors, then grabbed my camera and sauntered over to the building. I trotted down the hill, careful to stay away from the closest windows in case anyone happened to look out. There were just enough trees to give me some cover, even without their leaves. Walking by the windows, I spied a kitchen, a bathroom, and a bedroom. They seemed unoccupied. I went around to the back of the house, where I was exposed to more neighbors. But no one seemed to be home from work yet.

At the rear of the building there were two large windows revealing a dining room and a living room. The living room furniture looked a lot like my own—lots of hand-me downs and thrift-store finds. And there, sitting on a serviceable but hardly impressive sofa, sat my judge. He was still wearing his coat, but he was seated. He looked unhappy. There was a woman in the room with him, pacing back and forth and occasionally waving her arms around. She looked to be in her mid-thirties—nicely dressed, good haircut, pretty face. She seemed confused or upset by something. My guess was that the judge had confronted her about the love note, and she was letting him know that it wasn't from her. Was she angry because he was accusing her, or was she angry because she thought someone else was sending him love notes? It was hard to tell.

The judge tried to get a word in every once in a while, but it was hard going. Finally he stood up and walked to her, taking both of her hands in his. He was trying to explain something. She shook her head. He kept talking. She nodded. She took one of her hands out of his and reached up to brush away a tear. He lifted his hand to her cheek, and she leaned in to his hand. He was apologizing. He was explaining. She nodded some more. Then he took her into his arms, and she leaned her head onto his shoulder. He stroked her hair, saying reassuring words. She lifted her head from his shoulder, smiled, and kissed him. They stood that way for a nice long while.

And lucky me—there was just enough light to take some pictures.

46

Porkchop leaned forward, peering into his computer screen. From my end, all I could see was his large, nearly albino nose. We were meeting by webcam for his safety and mine, just in case the judge's beefy friends still had issues about my friendship with lawyers. I was holding up a printout of one of the photos I had taken the day before, since I didn't have a scanner at home.

"Nice," he said. "Some of your best work."

"Well, there was still some daylight. That always makes it easier."

"I generally prefer more skin," he said, sitting back in his plush office chair. "But that's just me."

"No skin," I said. "It was all very chaste. But I doubt his wife would see it that way."

"Indeed," he said.

"You recognize the man?" I asked.

"No comment," he said. "I'm just glad no one can take a picture of *us* together, talking about him."

"You got off easy, last time," I said, referencing my healing schnoz.

"I get off easy *every* time," he said. "That's my rule. But let's get down to business, before my secretary comes in for my 4:00 blow job."

I rolled my eyes.

"I saw that," he said. "You doubt me?"

"I doubt nothing," I said. "You have mad skills."

"So," my quasi-attorney said. "I'm curious. What, exactly, are you planning on doing with these pictures? Usually you take things like this for a client, because she's looking for evidence of that particular act."

"That's true."

"But this act is secondary and maybe even irrelevant."

"I don't think so."

"More importantly, do you even *have* a client anymore?"

"Not so much," I admitted

"So…not to be dense, but…what's the point of all of this?" He leaned back in his chair in a pensive pose.

I explained my theory of the case: Three years ago, the judge was having an affair with this young woman, who lived on a side street off Boulevard Drive, south of Ponce de Leon. One winter morning, after spending the night with her, the judge drove home too quickly on Monroe Drive and smacked into Giselle, who was careening down Virginia Avenue on her rollerblades and drifted as she made a right onto Monroe. A police report putting him at that location so early in the morning, far from both home and office, would look mighty suspicious to his wife and others. So, in fear of divorce and his larger reputation, the judge called in some favors with the precinct and made the case go away.

Porkchop listened carefully, nodding. Then he started firing more questions at me.

"Who's his girl?"

"Don't know."

"Can you prove an affair three years ago? Or just a kiss yesterday?"

"Just the kiss."

"Can you prove he was with her on that particular night?"

"Nope."

"If he *was* with her that night, and he was with her all night, where was the wife?"

"What do you mean?"

"Well, either she's at home, waiting for him and wondering where the hell he is, in which case speeding home in the morning is hardly going to save his ass, or she's out of town, which lets him spend the night safely, but doesn't give him a reason to race home at dawn."

"Hm."

"Hm indeed."

"I'll have to work on that one."

"Last question. Do you have any evidence placing him at the accident site?"

"Just the hood ornament."

"So you've got nothing."

"Well, I sure as hell don't have an indictment. But that's not my job."

"What *is* your job?" he asked. "And again—*who* are you working for?"

I paused. It was an excellent question.

"I'm just trying to tie up loose ends, counselor."

"Compulsive neat-freak that you are."

"Something like that."

He nodded. "Which brings us back to the picture and my original question. What's it good for? What does it get you?"

"An opening, maybe. A conversation. When we first talked about this, you said something about blackmail."

"Oh, I don't think so. That doesn't sound like me at all."

"Not real blackmail—just the threat of it."

"I'm sure you're mistaken. I'm a serious professional and a member of the Georgia bar. But whoever said such a thing to you was probably thinking of a ruse to make your suspect give himself away, because he thinks you know the whole story already."

"Exactly."

"Which, obviously, I condemn in the strongest possible terms."

"Sure, sure."

"And let me just say, whoever suggested this idea to you was talking out of his ass. That's a very dangerous business. What's to stop him from beating the shit out of you again? Or worse?"

"Well, my father *is* his best friend."

"Yes, that seemed to mean a lot to him last time. Jordy, you know that old saying about how if you're going to hit at the king, you'd better kill him?"

"Sure."

"If you show this particular gentleman that particular picture, or hint that you even have such a picture—if you pretend you can place him at the hit and run—you're going to put him with back to the wall, and he's going to strike out any way he can, no matter who your daddy is. This guy has way too much at stake. You can't afford to dance around him and hope for the best, see where it leads. Not this man. You take a swing at him, you get one swing, and it has to be a knockout punch. Down in one. You get what I'm saying?"

"Yeah, I do," I muttered. "But I don't have a knockout punch."

"Well, you'd better get one. Also, you have to be very careful how you introduce the picture. If you say anything about a deal, or a quid pro quo, or money changing hands, that's blackmail, Jordy—actual blackmail, not pretend. No one will care what you were really, secretly going to do. If you put it out there, it's a crime."

"But if I just hint around it? Never say it, but insinuate it?"

"The goal is to make *him* say it—all of it. And you remain non-committal." Then he shrugged. "I don't know—maybe it doesn't matter. In the end, it's going to be his word against yours, and you're not exactly on equal footing."

"I could arrange for witnesses."

"If you can do that without making him run for cover, it's not a bad idea. It wouldn't be admissible evidence, but it might give you some protection." He pondered for a moment, then said, "I guess the question here is, what are you looking for out of this? Do you just want to know, once and for all? Or do you want to put him away?"

"Both."

"Well. If you want to put him away, you're going to have to come out of this with something tangible and damning. And admissible. Something the DA can use to build a case."

"Even if he doesn't want to."

"Especially if he doesn't want to." There was a knocking sound on his end. "Sorry, Jordy—there's the girl for my 4:00."

"You knocked on the desk yourself, you idiot. But that's okay—you're a busy man. Thanks for the consult."

"My pleasure, dear boy. You'll get my bill. It's payable in beer."

He reached out towards his screen and the picture went black. Without his white face front and center, I was able to see my own face reflected in the screen—and behind me, Susannah, standing against the wall, arms folded across her chest. I turned around to look at her. She didn't seem happy.

"You're home early," I said, as breezily as possible. She said nothing—just walked up towards me and picked up the photograph of the judge and his lady friend.

"How long were you standing there?" I asked.

"Long enough," she said. She dropped the photograph on the table and walked out of the room.

"Shit," I said—to no one in particular—and went off after her.

I found her on the porch glider, wrapped up in her big, chunky sweater, her hands pulled up into her over-long sleeves.

"Come inside," I said. "You're gonna freeze."

"I like the cold," she said.

"You? The barefoot girl from Macon, Georgia?"

She looked up at me, then away. "You know what?" she said. "I don't want to banter right now."

I closed the door and sat next to her. She didn't move.

"Why are you doing this?" she asked.

"I have to," I said.

She looked at me and said, "Explain it to me."

I sighed, but said nothing.

"Seriously," she said. "Explain it to me. Because I don't understand. Your father told you to quit. Carter told you to quit. I *begged* you. Even your client told you to quit. All you're going to do is get yourself killed. And then I'm going to be here alone, sitting on this stupid, rotting porch, never knowing why."

"Susie…" I started.

"No, that's how it's going to be. I'll be sitting here—right here, on this glider you bought for our anniversary. I'll be sitting here alone, looking out at the street, and no one will ever come by, because they'll be too embarrassed and they won't know what to say. Oticha, Mel…they'll try and be friends for a while, but they'll drift away. Everything I have with you—everything I love—it's all going to drift away, and I'll be left here alone, never knowing why."

"I'm not going to get myself killed," I said.

It was completely the wrong thing to say. She slapped at me with her sweater-covered hands, then punched at me—arms, chest, whatever she could reach.

"What the fuck is going on?" she yelled. "This isn't you. You never give a shit about *anything*."

I grabbed her arms—mostly to keep her from whacking me in the nose by accident. I looked her in the eye and said, "I give a shit about you."

She calmed down a little. "Then *talk* to me," she said. "Who *is* this girl?"

"I told you—"

"No. You told me shit. This isn't some old girlfriend. You don't risk your life for some old girlfriend who isn't even alive anymore. Who the fuck was she? Why do you care so much?"

I didn't say anything at first. She waited. Then she pulled her arms out of my hands and wrapped them back around herself for warmth. We rocked back and forth for a while, each in our own heads. The usual non-answers weren't going to work anymore, and the real answer…the real answer was something I hadn't ever said out loud. To anyone.

"I swear to God, Jordan Greenblatt," Susannah said quietly, but with finality, "if you don't tell me what's rolling around in that head of yours, I'm going to split it open and find out for myself. And you know I can handle an axe."

So I told her.

47

It started the morning of graduation. Everything went wrong. My band was supposed to accompany the school chorus on a couple of songs, but the sound system out on the football field fell apart, and two fat guys in an old van had to drive out and park in front of the podium, right in the middle of the ceremony, to fix the microphones. Then the parents started acting like drunk idiots at a football game, yelling "siddown" and "shaddup" at each other. They were yelling because people kept standing up and moving around. As soon as a kid got his diploma, his parents packed up their stuff and started heading out of the bleachers. So there was constant noise and churn and chaos on the field all morning. And to top it off, our genius assistant principal had arranged for the chorus and my band to receive our diplomas last—after the rest of our class—so that we could remain in place to provide music. Which was a great idea in theory. But by the time we walked across the stage, there was almost no one left in the audience to applaud for us when we got our diplomas. Poor Rachel Zuckerman in the chorus heard crickets when she walked across the stage.

My parents, of course, were not yelling at people to siddown and shaddup. They were far too educated and cultured for that. Instead, they just bitched about it on the drive home, yammering on and on about how low-class everyone had been. As though they were the cream of Long Island society—my law-professor father and my housewife mother.

"You know, this is why I never had any friends," I growled at them.

"What are you talking about? You had plenty of friends," my mother said.

"Yeah, as long as *their* parents took us places or let us do things at *their* house."

My mother sniffed and said, "This is a ridiculous conversation."

That was my mother's way of arguing. Instead of meeting you head on, she would just reduce you to nothing by telling you that your issues were ridiculous and not worth discussing. She kind of defined you out of existence. And my father was no help when I got into arguments with my mom. He was always grading papers or something. He only engaged in the higher-order arguments, things involving history, or the law, or philosophy— and then, as I mentioned earlier, he was always right. So he was no fun to argue with, either.

I used to wish for a brother, just so I'd have someone else who understood my parents. But I didn't have a brother. Instead, I had a bass guitar and an amp.

Later, I drove four of my friends from party to party, fulfilling my usual role of designated drunk driver. The parties were all stupid. I don't know why. Everyone else seemed to be having a good time, but I couldn't get out of my head. I hung back, drinking beer, watching everything and narrating the scene to myself. Playing accompaniment, as usual.

After the fourth party, we were on some road in the middle of Nassau County—God knows where—when Evan Silverman and Jake Mazilla decided to sing some made up words to "Pomp and Circumstance" at the top of their lungs while leaning out of the car doors, which they had flung wide open. Josh Lipton, in the middle, was singing with them and holding onto both of them, to keep them from falling out of the car. But Josh was too scrawny to anchor them, and they were all too drunk to focus, and when I came around a sharp curve, Jake flew out of the car.

"Holy shit—Jake's gone," Josh yelled.

I pulled over to the shoulder and we all fell out of the car to look for him. He was lying on a grassy embankment by the side of the road, perfectly happy and totally unharmed, looking up at the stars.

"That's it," I said. "We're done." I had had enough. No one argued with me.

I drove them all home and then pointed the car back towards my own house. But I didn't go home. It was only eleven o'clock, and it was graduation night, and I felt surly and miserable. It wasn't right. It was all over and it was ending the wrong way. I was the only guy I knew who was going to be alone next year. Everyone else was going to school with at least a few other Hempstead kids, or staying home to start a job or go to Adelphi. Me—I was heading down to Atlanta, Georgia, a place I'd never been. And no one in my class was going with me. I felt like I was going to leave Long Island and it would all disappear behind me forever, and there'd be no turning back.

I didn't want to be alone, but I didn't want to be with my usual idiots, either. Here it was, graduation night, and I didn't feel celebratory, and I wanted to. I wanted to enjoy something without thinking it to death. I wanted my last night to be something memorable—something wonderful. And nothing in my life had felt memorable or wonderful. Not since that last time I had driven Giselle home.

Giselle. That was it. I needed to see Giselle again. I needed one last chance with her. I had tried to call her once or twice in the months since the SAT class had ended, and I had always chickened out and hung up. But I still knew her number. So I stopped at a 7-11 to use the pay phone, and I called her house.

Her father answered angrily, and asked me if I knew what time it was. I told him I wasn't sure. He yelled at me for another few minutes.

I was finally able to ask him if Giselle was at home, and I found out she wasn't. It was graduation night for her, as well. She was at a party somewhere. Greg Zeitlan's house, maybe? He wasn't sure. I heard him bark something to his wife, away from the phone, and heard her yell something back. Yes, that was it. Greg Zeitlan's house. And he threw some Great Neck street name at me.

I was in a foul mood now. Giselle was off with her rich kid friends at some rich kid's house. They were all talking about Harvard or Yale. Even when I was a doctor, someday, those assholes would still outclass me. I'd be seeing patients, or doing surgeries, or whatever, and I'd still have my thick accent, and one of them would look up at my wall and see my diploma from Candler, and they'd say, "Oh, that's in Alabama somewhere, isn't it?" Condescending fucks.

I aimed my car north and decided to see what a condescending fuck's graduation party looked like.

I knew my way to Great Neck, and I knew the address well enough to know what neighborhood it was in, but that was it. Since this was pre-cell phone and pre-GPS, I stopped at a gas station and asked for directions. Not like I really had to bother. The party was huge, with a line of parked cars snaking away from it in every direction for half a mile or more. Good, I thought— easy to get lost there—no one will ask who I am.

I was disappointed at first. It was the same dumb, loud music, the same plastic cups of beer littering the lawn. Of course, the lawn was much bigger, and the bathrooms inside were much nicer. I wandered around, picking up shreds of conversation here and there. No one was talking about Harvard or Yale. It was exactly the same stupid shit that my friends in Hempstead was saying. None of it mattered. None of it was worth being a part of—or leaving.

Someone shoved someone else, and a body stumbled and fell into me, spilling beer on my shirt. I shoved him away from me, and he wheeled on me, angry, ready for a fight. He was tall and scrawny, with long hair and a stupid, Axl Rose headband. He looked me over for all of a second and decided I wasn't worth his time, so he waved me away like the hired help and turned back to his friends. I don't know if it was my clothes, or my haircut, or the fact that I was four inches shorter than him. But I didn't care—I didn't like being dismissed. So I shoved him in the back, which knocked him into yet another partygoer, spilling even more beer. Now Axl Rose was angry. He wheeled on me and yelled, "What the fuck?"

I said nothing. Axl looked me over again, laughed, and held his arms out in invitation, "All right, midget—what do you want?"

Now a crowd was forming. Axl made some feints in my direction, to see if I would flinch. I didn't move. It was the primate dance—the gorillas pounding their chests and circling each other—the ritual of fighting that we string out as much as possible, to avoid the reality of hitting each other.

Suddenly, I heard a voice calling my name from across the lawn.

"Jordan?"

I felt a hand on my shoulder. I turned around. It was Giselle.

"You know this fuck?" Axl said.

"Yeah, I know him. He's a friend of mine," she said, challenging him. "So what?"

"So nothing. Just get him the fuck away from me."

He turned away and went back to his friends. I made a move in his direction, but Giselle grabbed my arm and pulled me away. "Come on, tough guy," she said. And she led me away from the crowd to a ridiculous concrete fountain up by the house. We sat on the edge together. I scooped up some water and threw it on my face to cool off.

"What was *that* all about?" she asked.

"Who knows?" I said. And she laughed. She laughed—and I smiled for the first time that day.

"What are you doing here, Jordan?"

"I came to see you."

"Are you serious?"

"Sure, why not?"

"I don't know. It's just…weird. Isn't it? Why me? Why tonight?"

I shrugged. "I don't know. I wanted to call you, like a million times, and I never got up the nerve. But now, you know, it's graduation, and everyone's going to leave, and…I wanted to see you."

I dared myself to look her in the eye. She was looking straight back at me, and there was nothing dismissive about her.

"You want to go for a drive?" I asked.

She laughed. "What, and miss all this?"

So we went for a drive. We drove around aimlessly for a while, with the windows rolled down, listening to the radio, just like we had done months before. Then I drove her down East Shore Road, away from people and noise.

"Do you know any place where we can walk down to the water?" I asked.

"How about right here?" she said.

Right here was nowhere, but what the hell—it was her town. So I pulled off onto the shoulder and we climbed over the low railing and down through some trees to the long slope of the grassy beach. I looked out at the lights twinkling across from Manhasset.

"Hey," I said. "It's the green light."

"What?"

"The green light. Like on Daisy's dock." I looked back at her. Nothing. "What—you didn't have to read The Great Gatsby last year, like the rest of the world?"

"I read it. So what?"

"Never mind."

I wished we could be at an actual beach, where we could sit on the sand and listen to the breakers crash against the shore. Instead, we had this flat, lifeless sliver of Long Island Sound. But I was lucky enough to have that, right now, and I knew it.

"Didn't you bring a blanket or anything?" she asked, a little petulantly.

"No," I said. "I didn't plan ahead. I didn't think—"

She shrugged, said "Whatever," and sat down on the grass, looking out at the dull water and the lights beyond. I stood there, doing the same.

"You gonna sit down, or what?" she said.

I said nothing, but I sat down next to her. Her voice was harder than I remembered it, and she seemed a little whiny. But maybe it was just the night, and the drink, and the strange feeling of being at the end of one thing and not at the beginning of the next thing yet. I was probably a little hard and whiny myself.

I caught myself being locked in my head, and tried to stop it. Here I was, with the girl I'd been thinking about for months, and all I could do was talk talk talk to myself. So I told myself to shut up, and I took a deep breath, and I put my arm around her—this girl I hadn't spoken to in months. And she leaned her head on my shoulder.

Maybe we *hadn't* lost that spark—maybe I could pick up right where we left off when her father interrupted us. Because nobody was going to interrupt us here. Nobody could even hear us.

I leaned down to kiss her, and she kissed back.

"Mmm," she said. "*So* much better than doing fucking beer bongs with Greg Zeitlan."

"You do a lot of those, tonight?" I asked, kissing her again.

"Enough to be out here with you," she said, laughing.

I pulled away a little bit. "What does that mean?"

"What? Nothing. I was joking. Come on." And she pulled me in for another kiss.

And I was back in my head again. What—she needed to be drunk to come out with me? Why? Because I wasn't a rich prick like her Great Neck friends? Because my father was a professor instead of a psychiatrist or a lawyer?

Lost in my angry thoughts, I started kissing her more aggressively, pushing her back on the grass. She reached up and wrapped her arms around my neck.

"Oh, yeah, tough guy?" she said. "You want to push *me* around too? You want to fight?" And she pulled herself up against me and kissed me hard, biting me on the lip.

"You think I can't take you?" I said.

"Yeah, you're bad." She laughed.

Was she making fun of me, or did she think I was the kind of guy who picked fights at strange parties—which I totally was *not*…even though that's what I had just done? Is *that* why she had come out with me? She thought I was something risky? Something dangerous? Did she even like me, or was this just something to piss off her parents? Did I care?

I reached up under her t-shirt and unhooked her bra. She purred and reached under my shirt to scratch my back. The touch of her skin felt amazing—better than I had dreamed. My other hand found the button on her jeans. But that hand got pushed away. I reached again, and again she pushed me away.

"You want to fight?" I whispered. "We can fight."

"Too much."

"Come on, isn't that why you're out here with me?"

"Jordan, no—"

"You want to be the bad girl? Come on." I grabbed her button and tugged it loose before she could pull my hand away. I unzipped her jeans.

"Jordan, no—that's enough—" Pushing on my chest.

I didn't say anything.

"Jordan—don't—I said—" Trying to squirm away from me.

I didn't say anything.

"Please…" Crying.

I don't remember the rest of the words. I wasn't listening.

48

Night had fallen by the time I finished talking, and it was genuinely cold now out on the porch. Susannah had pulled her knees up to her chest for warmth. I was shivering, but I barely noticed. The glider had stopped rocking back and forth.

"I saw her lying there," I said, "crying, her clothes all grass-stained, her hair all messed. And it was like I had just gotten there—like 'what happened?' Because, you know…how could *I* have done a thing like that? Except I had. She got dressed and she went back up the hill. She didn't say anything. She didn't say anything, the whole way home—she just stared out the window and cried. I didn't say anything either. I didn't know what to say."

From Susannah: silence.

"I tried to call her all summer, to apologize, to…say anything. But she was gone—working as a camp counselor or something. And her father wouldn't tell me how to reach her. He wouldn't tell me anything. I don't know what she told him, but he definitely treated me like I was bad news. After a few times, he just started hanging up on me. And then…it just got to be too late, I guess."

From Susannah: nothing.

"Say something," I pleaded.

"What do you want me to say?" she said quietly.

We sat there in silence for a minute.

"How could you not tell me about that, Jordan? All this time? All this time we've been together?"

"I never told anyone."

"I'm not 'anyone.'"

"I know. It's just…not something I really wanted to share."

"So what, Jordan? You know? I've shared shit with you that isn't pretty. We're married."

"I know."

"You know. You know—except you keep a thing like that from me—a thing that changed your whole life."

"It didn't —"

"Shut up," she said quickly. Then: "Seriously? You seriously think this shit hasn't been working on you, your whole life?"

"I guess."

"You guess. Didn't you fail half your courses when you went to college? Didn't they put you on probation? Didn't your goddamn parents have to move down here to babysit you?"

"That's not—that's not what it was. I mean …" I let it trail off into nothing, not sure what I was trying to say.

She sighed. "You don't know one single thing about yourself, that's your problem. You investigate everybody else's shit, but you never look at your own."

"I ruined her life, Susie."

"You ruined your own."

"No. I talked to her roommate, her husband. She was never the same person after that. She was lonely and closed-up. And I did that do her."

"You know that for a fact? You're the cause of everything? After you, nothing important ever happened to her again?"

I didn't understand what she was doing. "I'm not the victim, here, Susie. She is."

"Victim. I hate that fucking word."

"This isn't about her; it's about me. She didn't—"

"How could it not be about her?" she said loudly. "She was there, wasn't she?"

"Of course she was there."

"Then it's about both of you, Jordan. For Christ's sake." She got up and walked away from me, looking out at the street.

"You think bad shit never happened to *me*? You think I never had uncles rubbing up against me, teachers looking down my shirt, football players trying to get my pants off after a game? I'm a girl from Macon fucking Georgia, Jordan. You know the shit I went through. I told you everything."

"I know."

"I told you everything, and you told me nothing."

I couldn't deny it, so I didn't say anything.

She turned back to me. "But I'll tell you one thing I *never* did—I never got myself drunk and then wandered out in the middle of nowhere with some guy I didn't hardly know. My daddy didn't have as much school as yours or that girl's, but he had brains enough to teach me how to survive. And how to kick a man in the balls when I had to."

"You're saying this was *her* fault?"

"No!" She turned away again. "Maybe. Shit, I don't know." She stood there for a long moment, watching the traffic go by. A long moment. I could feel how upset she was—I could feel it in the air between us. I wanted to go to her, put my arms around her. but I felt like I had lost the right. So I waited.

Finally she came back to the glider and sat next to me. "Look, here's the thing," she said, calmer now. "I didn't know her. I know you. So I'm going to be biased, all right? Even if I'm pissed at you. And I'm sure as shit pissed at you right now. But I'm still gonna be on your side. That's just how it is. I don't have to defend it."

"Okay."

"The other thing is…" She stopped. I could hear her taking deep and slow breaths.

"What?"

She shook her head after a moment, and then sat back, defeated. "Nothing." She sat there for a moment, looking out into the night, and then said, "Just…you should have gotten help for it. Forever ago. You both should have gotten help."

We rocked back and forth for a moment.

"And you should have fucking trusted me," she added quietly.

"I didn't want you to think I was a bad person," I said.

She turned to me. "I know what kind of a person you are."

"Now you do."

"I always did."

"But it's different now. Isn't it? Doesn't it have to be?"

She shrugged, and looked away. "I don't know.."

"Anyway," I said. "That's why I can't let this go."

"But there's nothing you can do for her," she said softly. "I get that you feel like you owe her, like you need to pay it back, but it's too late."

"I just want to make things right."

She looked at me, closely and for a long time. "Bu you can't," she said. "It's too late."

I winced. "I could. A little. I could give her some justice. Not for what *I* did to her, maybe, but at least for how she died."

"You can't give her anything, Jordan. She's dead."

49

The thing about knowing something no one else knows is that you control the switch. You know if you keep your mouth shut, the train is going to keep going in the same direction it's always been going. But the minute you say the thing no one else knows, the switch gets thrown and the train goes off in a new direction. You can't be sure what direction it's going to go in. All you know is that once people know this thing, they're going to see you differently—think about you differently. And you know that there's no undoing it—once the switch is thrown, it's thrown.

Getting engaged was like that. There was a period where some people knew I had asked Susannah to marry me and other people didn't. And I could see that I was suddenly somebody slightly different to those people who knew, but I was the same old person to everyone who *didn't* know. And I controlled the switch. The minute I told people, something would change forever. And if I didn't tell people, that something wouldn't change.

It was the same thing when I failed all my pre-med classes. My parents were still up in New York, so if I didn't tell them, they wouldn't know. For two weeks, they kept on believing that "my son, the doctor" was going to be real. And the longer I didn't tell them, the more I wanted to be able to keep them from knowing. Until the dean wrote to my parents to tell them I was on academic probation.

That bucket of shit came crashing down on my head, and I survived. But this one? Could I survive people knowing about this? I had barely survived knowing about it, myself. Ever since that night, I've wished I could stop being the guy who did what I did. I never wanted to be that guy. I never thought I *could* be that guy. But I was wrong.

I told you earlier how Pete likes to say you never know who you are until you're in that moment of truth, when you're tested. And I told you how I like to laugh it all off and make a joke about the whole thing. But it's not a joke, and I can't avoid thinking about Giselle whenever he says it. Because there was a moment of truth for me with her, and I failed it. I was the guy who raped his dream girl on graduation night. I can't even type the word without deleting it five times and trying to figure out how else to put it. But there is no other way to put it, because that's what it was. That's what I did.

So I never told anyone. Because I didn't want people to change the way they saw me, in that way you can never change back. Especially not Susannah. Please, God, not Susannah. The idea that she might somehow find out…might see me differently…it had scared the hell out of me for years. Because I liked the guy I saw reflected in her eyes. I needed that guy.

But now I had thrown the switch. I had told her. And now everything would change. Now she would never be able to look at me or think about me without including that night as part of the story of who I was. How could she? How could she love me, knowing all that? She couldn't. No one could. Maybe she'd put on a brave face for a while, but it wouldn't last. She wouldn't be able to live with this. And some day she would leave me. It was inevitable. It was what I deserved. I just had to wait and wonder, every day, if tonight was going to be the night.

The day after my confession, she went off to work, same as usual, and I stayed at home, practicing some Ray Brown bass lines and dreading her return home. Would I see it in her eyes right away? Would it be tonight?

But she came home that afternoon, and she seemed fine. Normal. She didn't look at me strangely. She didn't say anything about it. On the other hand, she didn't say much of anything.

While we were eating dinner, though, she got an apprehensive, worried look on her face. I dreaded asking her what it was about, so I didn't. I acted oblivious. If she wanted so say something, let her say it.

Finally, she did. She put down her silverware, looked me in the eye for the first time that day, and said, "I want to be there."

"Where?"

"Wherever. When you talk to the judge. When you show him the picture."

That wasn't what I was expecting, so it took me a minute to process the idea. Then: "Hell no. Are you crazy?"

"Yeah, I'm crazy. You're going to get yourself killed and I want to protect you, and *I'm* the crazy one."

"I'm not going to get myself killed, and you can't be there. If he thinks anyone is there besides him and me, he's going to run."

"Lee said you should have witnesses." For some reason, Susannah had never felt comfortable calling my friend Porkchop.

"If they stay hidden, he said."

"Fine, so hide me."

"Susie, I haven't even figured out how to talk to him, much less where to have the meeting or where to hide people."

"Well, when you figure it out, let me know. Because you're not doing it if I'm not there, and that's all there is to it."

"Susie—"

"No. That's my final offer. No negotiation." And she picked up her fork and returned to her food.

I watched her eat for a moment, amazed at her. I wondered if I should tell her, but then I figured I had nothing left to lose.

"There's one more thing you should know," I said.

"Jesus Christ, Jordan," she said, dropping her fork loudly. "I'm trying to eat, here."

"I know, but...it's part of the whole equation here, so you should know."

She nodded. "All right, what is it?"

"He got my license pulled. The judge did. I'm not a PI anymore. I'm just a…guy."

She stared at me, waiting for me to explain what it all meant.

"So whatever I do now," I said, "whatever *we* do, it's going to be totally illegal. I've got no cover."

She kept staring at me. Then she nodded, picked up her fork again, and said, "Well, then, you'd better nail the fucker."

50

Porkchop had said if I hit at the king I would have to kill him. Susannah had said the same thing. And I knew they were right. It was all or nothing now. But I wasn't sure how to do it.

I had a feeling I could use the photograph to pull him out of the shadows and into a meeting with me, and I felt sort-of sure that I could get him to admit the hit-and-run to me if I pushed him hard enough. But that was the limit of my sure-ness. If he admitted it to me, then....I'd know. But I already knew. I'd just know better. And so what? What would that give me? What would that change?

I spent days trying to think my way through it, but nothing came. The week wound down, and the band descended on our house for rehearsal, which was a more elaborate process now that the cold weather had come. We had to move furniture around the living room, roll up rugs to keep them from getting ruined—a whole production. Oticha couldn't host rehearsal when his kids were sleeping, and now that school was in session,

273

the two younger kids had to be in bed earlier. Pete couldn't fit us in his tiny apartment. As for the drummers…well, none of them were invested enough to make room for us in their lives.

So it fell to me. I got the room ready with help from Oticha's older daughter, who was hanging out with us for the evening. Susannah broke out the tequila and beer, and the boys set up their instruments. We ran through a couple of old numbers, and then started working through "Stardust," which had been requested by an elderly neighbor of Oticha's who had hired us to play for his 50th wedding anniversary. There are dozens of recordings of "Stardust," but since we're a trumpet-centric universe, we decided to follow the Louis Armstrong version, without the growly vocals. We don't do vocals.

Louis' arrangement starts with some plinky piano, and then the trumpet sneaks you into the melody with a long introduction that makes you wonder where the actual song starts. Oticha played it smoothly and languidly, like he does. When the actual refrain kicked in, the drummer du jour and I came in with some simple accompaniment. On skins tonight was an aging hippie named Damon, who lived down the road in Little Five Points. He had long grey hair tied messily into a ponytail, with fuchsia-tinted granny glasses and a leather vest worn without a shirt underneath, which I found truly perverse in this bitter weather. But he was a solid drummer and he tolerated our sloppy work ethic, which consisted of short bursts of intense concentration broken up by long periods of beer drinking and chatter.

The opening was good enough, although you could feel the lack of a second brass. Peter tried to give Oticha some counterpoint on the keyboard, messing around with his various sound effects and fake instrument options, which most of us usually hate. But we needed some options. Louis goes through the melody only once, but we like to stretch things out a bit when we play live. It gives us fewer songs to learn, and without vocals, some of these songs can be pretty short without stretching. So Oticha wrapped up the refrain and let Pete take over. As usual, his solo began well—lovely, lush, and romantic—and then slowly veered off into the weird. Suddenly there were birds chirping in the background, and then the birds were chirping in rhythm with the piano, and then, somehow, the birds became the piano.

"All right, all right, hold up," said Oticha. "What the what, boy?"

"You don't like it? You never like it. What about you, Jordo?"

"I was with you during the Snow White part, when it was like the birds were singing with you, but then you lost me."

"Yeah," said Damon. "What the hell was that?"

"I programmed the birdsong into the computer, matching a different sound to each key on the keyboard. So they start as regular birds, and then they're singing along with the piano, and then they're singing instead of the piano. It's like a transformation."

"I'll tell you what it's like," Oticha started, but I stopped him.

"I was going for something magical," Pete said. "Cause it's an anniversary. It's the guy's 50th. That deserves something magical."

"Well, let's stay on key for once. That'll be magical enough for me," Oticha said.

"I thought it was cool," said Damon with a shrug. "Weird, but cool."

"As the resident Jew, descendent of King Solomon and all," I said, "I have a solution that is wise and just."

"You want me to cut the piano in half?" Pete said.

"No, just the solo. Take the transformation halfway, so the birdsong morphs into the birds singing in time with you—but then leave it there. I thought that part was kind of pretty."

"Yeah, but will anyone even notice what I'm doing?" Pete asked.

"Not if we're lucky," said Oticha.

"Yeah, actually, I'm with Oticha on that," I said. "I think the subtle effect is better."

Pete nodded and said, "Let's give it a try." That's the great thing about Pete—he's up for anything, and never seems to have ego tied up in what he's doing. Of course, when you live alone, padding around in your socks on a Cheetohs-encrusted carpet, I guess you learn to be humble.

We nailed down the basic outline of Pete's section, and then Oticha pointed at me.

"Nah," I said. "No one can hear a bass solo at a party. It'd be a waste."

"Man, you always got some excuse."

I shrugged. "It's too quiet. And anyway, if they *could* hear it, It'd just bring the energy down."

Oticha shook his head and then threw up his hands in defeat. "Moving on," he said. "We'll go Pete, back to me, throw to Damon, then back together to finish it up. Yeah?"

"Skip me," said Damon. "I don't think you want a drum solo here. It's a romantic song. I think it's a handoff back and forth between you two, many times as you like."

Everyone agreed, and we gave it a try. And it sounded good…except something was nagging at me. I wasn't distracted, or dreamy, or anything. God knows, I'd been having enough of that, lately. No, I was fully present. It was just like there was this thought I wasn't quite having but knew I *should* be having—like a little itch in some corner of my brain that I couldn't reach. We ran through the song twice, and it never left me. Then we broke for a shot of tequila and a beer, and I retreated to one side of the room to try to puzzle it out.

Susannah came up and put her arms around my neck. "Everything ok?" she asked.

"Yeah," I said, non-committally.

"What's going on?" she said.

"Dunno. Can't put my finger on it."

I heard birdsong again, and looked over at the keyboard. Pete was showing off for Oticha's daughter—making the recorded bird noises sing the Barney theme song and other kiddie atrocities that made the girl laugh. I wandered over to watch.

"Where did you get the bird tracks?" I asked him.

"I recorded them," he said. "Up at the Botanical Gardens a few months ago."

"And you were able to isolate the other stuff—car noises, people, all that?"

"Sure. Easy. Anyway, I didn't have all that much background noise—I used a directional mic, and I had it right up in the trees on a boom. The recording was super clean to start with."

You know how you feel when you finally reach an itch that's been driving you crazy? That's how I felt, right then. All of a sudden, the thought I'd been trying to think exploded in my head, and I felt like an idiot for not realizing what it was I'd been trying to get to. I pulled Pete away from the keyboard and the crowd.

"When you do theatre jobs," I asked, "is it just music and sound effects, or do you rig the whole sound system?"

"Depends what they need," he said. "Mostly it's tiny performance spaces, so they don't need much. You know— music, effects, no real amplification or anything."

"But sometimes you rig mics for actors? Body mics?"

"Sure. For trade shows, especially."

"Do you own all that stuff, or do you use what they have?"

"I've got my own stuff. Sometimes they've got; sometimes they rent. What's all this about, Jordo?"

I nodded to myself. A dumb, self-satisfied smile spread across my face. Why hadn't I thought of this before?

"What?" he asked, baffled.

"Peter, old man, friend of my childhood," I said, putting my arm around his neck, "You and I are going to put on a little show."

51

Later that week, I paid Pete a visit and sat at the dining-room table in his dimly-lit apartment, while he rummaged around in a closet for the sound equipment he wanted to show me. I say "dining room," but it's really just one of those dining-area configurations—a small space in front of a cut-through window to the kitchen, with a kind of bar top in the cut-through for serving food. Or for displaying your Star Wars action figures, if you were Pete.

Susannah was sitting next to me, and she was looking around the apartment with barely-disguised dismay. "Do you think I'm the first woman who's ever set foot in this place?" she asked.

"Yes," I said. He's my friend, and all, but there's no point in pretending.

Pete emerged from the dark recesses of the hallway with an old, square, cardboard box filled to overflowing with gadgets and cables. He plopped it down in the center of the table and then took a seat.

"Pete," Susannah said. "Is it okay that I'm here?"

"Did you touch anything?" he asked.

"No."

He shrugged. "Then it's fine." He reached into the box and began pulling things out. "Okay," he said, "here's what we're going to use with you." He held up a tiny, black object. "I was thinking directional, like we first talked about. But if it's outside, on the street, there's gonna be tons of ambient noise and I won't be able to get close to you with a directional mic without it being obvious. I can still rig one for backup if you want, set back a ways, but I think you're safer with a body mic. So...this is what you wear. Wire comes down to this little box."

"I thought it connected wirelessly," I said.

"The connection to me is wireless. We'll have to test out safe distances to make sure I set myself up in the right place on the actual night."

"And me," said Susannah.

Pete froze, his hand in mid-reach towards the box.

"Yeah, I didn't mention that. Susie's going to be there with you."

"In the car? With me?"

"Take it easy," she said. "I won't bite."

He laughed, but it was a nervous kind of laugh. First I bring a woman to his sanctum sanctorum; now this.

"Anyway," he said, trying to soldier through, "You wear this—anywhere. Usually I place it over the ear, but for this kind of thing, where you don't want anyone to see it, under the shirt is probably best, as long as you don't move around too much. The more your shirt rubs against it, the more noise you're going to create."

"Do I need to shave my chest or something?" I asked.

He stared at me for a minute.

"If I have to tape it to my chest…"

"You can tape it to your undershirt."

"If I wore an undershirt, I could."

He stared at me for a moment. "You know what? Do whatever you want. Just don't move around too much."

"Got it."

He hauled out an electronic box and placed it in front of himself. "This," he said, "is what I'll be recording on. Totally digital—I can transfer it to any format you need."

"And how do I hear you?" I asked.

Again, he stared at me.

"In case something goes wrong and I need to talk to you," I said.

"If something goes wrong, why the hell would you want to talk to *me*?" he asked.

"Good point," I said.

"If something goes wrong," Susannah said, her hand on my leg under the table, "You run like hell."

"Forget I asked," I said. "Anyway, nothing's going to go wrong."

"Famous last words," said Susannah.

"Actually," said Pete, "for men, the most common famous last words are: 'Hey, watch this.' I read that somewhere."

"Thanks," she said. "That's a big old comfort."

He changed the subject nervously. "So where's this intersection you want to work?"

"Corner of Monroe and Virginia."

"Woody's Cheese Steaks? That's not exactly remote."

"No, but if we do it late enough, it should be fine. And he might feel safer, out in the open."

Susannah said. "He'll feel safer, coming to meet you at the scene of the crime?"

"Safe is a relative term," I said.

"Oh!" Pete said, suddenly remembering something. He dug around in the box and pulled out a beaten-up old Walkman. "Here's the tape player you asked for. I wasn't sure I still had one. It's pretty old school, but it should work with some new batteries. And a new tape," he said, popping out the old one and looking at it. "Flock of Seagulls. Yeah, you should probably pick up a new one."

"Thanks," I said.

Susannah looked confused. "What do you need that for? Don't you trust Peter?"

"I trust him with my life," I said. "This is just a prop."

"A prop? Jordy—"

"Nope. No questions. I can't give away all my professional secrets."

"Professional secrets," she snorted. "The only professional secret you've got is how you manage to pay the rent every month."

I blew her a kiss.

"All right," Pete said with a cartoon-ish little cough. "I actually have some work to do tonight, so…"

Poor Pete.

I thanked my friend, gathered up my new equipment, and we made our exit.

52

Me:

Judge Harper?

Him:

Yes?

Me:

Thank you for taking my call. I'm the guy who left that photograph with your secretary this morning.

(pause)

Him:

Jordan...

Me:

Just a concerned citizen, your honor. No need for us to be on a first-name basis.

(pause)

> Him:

What do you want, Jordan?

> Me:

Well, I thought it was about time we talked, you and me. We've got some things to talk about, don't you think?

> Him:

No, I do not. Now, if you'll excuse me—

> Me:

Sure, sure, you don't have to talk to me. It's a free country. I get it. But I've got to tell you, Judge—I'm a lonely guy these days, now that I don't have a job anymore. And when I get in the mood to talk to someone, I've just got to talk to someone. You know how that is? And I think I've got some friends from college who work for the Journal-Constitution, who'd love to hear from me.

> Him:

Young man, are you seriously threatening a federal judge?

> Me:

No, sir, I'm threatening a guy who leaves dead girls on the side of the road. Sorry if there was any confusion about that.

(pause)

Him:

You're playing at a very dangerous game, Jordan. Does your father know—

Me:

No—maybe we should call him together. What do you think?

See, I don't think it's all that dangerous, Judge. Not for me, anyway. I mean, you made sure I've got nothing left to lose, right? Not sure what your strategy was, there, but it seems to me I've got nothing to lose now.

Him:

Now, hold on—

Me:

No, you're right. We should dial it down a little. No need to get crazy. I'm not trying to threaten you. I'm just making a friendly phone call. Trying to get together with a family friend, someone who has mutual interests.

Him:

Jordan…

Me:

Of course, if things *were* to get dangerous for me….if anything bad were to happen to me after this call—say, if you happened to send another "message" my way, it's possible I might have made

287

arrangements with some friends who are under strict orders to send copies of this picture to the paper, the TV news stations, and *your* friends. Starting with my father.

Now, let's talk about how dangerous this is for *you*. Because it is.

Him:

Go on.

Me:

No, sir. Not at work. I know you're a busy man, and I know it's not a place you can speak freely. We'll meet in person, away from work. Tonight, in the parking lot at Woody's Cheese Steaks. Monroe at Virginia. I think you know the intersection. Be there at midnight.

Him:

Jordan, I am not going to meet you anywhere, and certainly not at *midnight*. This is absurd.

Me:

Well, I'll tell you what. *I'll* be there at midnight. And if I don't see you by there by 12:30—or if I see any of your persuasive friends—or if I see the police—the picture goes out, and you can kiss your career goodbye. And maybe your marriage, too—who knows? Then you can decide how absurd this all is.

Him:

That's blackmail, young man.

Me:

Not yet, it isn't.

(Hang up. Breathe. Run to bathroom. Throw up.)

53

Midnight. I stand alone in the dark parking lot, looking down at Monroe Avenue and the place where Giselle died. Cars break the silence every once in a while, whooshing by, but there aren't many of them, and most of the time, it's dead quiet.

It was dark and cold and rainy the morning Giselle died. It's dark and cold tonight. How many times have I been here during the day, thinking about her, imagining what happened to her? But only tonight does it feel the way it must have felt for her. The only thing it needs is a freezing rain—and we just might get that. The sky has been heavy and overcast all day.

Pete and Susannah are sitting in a car parked up the street, just in case the judge or one of his minions snoops around before the appointed time. I can't see them or hear them. I assume they can hear me—my breathing, my shuffling sounds, as I try to keep warm.

Winter in Atlanta is depressing. You get bursts of sunshine and warmth every once in a while, but most of the time it's just grey and wet and cold. It rarely gets cold enough to snow, so you don't get the bright, white, clean kind of winter feeling you get up north. But it's cold enough to be uncomfortable. And it's grey.

12:15 comes, and still no judge. If he cared enough about his marriage to cover up the accident, surely he cares enough to stop me from sharing the picture I took. Unless it meant nothing—unless it was his daughter I saw him with, or a niece, or something.

No—they kissed. It wasn't a family thing. And if it had been a harmless meeting, he wouldn't have cared about the photo. He would have called my father and said, "Your son has gone off the deep end."

No—he's coming. He's just going to wait until the last possible second. Make me stand out here in the freezing cold. Because he's a judge—he lets people sit around, waiting, until he's good and ready to make his entrance. And when he enters, everyone leaps to their feet. That's his world. Twenty bucks says he shows up at 12:30.

I want to pace, or hop up and down—anything to get the blood moving and stay warm. But I'm not going to do that. I don't want to look weak. I need to appear still and centered. Implacable.

What I'd really love to do is run over to Pete's car and warm up for just five minutes—have some of the coffee they brought in a thermos. And not be alone.

12:28 by my watch. A car slides down the quiet street, coming from the north. It slows down just above the intersection, then stops in the shoulder, right by the high school football field. It's him. It must be him. There's nothing else to stop for at this hour.

Interesting that he doesn't want to park up here in the lot. Why? Does he have a friend waiting and watching, like I do? Or does he just want to make sure he doesn't get ensnared, somehow? Leave himself a safe getaway if he needs one? Or maybe he's not even the judge.

No, it's him. Even in the shadows, in his heavy coat, I can recognize him. The mole has come out of his hole.

He crosses the street and heads up the slope of the parking lot. I stand in the only pool of light available, to make sure he sees me.

He walks straight up to me and stands in front of me. He looks up at the lamppost and takes three steps back, to get out of the light. He expects me to yell my conversation…or to step into the shadows with him. I follow his lead and step out of the circle of light. Susannah will not be happy.

"What do you want?" he asks. "Money?"

"Did I ask for money?" I say.

"You said you wanted to talk."

"That's right."

"I've known you for years, Jordan. This is insane."

"Talking is insane?"

"You've been following me. Spying on me."

"You're a fascinating man."

He shivers. "All right. Let's get this over with. I'm freezing. Tell me what you want."

I nod. "Fair enough. Let's start with the woman in the picture. Who is she?"

"That's none of your...do we really need to go through all of this?"

"That's none of my business, you were going to say?"

"I was."

"But you know what I am, Judge. I'm a snoop. It's exactly my business. Could be it's your wife who's paying me to snoop."

"Is it?"

"Snoop-client privilege, Judge Harper. You know how it is. So who's the lady?"

He looks around nervously. I can just make out the whites of his eyes.

"Come on, Judge. I'm going to find out, one way or another. The question is whether it stays with me or not. Maybe you can influence that."

"Her name is Marion. She was one of my clerks, several years ago."

"And slightly more than that."

"Yes, slightly more than that."

"For how long?"

"On and off for about four years. I tried to end it…many times."

"So it was her you were seeing, the night you hit that girl."

He pauses. Maybe he's never admitted it to anyone. Maybe not even himself, out loud. I know how that is.

"You want to deny you hit that girl? Giselle Palmer? Right down there at the intersection?"

"I don't know what you're talking about."

"Really?" I say, getting irritated. "You want to see the hood ornament from your old car? The one with your fingerprints on it?"

He snuffs. "You don't have any hood ornament."

"Maybe I do, maybe I don't. But I know about it, don't I? Which is bad news for you. And let's be honest—do I really *need* to have it? Or do I just need this photograph getting sent to the press, along with a wild story about how you covered up your involvement in a hit-and-run accident to hide your affair?"

"Wild stories aren't evidence."

"Your world turns on evidence, Judge. For the rest of us, smears and accusations do more than enough damage."

He pauses for a moment.

"Why do you want to know all of this?" he asks.

"Because someone hired me to find out."

"So you think you know something. Why don't you just tell your client and be done with it?"

"I could. Give him your name and wash my hands of the whole thing. I could do that. But maybe I don't care about the client anymore. Maybe I think my client is an asshole. Maybe I want something more."

He nods and reaches into his pocket. The hand comes back out again with a thick wad of cash, straight from the bank, with the paper band still around it.

"That's ten thousand dollars," he says.

"Interesting," I say. "And just so we're clear, what is it you think you're paying for with that?"

He pauses for a moment, then says, "Silence?"

"Silence. That's good. That's one of my top three things, actually. But silence about what, exactly?"

"Everything."

"Everything meaning...the girlfriend?"

"The girlfriend, the accident—everything. Stop playing games with me!"

I breathe out and relax. Finally. It's what I've been waiting for. "Thanks, Judge," I say. "That's all I wanted. You can put your money away."

He pushes the money towards me. "No—take it. Please. I want to put this behind me. Take it."

"I don't want your money," I say.

He's flustered now. "Well, what…what *do* you want? If this isn't about money, then what? You say someone hired you, but you don't want to give up my name. You live in a degenerate part of town with a laughable job, but you don't want my money. What are you playing at, Jordan? What are you trying to do?"

"That's easy," I say, reaching into my coat pocket and pulling out Pete's old Walkman. "I'm trying to put you in jail." And I hold the device right up in the judge's face, so he can see the little gears turning.

Time stops, just for a second. I can see that he's horrified. I can see that he's trying to think his way through this.

"You think you can just do what you want to and walk away, clean?" I say, my voice getting louder, but mostly because I'm scared. "Leave your messes for someone else to clean up and never have to pay for it?"

"Jordan…I…"

"No. You want to know what I am, Judge?" I say, louder still. "You're right—I'm not a blackmailer. I'm not a cop. I'm not even a P.I anymore, thanks to you. But right now, Judge, I'm the sword of fucking justice. That's what I am. And you are going to pay for what you did."

"Jordan, listen to me…"

"We're done here," I say.

"What good does it do to have me in jail?" he says, spinning fast, looking for an angle. "Now? After all this time? Think about it, Jordan. Don't I do more for justice sitting on the bench, trying cases? Even after all of…this?"

"I said we're done." I start to put the recorder back in my pocket, but suddenly he's moving, and I can't quite see what he's doing.

"Give it to me," he says.

"Not gonna happen," I say.

He pushes me—hard—on the chest, making me fall back a few steps into the light. He steps forward after me, so that I can see him. And I see, now, that he's holding a gun.

I'm thinking, "Seriously?" But I say, "Shit."

"Give it to me," he says. "Now."

I wasn't expecting this, so I don't play games. I reach out to him slowly and hand him the Walkman. He pops the cassette out and starts ripping the tape out of it, wrapping it around his hand. He does all this while keeping his gun more-or-less pointed at me, and I really wish he wouldn't try multi-tasking like this.

"It was an accident," he hisses at me, shaking the gun dangerously. "You understand? A stupid accident. I broke up with her, but she called me, crying, and I went over, and we ended up spending the night together. Stupid. With my wife already suspicious. And I was worried about coming home so late, trying to come up with a good excuse, a good reason, and I was driving too fast. A stupid accident!"

"All right," I say. "Just—"

"She came out of nowhere!" he yells. "Out of nowhere. She came flying into the street. That's my fault? I should be punished for that? Lose everything? My whole life? For *that*? No," he says firmly. "This goes nowhere. This stops here, tonight." He stuffs the ruined tape in his pocket.

"I do still have the pictures," I say, keeping very still. It's a stupid, cocky thing to say, but something in me doesn't care anymore.

He looks up at me, narrowing his eyes, and he keeps his gun pointed at me. He's weighing the odds, considering his options. He's thinking, maybe I did instruct someone to send out the pictures if I got hurt or killed…and maybe I didn't. Am I bluffing? Is it worth the risk?

"What are you gonna do?" I ask. "You gonna shoot me? You think they'd bury that little accident for you, too? You think they'll do *anything*, just because you say so?"

The judge considers this, and I can see that he can't let it be over. He can't handle it being over. And I'm not sure where that leaves me. And I realize, strangely, that I don't care. It occurs to me that I should be shitting my pants right about now, but I'm not. I'm just here—fully here, in this moment, and I am standing my ground.

"Go on, then—do it," I say. "You'd be doing me a favor."

Suddenly there's a flood of light in the parking lot, and there's a voice on a bullhorn telling the judge to drop his gun. He whips around in a panic, looking for the source, then back, meeting my eyes with a look of utter betrayal. I'm just as shocked as he is, and he can read it on my face. He bolts. The voice on the loudspeaker yells for him to stop, but he doesn't stop. He races down the sloping parking lot towards his car, screaming "Leave me alone!" Shots ring out from behind me, and I hear footsteps, running. The judge turns back, still running, and fires back—three, four times. I can't tell if he's aiming at the voices or at me, but it's me he hits. I feel a searing pain in my leg, above the knee, and a white hot burning feeling radiating out in every direction, and then my leg collapses out from under me, and I'm eating gravel again.

Lying on the ground, groaning in pain, I can see the judge race towards his car, looking back over his shoulder to see who's following him. He doesn't see the car coming north on Monroe, and the car doesn't see him run into the street, and suddenly there's a horn blasting, and tires screeching. The judge smashes into the grill, then rolls up onto the hood, then rolls off sideways, onto the ground—all in a matter of seconds. Then he stays on the ground, not moving.

I see uniforms swarm around him, and the driver race out of his car to see what he's done. I feel a hand on my shoulder, and I look up. Carter Wiggins is there, kneeling beside me.

"What the fuck are *you* doing here?" I ask him through gritted teeth, trying to keep from crying.

"Trying to keep you out of trouble," he says. "I've been following you since you got that beat-down."

"Fantastic," I say. "Good thing you were here. Otherwise, I might have gotten hurt." I'm not sure if my sarcasm is getting across.

I hear more running. Susannah is by my side, crying, asking if I'm all right. Carter tells her he's already radioed for an ambulance. They're saying more to each other, but I can't follow it. I can see Pete standing there near them, looking helpless and confused. I call his name and he looks down at me.

"Did you get it?" I ask. "All of it?"

He nods.

"Good."

"Nice bluff with the cassette," he says.

"I have my moments."

I turn my head to the street, where a crowd has gathered around the judge's body. Three cops are kneeling by his side, along with the driver of the car and his wife, who both look upset. I try to keep them in focus, even though my eyes are starting to get blurry. I can tell I'm going to pass out from the pain any minute.

"Look," I say to Carter, trying to get his attention. "Look. You see? They stopped."

"Yeah," he says. "Course they stopped."

"Course they stopped," I repeat, bleary, knowing that my words are slurring. "Cause that's what you do. That's what you do when you hurt someone. You stop. You go back. You make sure they're okay."

Susannah wraps herself around me, crying. I can hear the siren of the ambulance, far off, coming to get me. I wonder if they'll put me in the same rig as the judge.

And then, of course, it starts to rain.

54

I woke up slowly, unsure where I was. It was the middle of the night. Was it the same night? Or a day—or days—later? I had no idea. I was in a hospital bed, and my leg was in a cast. Surely I had been awake for that. But if I had been, I had no memory of it.

Suddenly, my body decided to remind me that my leg hurt like hell. I groaned.

"Hey," said an angel's voice. "You're back."

"Am I okay?" I asked, equally blearily.

"You will be," she said.

I pulled up my head and saw that Susannah had been sleeping in a chair pulled up next to my bed.

"You're here," I said.

"Where else would I be?" She leaned forward in her chair and took my hand.

"And you're not going to leave?"

"No, Sweetie, I'm not going to leave."

I started to cry, barely able to hold myself together. And I said, "Why?"

"Shh," she said, putting a finger to my lips. "Enough now. It's enough."

"It's not."

"Yes, it is," she said quietly. "It will be." She got up from her chair and lay next to me in the hospital bed.

And I fell back to sleep.

55

The next time I woke up, it was daylight. There were flowers in the room, and my father's girlfriend, Amina, was sitting in a chair, listening to Susannah tell the whole story of our midnight adventure. Hearing it made my leg hurt, and I moaned sufficiently to break up the conversation.

"Look who's up," Susannah said.

"Hey," I said, hoarse and sleepy.

"Your father wanted to come," Amina said. "This whole thing has him very upset."

"I'll bet," I croaked.

"I'm afraid he's not up to a hospital visit, though," she said sadly. "It brings back too many memories, he said. The smell, especially."

"I know what he means," I said. "I'd rather not be here, myself."

"We'll come spend some time when you're at home," she said.

That didn't sound good. "How long am I going to be laid up?" I asked Susannah.

"I think I can take you home tomorrow or the next day," she said. "But it's going to take a while. You're going to need physical therapy once the cast comes off. You shattered some bone or other."

"Shattered? I don't like that word."

"Yeah, I wasn't crazy about it either."

Up above their heads, I could see the news playing out on the tiny, hospital television. I saw the judge's face on the screen, and asked Susannah to turn up the volume.

"…no significant injuries," the anchorman said. "Meanwhile, police spokesmen refuse to comment on what investigation brought them to the scene four days ago and led to the shootout that left one man wounded and—"

"Four days ago?" I asked. "Seriously?"

"Yes. And no one's saying a word. Carter says it's all going to blow up in a day or two, though."

"Carter's been here?"

"Every day," she said.

"Huh," I said. "I wouldn't have expected that."

"People can surprise you," she said.

"True that," I said.

56

I went home the next day and returned to my cocoon on the couch, where I had holed up after getting beaten by the judge's friendly messengers. It was becoming a bad habit.

Over the next week, a steady stream of visitors came to see me. They all brought food, like they were sitting *shiva* or something. I tried to make it clear that I wasn't dead yet, but they kept coming, with platters. And we sat around, eating, talking, and watching the story play out on the TV news.

At first, the coverage was exactly what Carter had predicted: allegations and rumors of entrapment, blackmail, even racist conspiracies to destroy the Black power structure of the city. An investigation had uncovered that the wounded man who had set up the sting operation had long-standing ties to racist organizations.

That one made me sit up and take notice. "What the hell?" I said to the room. "Where'd they get that one?"

Carter, who happened to be visiting that afternoon, leaned back in his chair and laughed. He took a long swig of beer instead of answering my question.

"Did *you* tell them that?" I asked.

"No, sir, I did not," he said, still laughing. "All I gave them was your name. Billy Barnes, formerly-licensed private investigator. Thought it might be a good idea to protect your privacy, knowing what was coming."

"They think *Billy Barnes* was a racist?" I asked.

Carter pointed to the television and said, "More than think."

I looked at the screen and saw an old picture of Billy—a much younger Billy—posing in a white sheet, hoodless, with some good old boy pals of his, in days gone by.

"Damn," I said. "Who knew?"

"Aw, don't worry about it," said Carter. "They may not be much in the brains department, but sooner or later, they'll figure out the real Barnes is dead."

"Meanwhile, the judge is out of the hospital and happily at home."

"Well, now, I don't know how happy he is," said Carter. "But yeah, he ain't exactly in jail."

"So this whole thing was a waste," I said gloomily.

Carter shrugged. "Fat lady ain't sung yet," he said.

"You fucking hick," I said. "Stop being inscrutable and go arrest somebody."

"I'm off duty," he said with a smile.

But he was right. The fat lady had not sung yet. The question was: would she ever?

All I had wanted to do was get a recording of the judge confessing. That was all I wanted. Then I could send it up to Palmer and say, "I did my part. You do yours." And it would be out of my hands. He'd never be able to use the recording as evidence in a trial, but he could use it to prod Carter's captain into action. Or pass it over to some interested journalist. He could have done something.

But now, with the judge injured and the police involved, the whole thing was toxic. The case was firmly out of my hands and out of my control. Pete had turned the tapes over to the police, as requested. Demanded, really. And the police, predictably, were doing nothing. If anyone was talking to anyone, no one was talking to me.

Had the judge made the right phone calls again? Leaned on the right friends again? Was the whole story going to get buried? It sure seemed that way.

But then, one day, about two weeks later, I heard my voice on the evening news. As usual, there was a group gathered around, eating and joking and keeping me company. But everyone got quiet when they saw my face float up next to the news anchor, and heard my recorded voice:

> *I'm not a blackmailer. I'm not a*
> *cop. I'm not even a P.I. anymore,*
> *thanks to you. But right now, Judge,*
> *I'm the sword of [bleep]ing justice.*
> *That's what I am. And you are*
> *going to pay for what you did.*

"Very dramatic," said Porkchop. "Nice use of imagery."

"Oh, my god," I said. "Did I really say that?"

Everyone laughed.

I grabbed the phone and called Pete. "What the hell are you doing?" I yelled at him.

"I have no idea what you're talking about," he said calmly.

"No idea what I'm talking about? I'm hearing my voice—right now—on 11 Alive. Did you send them a copy of the—"

"I'm sorry, I have no idea what you're talking about."

"Pete, what the fuck, man—"

"Pete? I'm sorry, there's no one here by that name."

And he hung up.

"Son of a *bitch*," I said.

Next came some video of Carter Wiggins, at his desk, being interviewed by some pretty blonde. "Billy Barnes?" he said, leaning back in his chair and pretending to be wise. "Let me tell you something about ole Billy Barnes. That boy is tenacious. He gets his teeth on a case, he don't let go for nothing. I tell you what, that boy is a *bulldog*."

It's a good thing he wasn't visiting that day, or I would have thrown something very hard at him. It's bad enough I had five or six other friends over. They all started barking and growling at me. I was humiliated.

Now they had the judge's face up on the screen. The room got quiet as the anchor played another audio clip:

> *It was an accident. You understand?*
> *A stupid accident. I broke up with*
> *her, but then she called me, crying,*
> *and I went over, and we ended up*
> *spending the night together. And I*
> *was worried about coming home so*
> *late, trying to come up with a good*
> *excuse, a good reason, and I was*
> *driving too fast. A stupid accident…*

That was the fat lady, singing.

57

The judge turned himself in to the police two days later and made a full confession. He was fired and disbarred immediately, and charged with everything from reckless endangerment and fleeing the scene of an accident to attempted murder. The case dragged on for weeks, with lawyers on both sides angling and positioning and arguing to see what, exactly, was going to happen to the Great Man.

But it didn't matter. He was ruined.

The day they finally sentenced the judge, my father and Amina were visiting. I tried to read my father's feelings about the whole thing, but his face was like stone. I shut the TV off and let silence settle over the room.

"Well," he said finally, "Looks like you were right, after all."

"I'm sorry it had to be your friend," I said.

"So am I, Jordan. So am I." He shook his head sadly. "I don't understand it. He could have come to me for help. He could have come to any of us. There were so many people who could have helped him—who *would* have helped him."

"I know. It's weird," I said. "I guess people do dumb things when they're in trouble."

Susannah gave me a meaningful and loaded look, which I chose to ignore.

"But, you know," I said. "He *did* go to you for help, in a way. He just couldn't do it face to face."

He looked at my quizzically. "What do you mean?"

"You told me about it months ago, but I never put the pieces together. You had some party at your house. Valentine's day, maybe, or a few weeks after. And you found him in your garage. Remember?"

"Yes—he was in the garage. He stumbled and snapped the hood ornament off my car."

"Off your Mercedes."

"That's right."

"Kind of a convenient stumble, don't you think? Given the fact he had lost his own hood ornament recently?"

His eyes widened. Then he sighed, and shook his head. "The things people do."

"We're a hell of a species," I agreed.

He nodded. "But you built the case," he said. "You got your proof."

"Yes, I did."

He looked at me. Not in my direction, but *at* me—with those lawyer's eyes. He looked at me for a long time. And then he smiled, and he said, "Good job."

And that was the end of it.

Except...

Except it didn't really end. All of a sudden, I was a Name. Well, Billy Barnes was the name, but you know what I mean. I was talked about in the papers. I was talked *to* on local TV shows. Suddenly, everybody wanted to talk about Giselle Palmer. She stopped being a Nobody who died in the rain, and became a person again.

My friends teased the hell out of me about the "sword of justice" line and Carter's bulldog crack, but the reporters loved it. So even once the Palmer case died down, I kept getting requests for interviews. I had magically turned into some kind of Resident Expert on bad behavior.

And once my license got reinstated, with profound and embarrassed apologies from the state board, my voice mail started filling up with calls—and not just from suspicious wives, anymore. Now parents were calling me, asking if I could track down children who had run away. Environmental groups were calling, asking me to investigate chemical dumping. All sorts of people were calling—people who needed someone who wouldn't give up, someone who wouldn't let go, someone who kept on going, even when common sense told them it was time to quit.

It turns out there a lot of folks out there who need someone like that—someone who's too stubborn to give up on lost causes. And strangely enough, that someone turned out to be me.

I am Bulldog Barnes.

58

So that's my story—and to tell you the truth, if I had known how much work it was going to be, I wouldn't have started the damned thing. I thought it would keep my mind off things while I was laid up in the cast, but it's dragged on for months now. Months. Now it's August again—a year since Ted Palmer called me and set this whole thing in motion.

Susannah is standing behind me, hands on my shoulder. "Well?" she asks. "You're all done. Are you happy?"

I sit back from the computer and stretch. Then I say, "I'm working on it."

She laughs at my feeble answer and says "Oy vey," in that southern accent of hers that makes Yiddish sound so adorable. And off she goes to prepare her tray of tequila shots.

I'm late for rehearsal—I can hear the guys warming up outside, waiting for me. I can hear Oticha working on the Tiger Rag for an upcoming Clemson alumni party. The song really ought to have a trombone to go with the trumpet, but we make do with what we have. While Oticha plays it, I can hear the bass line in my head. My fingers are aching to join in.

In a minute or two, I will turn off this computer and walk out onto the old porch, and there they'll be—my friends. The boys will be in place. Melanie will be sitting on the glider with Susannah, yakking away and laughing while they watch the kids race around on the front lawn or dance to our music. People taking a sunset stroll down our street will pause to watch us for a few bars. I'll grab a beer, limp over to my stool, and lean the bass into my chest. The leg isn't bad anymore—it's just stiff when I've been sitting for a long time. And I've been sitting for a *long* time.

We'll rip into the song, and Oticha will blast out the melody.

> *Where's that tiger! Where's that tiger?*
> *Where's that tiger? Where's that tiger?*

There's something about that tune that makes you want to get up and move. Not dance, maybe, but move. Walk. Run. Do something. Race ahead with your arms outstretched, to grab whatever's out there. It is, after all, a fight song.

> *Hold that tiger! Hold that tiger!*
> *Hold that tiger! Hold that tiger!*
> *Grab that tiger, never let him go!*

Oticha will finish up the melody and throw to Pete, who'll do some good old-fashioned stride piano. Ray will do a short drum solo and throw it back to Oticha, who'll do a variation on the melody for a while. Then he'll pull the horn from his mouth, point across the porch to me, and yell, "Jordy G—take it!"

And I'll take it.

"Are you happy?" she asks me. Seriously, what kind of a question is that?

I figure there's probably just three things you need in life to be a happy man. There's always just three things. And I already know that patience is one of them.

When I figure out the other two, I'll let you know.

Coming Soon:

The Cat Came Back

After ignoring a college student's warning about strange goings-on on campus, Jordan goes undercover at his alma mater to uncover a drug dealer selling lethal merchandise. But his old school holds unpleasant memories and too many temptations. It's a job that's easy to get into…but may be hard to get out of.

"I don't buy it," said Carter, watching me from his desk. I was pacing back and forth, spooling out my story, and he was watching me, leaning back on the back legs of his chair, chewing gum, and saying little.

"He didn't do drugs," I insisted. "Ever."

"That's what he said."

"I think he was telling the truth."

"And that's what *you* say."

"Come on, Carter…"

"Maybe he didn't never do it but that one time. You don't know."

I paced some more, shaking my head. "You should have heard the way he talked," I said. "How his dad was an alcoholic, how he always had to be the one who cleaned up after him—picking him up off the floor. Now he's here at college, doing the same thing for his friends. This is the poster child for Just Say No. This is not a kid who suddenly starts using."

"Except he did," Carter said, trying to be patient. "They tested his blood. It's drugs killed him, sure as shit."

"Then somebody gave it to him."

"Course somebody *gave* it to him. Nobody thinks he was brewing shit in his room."

I groaned. "It doesn't make any sense. There's something else going on here."

Carter puffed out his cheeks, thinking, and slowly let the air out, like a dying balloon. "I see two ways this goes down. One: accidental OD. He's a user and he fucked up. Maybe he's habitual, maybe he's a first-timer. Either way, he fucked up and it's an accident. Two: he got depressed and he offed himself. Did it on purpose, we don't know why. He never used before…or he did use before…but either way, he knew what he was doing and he did it for a reason. Either one of them's possible, and both of them fits the evidence, and neither one of them's a mystery you got to solve."

"I know, I know."

"But you don't like either of them stories. I can see that. So what are you looking for?"

"I don't know. Whatever he was looking for. Whatever he came to me to talk about."

"Well, if there's anything there, you ain't gonna get your hands on it," Carter said, "Cause unless you get the parents to give you permission, this thing's shut down tight.. They don't even want to know suicide or accident—they just want to go home."

I gave up my pacing and sat down across the desk from him. "Look, he comes to me and he says they're all on some new drug, he says they're all paranoid and defensive and sick, he says he's going to bring me evidence. Okay, I never hear from him. I don't care. I didn't think he was going to do anything. Maybe he never was going to. But what if he *did* start poking around, making trouble. What if he was going to come back to me, and he just got in someone's way?"

"What if, what if," said Carter with a shrug. "You ain't got a shred of evidence."

I shrugged. "That's never stopped me before."

ABOUT THE AUTHOR

Andrew Ordover is a playwright, novelist, and educator. He lives with his wife and two sons in northern Virginia.

For more information and downloads of Jordan's favorite music, visit http://crafting-a-life.com/c4c/

ABOUT THE COVER ARTIST

Mike Young is a graphic designer who resides in New York City with his lovely wife and two cats. His interests include Batman, single-malt scotch, American history, and writing in the third person. More of his work and his inane ramblings can be found at iammikeyoung.com.

www.ingramcontent.com/pod-product-compliance
Lightning Source LLC
Chambersburg PA
CBHW062026170626
46813CB00001B/301